DRAGON PRINCE

THE ROYAL QUEST - BOOK 1

KELLY N JANE

ASHLEY MCLEO

MERAKI PRESS

Dragon Prince, The Royal Quest series Book 1

Copyright © 2020 by Kelly N. Jane and Ashley McLeo

Published by Meraki Press

Cover by Carol Marques Cover Design

Editing by Jen McDonnell of Bird's Eye Books

ISBN (Paperback) 978-1-947245-33-4

ISBN (eBook) 978-1-947245-31-0

www.kellynjane.com

www.ashleymcleo.com

1

VIOLET

PLEASE, please, please let the plasma center still be open when I get there.

I swirled the dregs out of a French press and washed the glass container with care. I was in a hurry to get to the center, but I also needed this job, so cutting corners wasn't an option.

With its meditation music playing on a loop and prayer flags hanging from the ceiling, The Mystic Bean gave the impression of an über relaxed workplace, a place where the employees might light up a joint on their break. It was all a façade, the manager didn't take any guff. I only hoped that the shop would remain empty until Alan got back from break. Having to help customers would slow me down.

"Why do you look so glum, Violet? Isn't it your weekend? From both gigs, right?"

Llewellyn, my eclectic Wiccan co-worker, whose real name was Rachel, wrapped her arm around my shoulder. "You must have some *hot* plans!"

Her positioning made washing dishes more difficult, but I

didn't complain. Llewellyn was a friend and the reason I'd landed this job.

"Nope, nothing happening."

Except for donating as much plasma as they'd suck from me, and racing to St. Francis' Assisted Living Home to pay a bill. But after those errands, I really didn't have anything lined up for my days off. Making plans often meant spending money, and even with two jobs, I couldn't afford to do anything.

Llewellyn frowned.

"Except for going to the library," I invented an activity on the spot to make her happy.

She thought I didn't get out enough, which was true. But money problems aside, I'd rather stay in anyhow. Not because I was an antisocial hermit—I enjoyed people's company most of the time—but drowning out their inner voices in my head often exhausted me. Especially when the voices always seemed to belong to the biggest weirdos. People who, given my family history, I didn't want to associate with.

"Oh good, *the library*. For a second, I worried that you'd waste your most formative, experimental years doing something boring like smoking pot and overindulging in tacos or backpacking through Europe with five bucks in your pocket."

My friend rolled her eyes and brushed her long, silver hair, which had been artfully highlighted with copper, over her shoulder.

"I like your new dye job. It's unique," I said.

For a brief two-day period, she'd gone back to her natural brown color, which had been odd. I preferred the brighter look.

"Thanks. It's more me." She wagged her finger at me. "But don't think you can change the subject like that and get away with it."

I grinned sheepishly. It had been worth a try.

"You know you can join our coven circle, right? You might find it interesting." She narrowed her eyes as if she was peering into my soul. "I sense some witchy vibes from you."

Llewellyn had invited me to the circle at least a dozen times. I'd always declined precisely for the reason that she stated. I knew that I was different, but unlike Llewellyn, I didn't want anyone else knowing.

Because being too different got people locked in a padded room.

She sighed. "Whatever. Enjoy the library. But if you want to have some *real* fun, hit me up. This weekend, we're going to try to contact a different world. Ganon says that the stars are aligned, and another realm is close, so we might be able to peek beyond the veil."

I stifled a groan. Ganon, Llewellyn's boyfriend, was such a tool. His presence was yet another reason not to go.

Llewellyn didn't notice my disdain and kept chattering about other realms. I mostly tuned it out, intent on finishing my closing duties and getting out of there. But when she paused in her speech, I met her eyes to see if she expected me to answer. She tilted her head as if she'd had a deep thought.

"I hope they can understand us if we break through the veil. If they can't, I guess we can always fall back on body language. I should call Ganon and see if he's considered that." She whipped around and strode to the back office to get witchy business done.

I released an exhale. Sometimes when Llewellyn started talking, she didn't stop for hours. I'd gotten off easy.

Finishing the dishes, I grabbed a rag to wipe down the counters. Alan should be back any minute, and then I could leave.

I'd conquered half the barista counter space when the bell on the front door rang. A funny sensation came over me, and I glanced up. My breath hitched, and the rag fell from my hand as a guy swaggered into the shop.

With his defined, square jaw, thick black hair, perfect aquiline nose, and gorgeous brown eyes that seemed to blaze with a hint of cabernet red, he immediately intimidated me. By the way he walked and radiated power, you'd think he owned the place. And that wasn't even taking into account all the *muscles*. His freaking muscles had muscles. Putting aside the distracting, massive, crimson purse he wore, he was easily the hottest guy I'd ever seen. Which was why every other time he'd come in, I'd dashed into the backroom.

This time, however, I was the only one in the shop to help him. And unfortunately, he'd already caught me staring. My insides twisted, and I averted my eyes. The espresso machine officially became the most interesting thing I'd ever seen, but I could still feel his gaze burning through me. Demanding my attention.

All the nerves running through me made me drop the mental barriers that I kept up around my mind. The moment they fell, a voice emerged in my head.

Is the human just going to stand there? Or come and take my order?

My spine stiffened. What the hell? The *human*?!

4

I scanned the room for any aliens or animals that I might have suddenly developed the ability to hear.

Nope. Only the hot guy stood in front of me. Another man who resembled a weasel was coming in the door, but I couldn't have heard him from that far away.

Maybe the human doesn't see me?

Hot Guy waved his arm, and my mouth dropped open.

Holy crap. I'd heard Hot Guy. And he thought he was something other than human.

My eyes darted to the murse. I should have seen it coming. After all, I only heard weirdos.

"Hello?!" Hot Guy asked, as if I hadn't seen him wave li he was trying to guide an airplane onto the tarmac.

I hurriedly reassembled my mental barriers.

"Um, hi. Sorry. I had a brain fart."

Hot Guy's perfect features twisted into an expressic made me wonder if I had accidentally said that I ate m

"Errr, anyway." I shuffled up to the register. "Wr get you?"

Hot Guy glanced at the menu, which was con his history. For the past week, he'd ordered the every day. My co-workers commented on it each ti the order was so precise and bizarre.

A moment later, his eyes met mine, and I shiver.

"A sandwich with ten pieces of roast bee cheese, and hot sauce coating both sides o vegetables. And a mocha with a teaspoon of

"Coming right up," I said as if it wa wanted a disgusting amount of meat a

much cinnamon! What was he trying to do, anyway? Blast his taste buds off with spice?

"That'll be nine bucks."

Hot Guy nodded and twisted so that I could barely see his bag. He shuffled items around and cast a furtive glance in my direction. After a few moments of searching, he extracted a bill and handed it over.

That's when I noticed his tattoos. His right arm bore a line of them. Done in bright blue ink, they reminded me of Nordic runes that I'd seen in a book Llewellyn had shown me. My gaze shifted to his left arm. Tattoos were there too but done in a totally different style. A blue dragon had been drawn closest to his wrist, and a human, centaur, gryphon, and giant spider appeared as my gaze traveled toward his elbow. Each creature morphed into the next seamlessly, like on a totem pole.

They were the most unique tattoos I'd ever seen, which said a lot, considering my place of employment.

"This is enough, right?" Hot Guy grunted.

I blinked. He was still holding out the bill and waiting for me to take it. It was a fifty. Obviously more than enough for a sandwich and mocha.

He must be foreign.

"Yeah, plenty," I said, taking the bill and handing him back the change, which he stuffed into his bag.

"Interesting murse," I said. "Most dudes I see go for a neutral shade, but the bold color suits you."

Even though I thought the murse was funny, it was true. It suited him. Then again, I doubted that any hue would look bad on Hot Guy.

He grabbed the bag as if I'd threatened to steal it, and the items inside clinked.

I tilted my head.

"Whatcha hiding in that thing? Barbells?"

"Murse?" Hot Guy retorted as he held onto the bag for dear life.

"Yeah, man-purse. Murse. They're all the rage among hipsters nowadays."

"This is not a purse. It's a satchel."

I bit my lip. "Which is another word for a big purse."

His frown deepened.

"Errr . . . I'll have your coffee right out. The sandwich will be a few more minutes."

Hot Guy scowled and marched off without tipping.

My cheeks warmed. Note to self, don't make fun of a dude's murse.

I fulfilled the next guy's order—a black cup of joe—and set to work making the sandwich and mocha. When the order was ready, I called it out and scurried away. I didn't want to risk actually having to talk to Hot Guy again.

He took his food to a table, where he proceeded to eat slowly. The other dude seemed content to stare out the window, so I resumed cleaning the café. Every so often, Hot Guy looked up and scowled at me, obviously still salty about my comment.

I couldn't get out of there fast enough.

Finally, after what felt like a year, Alan returned from his break. I filled him in on what I'd done and had just removed my apron when Hot Guy stood, patted down his precious murse, and headed for the door.

7

I breathed a sigh of relief and released my barriers. When Alan and I worked together, I didn't need them. He wasn't among the odd sorts that I could hear. Heck, I probably didn't need them with Llewellyn either, but I kept them up as a precaution because she was a Wiccan. Who knew when she'd cast a spell that might make her aware of my ability? If that happened, I'd have a crapload of explaining to do, and I preferred to keep my secret.

I waited behind the counter to give Hot Guy a few minutes so he wouldn't think I was following him.

The dude who had come in right after him shot up out of his seat and rushed out the door, too.

Can't lose him like that idiot Sven did.

I jumped. Well, crap. Was Hot Guy still outside? The voice had sounded a little more high-pitched. But maybe he was just frustrated? I walked to the door and glanced out the window to check.

Hot Guy was striding north down the sidewalk, out of my range. Weasel Face headed in the same direction and looked to be in a rush. I shook my head, unsure what was happening with my ability. I was about to write the whole afternoon off as one strange mess when I noticed Hot Guy cross to the other side of the street. Weasel Face did, too. Not five seconds later, Hot Guy crossed the street again, back to the original side. Apparently, he was lost.

The other guy followed. When Hot Guy stopped, Weasel Face stopped. And then he hid behind a trash can.

My eyebrows knitted together, and I instinctively glanced at the table that Weasel Face had occupied. His cup of coffee stared up at me, untouched.

I sucked in a breath as I realized that the second voice had been Weasel Face, the man who'd entered the shop right after Hot Guy.

And judging by how strangely he was acting right now, I was pretty sure of one thing. Weasel Face was following Hot Guy.

2

RONE

"This blasted thing makes no sense!"

I shook the enchanted scale Virhan had given me. I'd been walking back and forth across the street, waiting for the triangular tip to glow and indicate the way I should go. But instead, the light kept wavering and disappearing like the wind, giving me no help.

Buildings on each side of the road were only two or three stories tall. I could see over them if I rose into the air, but I'd be incapable of reading the glittering object in my other form.

My targets should not be this hard to find.

I rested my hand against my satchel. The heat coming through the leather reminded me of my mission, giving me calm and strength.

Then I remembered the comments from the serving woman. She seemed to have a problem with my satchel, calling it something like a purse. I hadn't been in this realm long enough to learn all its customs, but the term she used was clearly derogatory.

In my world, someone in her position never would have judged me. They would have grovelled before me to show the respect due to my station—but not that girl. And annoyingly, I found myself caring about her opinion.

I shook my head to clear the image of the pleasing, purple streak that had contrasted with her fair hair.

Keep yourself together—remember the mission, I urged myself. I didn't have time for distractions, especially attractive humans who insulted their superiors.

Once more, I cradled the shimmery item in my hand and waited for it to signal the right direction. This area of town wasn't large, but among the handful of humans walking the streets, I should have found at least one carrying the ancient blood.

Yet, I'd found none.

It had been five human days since I'd stepped through the portal Virhan opened for me. When I left, a possible coup had threatened my homeland, and the danger weighed on my mind as I wandered this realm.

Had anyone died in my absence? Were they—

Someone yelled behind me, cutting my musings short. I twisted toward the sound, and my spine straightened in surprise. The cute serving woman was waving at me. Once more, I checked my bag, running my hand over each lump, counting. Six . . . none were missing.

She jogged in my direction, and I turned. The agitation on her face spoke to the soldier in me, rousing my protective instincts. Clearly, she needed my assistance. I pulled my eyebrows together as the woman began waving her arms and pointing to my left.

What was she doing?

From the corner of my eye, I saw a flash of movement before a body slammed into me. The force made me stumble to the side, but I quickly righted myself. Screams from other humans rang through the air, and I heard the scramble of footsteps as many hurried away. Only the scrawny male who had accosted me remained.

His beady eyes glinted as he sneered and leapt at me once again.

I jabbed my forearm against his chest, forcing the air from his lungs as he fell. He slammed into the ground with a satisfying *thunk,* but scrambled back up faster than I'd thought him capable. Instantly, he brought his fists up.

This man was quick and sneaky, but also a fool if he wanted to fight me.

A growl escaped my throat as I stared him down. Thankfully, he had not hit my precious cargo, or I'd have snapped his neck.

"Are you all right?" the woman called.

I glanced in her direction. She was still ten paces from me, but I could see how she kept darting her gaze between me and the fool.

There was no time for me to answer, as the man charged once again.

I gritted my teeth and let out a roar. Hesitation crossed the man's features before I reached for his throat, but the wily lout slipped under my grasp and twisted out of my reach.

I adjusted my satchel to rest safely against the back of my

hip, shoving the scale into a pocket and gave the rodent my full attention.

He cartwheeled to the side, ending with a backflip as if he were some court jester. Charging forward, he tried to leap again, yet I was prepared for him and grabbed his jacket. His feet dangled as I lifted my arm higher.

The next second, I was holding only limp cloth, as he'd succeeded in wiggling himself free of the coat. Tossing the article aside, I followed his movements as he tried to circle me. I needed to end this, but in a manner that left him capable of speech. There was a reason he attacked me. I needed to find out what it was.

He leapt again, but instead of coming straight at me, he scissored his legs and swiped my knee before he hit the ground and rolled over his shoulder. I fell to one knee, bracing myself on the ground with one hand. The bag slipped from my hip, but I grabbed it before it swung away from my body.

A foot caught me in the jaw, and for a second, stunned me.

Utilizing my training, I pulled myself together quickly, sucking in a deep breath and focusing a glare on my prey. Then, using my crouched position, I burst up and charged.

The man ran—straight at the side of the nearest building.

What a coward! I felt my lips curl as my muscles tensed. He had nowhere to go. I would get my answers.

Then he threw one foot up high onto the building and used the momentum to carry himself upside down over my head. He landed in a crouch behind me.

I spun to face him. "Who are you?"

I didn't expect him to answer, but frustration ate at me for allowing him to escape my grasp not once, but *twice*.

The sound of shuffling feet met my ears, and a quick glance to my left confirmed that the serving woman watched from behind a green metal box that reeked of refuse. It bristled that she had seen my weakness against such a lowly opponent.

The man said nothing, but an annoying grin flitted across his face.

My focus snapped into place as heat boiled in my veins. I let it take over as I rushed forward in an attempt to grab him. He dodged left, but aware of his cunning ways, I didn't take his bait. My observations proved valuable when in the next second, he pivoted right.

I let out a cry of victory and snatched him by the neck.

He swung his body, using his core muscles, and braced his feet against my chest. I chuckled. My grip tightened on his neck, and I used my other hand to trap one of his legs. If he tried to squirm out of my hold, he'd only break a bone—if I didn't snap his neck first.

"He has a knife!" the serving woman screamed.

A knife? I scanned the man and saw nothing.

Was she attempting to distract me? Were they working together? They would not hinder my mission. I couldn't allow the hatchlings to fall prey to ruffians.

My eyes darted back to her to assess if she appeared truthful.

The moment I took my eyes off the man, a glint of steel flashed as it sliced across my chest. Pain shot through me. As if in slow motion, I saw an athame—the black handle firmly in the palm of the wiry man.

The knife was a problem, but it was the symbol on the blade that chilled my fire as nothing else could.

My hold slackened for a split second, which was just long enough for the man to slip from me. As soon as his feet hit the ground, he sprinted away, disappearing down a side street. I was about to take chase when I heard the heavy slaps of footsteps approaching me from the other side.

His accomplice.

I spun to face the woman who barely reached my shoulder and weighed next to nothing, but had caused me a defeat in battle.

"Who are you? Tell me now or die!"

She skidded to a stop with a gasp. Then, impossibly, she *glared* at me.

A curl lifted my lip. She should have been folding herself onto her knees and trembling. Instead, I watched as her fists balled at her side.

"I saved your life, Asshat! Don't threaten me."

I leaned into my heels, sensing that she wasn't the threat she seemed to think she was. Though, an energy I couldn't identify did radiate from her. As I stared, she arched a brow and put a hand on her hip. The slight tilt of her head gave her an innocence that I instantly shoved from my mind.

"Why isn't your blood red?" She pointed at my chest.

I glanced down at my wound, which was already closing.

If that knife had been what it seemed, I would be on the ground convulsing by now. It was a fake, but who would have knowledge of that symbol? And how would they know I'd come here?

"Are you going to answer me, or just stand there like an idiot?"

I raised my stare to the feisty servant. My satchel still rested on my hip, and I checked that all was well inside. Assured that it was, I took a step closer, then another, closing the gap between us.

The boldness slipped from her face momentarily before she braced herself and stood tall.

I smirked.

Still towering over her, I pulled my shoulders back to make myself as intimidating as possible. The scent of hydrake flowers and apples blended with the pungent aroma of coffee from the shop as I leaned closer.

"How did you know he had a knife?"

Her throat bobbed as she swallowed, trying to keep her strong façade. Finally, she was showing signs of respect. Except that her wide blue gaze still roamed over my chest and shoulders.

After a moment, it stopped at where the athame had ripped my shirt, and she lifted her hand to touch me.

I grabbed her wrist, halting her.

"No one touches me without permission," I snarled. "Now, explain how you knew of the knife."

3

VIOLET

I GASPED. Hot Guy had touched me. No. He'd *grabbed* me—like he owned me or something.

Oh, hell no.

"The knife?" he pressed.

I yanked my wrist away from Hot Guy—who I renamed Anger Issues Guy—and took a step back.

"Are you freaking kidding me? I just saved your butt! Is this how you thank someone who helps you? By interrogating them?"

My eyes strayed once more to the place on his chest where Weasel Face slashed him. Seconds before I'd thought I could actually *see* it healing and although I'd thought I was crazy then, now I wasn't so sure. The injury had almost completely healed, leaving behind only a thin crevice of purple marring tanned skin.

Normal cuts didn't bleed purple or heal like that. I'd once had a paper cut that had persisted for a freaking week. But this dude had been slashed by a dagger.

An honest to God *dagger*!

This neighborhood was going to shit.

I crossed my arms over my chest.

"Plus, you never answered my question, and I asked first. Why isn't your blood red?"

He sneered. The expression hardened his handsome face and was intimidating—although, I definitely wouldn't let him know that. I'd grown up rough and tumble and had dealt with jerks way worse than him.

Well, unless he was an assassin. And judging by the way he'd fought off Weasel Face, I hadn't ruled that option out yet. But if that was the case, I was screwed anyway.

He must have realized that I wasn't going to budge, because he glanced down at his injury, which by now had healed, and wiped off a smear of blood.

"It's the mark of my kind."

The mark of his kind? What the actual hell?

"Like, where you were born?"

"And my race and high rank in society."

I narrowed my eyes. Talk about snooty! "*Okay,* where are you from then?"

He pressed his lips together. "My turn to ask questions. How did you know that man had an athame?"

"Athame . . . you speak strangely," Something was very off about him. "What's your name?"

Studying other cultures was a hobby of mine. Since I knew little about my own family's past, I overcompensated by learning about others and where they came from. As a result, I could often figure out a person's lineage, or at least a portion of it, from their surname. Plus, if I needed to report him, having a name would come in handy.

He grunted.

"If you answer me, I *might* tell you how I knew about the dagger."

He shook his head. "In my homeland, others do not order me around. I'm coming to realize that things might be different here."

Called it. Totally a foreigner.

"No question about that," I agreed. "Your name?"

"You may call me Rone of House Ignatius. I hail from Baskara."

That wasn't anywhere near Portland. We didn't have fancy family houses in the Pacific Northwest, just old money and rich tech transplants. It sounded like Rone might be Eastern European, and perhaps from a noble family. Both would explain the odd accent and how he obviously thought he was better than others.

"Well, Rone, I'm Violet." I sidestepped him as I spoke, hoping to ease away. "Just Violet, because I don't need fancy titles to feel important."

I had no intention of telling Rone that I'd heard Weasel Face think about a dagger before he attacked. As far as I was concerned, I'd saved his butt, and he should be grateful.

"Good to meet you. Anyway, I have places to be."

I took two steps before he grabbed my wrist again. A squeal ripped from my lips and I whirled around to tell him off but stopped short.

His eyes sparked with anger as he brought his face closer

to mine. "Tell me how you knew about the knife. And what you are."

My stomach dropped to my knees. What I was? How did he know that I was different?

I shook my head. Now wasn't the time to clarify. Now was the time to get the eff out of here.

"I saw the knife. In the coffee shop."

Rone's eyes narrowed. "You're lying."

"I'm not." My voice cracked. "And if you don't stop grabbing me, I'll call the police."

Laughter boomed from Rone, but he didn't let go.

"I'm serious!" I said, and wished that I actually had a phone to make good on that threat.

He glanced around the empty street before turning his attention back on me.

"How? No one is nearby. They all ran off while I fought that lout with the dagger. The same dagger that you somehow knew he had right before he attempted to maim me with it."

He leaned closer, and scents of cinnamon, pepper, and wood fire washed over me. If he wasn't interrogating me, I'd happily sniff him all day. If that wasn't weird, that is.

"Tell me how you knew of the athame, or *I* might have to bring in those police you speak of. Perhaps you and that man worked together to attack me? You saw the funds I carried when I paid at your shop." With his other hand, he reached into his pocket and pulled out the change I'd made for him.

My mouth fell open at his nerve. "I'm sorry, but you think I'd rob you for *forty dollars*? Well, actually twenty after Weasel Face and I split it?" I rolled my eyes. "Geez, dude. I'm hard up, but I'm not a criminal. And if I were one, I'd definitely steal more than a twenty!"

Rone's lips tightened.

A shiver spider walked down my spine as he repositioned himself to loom over me.

"You *will* tell me."

My chest constricted, and something inside me shifted. An overwhelming sensation made it hard to breathe. Blinking, I noticed that my vision had begun to blur.

Rone's hand gripped me harder, and the discomfort intensified. Panicking a little, I allowed my mental barriers to drop.

Even if I have to use fire, I'll make her tell me.

Fire!? Holy balls! I had to get out of there.

I tried to pull my hand away, but Rone was too strong. So I did the only thing I could think of that might get him to drop his guard.

"I can read minds," I screamed.

As I thought it would, Rone's grip on my wrist loosened. I ripped out of his grasp and sprinted away.

"Violet! Wait!" Rone yelled.

Hell no, I wasn't an idiot. I picked up the pace, and made it around the corner before Rone caught up with me. I nearly ran into a wall as I darted to the side, trying to put space between us. My eyes narrowed as I glared at him, which was when I noticed that his breathing was measured, not ragged and fast like mine.

Ugh, of course, he could run without being winded. He might be crazy, but physically, the guy was perfect.

"Violet! You said you can read minds?"

"Yes! I'm a freak!" I wheezed as I pushed harder to get away. "Now leave me alone!"

I waved my arms as we ran by a group of people. I hoped they'd notice how frantic I was and would call the cops for me.

But Rone didn't leave. He didn't even look bothered by my antics. In fact, he did the exact opposite of backing off, and threw his body in front of mine, making me grind to a halt.

"And you heard him think about the athame?"

Unable to suck down enough air to form words, I nodded.

Rone had one hell of a single-track mind. Maybe if I gave him what he wanted, he'd leave me alone?

He glanced around as if he didn't want anyone to over-hear. "Can you read everyone's mind?"

My stomach screwed up tight. This was one of my most guarded secrets. Only Mom knew what I could do, and now I'd blurted it to a total stranger.

And yet, this stranger wasn't looking at me like I was insane. He looked . . . curious.

"No. Just some people's. They're usually weirdos like you."

"Violet . . ." Rone's tone had softened, and his eyes roamed over me like he was trying to figure me out.

His mood swings were almost enough to give me whiplash. Although, there was an upside to this reversal. Now that his anger had dissipated, a wave of attraction replaced it, rolling over me, and soothing the frantic adrenaline rush.

"Uh, yeah?"

I was suddenly mesmerized by the changes in him. Espe-cially the way his cabernet eyes seemed to light up as he looked at me.

"You're a supernatural, aren't you?"

I jerked back. Oh, hell. He was as crazy as Mom.

"You're the first I've come across in this world," Rone continued, oblivious to my incredulity. "Are you a witch? Or of the fae-born?"

"Sure. I'm a supernatural, and you have wings." I rolled my eyes. "Stop talking gibberish."

His eyebrows knitted together as he cocked his head. "I can't access my wings in this form."

I threw my hands in the air. There was always something wrong with the hot ones, and Rone was clearly no exception.

Counterintuitively, knowing that he had a few screws loose instantly made him less scary. After all, I had plenty of experience with mental instability in my life. My mom . . .

My heart stopped as what I'd planned to do after work came rushing back. I glanced down at my watch, one of Mom's old ones that made me remember better times, and gasped.

Crap! The plasma center was closed.

But I still needed to visit Mom . . . she expected me around this time every week. Hopefully, I could dodge Micah and pay back what I owed him next week.

My eyes lifted to meet Rone's. I didn't have time for this nonsense anymore.

"To be clear, I'm a basic human. But I'm also a basic human who has to catch her ride. So this is where I suggest that you seek a therapist, and leave you. Good luck with. . ."

What? Living in crazy town? Random street fights? Your gross sandwich orders?

"Your life," I settled on, and stomped off to catch my bus.

4

RONE

THIS WOMAN, Violet, had connections to the supernatural world, even if she denied it. I'd have to investigate the reason for her lies another time. For now, I could use her help.

A good warrior and leader learned to use all parts of his surroundings to his advantage. I needed to keep that bit of training at the front of my mind because I believed she had the ability to help me with my quest.

The blood of the dragons—my people—should be present in a significant percentage of the human population. At least, that's what Virhan explained to me when I left my world, and I trusted his opinion.

He was the most respected High Mage of all time and had served the royal House of Ignatius through three crowning cycles. No mage alive was as intelligent, skilled, or better informed about Draessonia's history than Virhan. So if he said there were dragonbloods in this realm, there must be.

I must simply not be using the scale he provided correctly, but perhaps this woman could help me.

Keeping that in mind, I followed Violet. She shot me a few furtive glances, so I increased the distance between us a bit. When she sat on a bench on the side of the road, I approached slowly and stopped a few paces from her.

Glancing up and down the street, I saw no sign of the contraptions humans rode in nearing our position.

"Does your driver meet you at this spot? Why is he not waiting for you? Have you called for him?"

Violet twisted to look at me. Her gaze narrowed as if my question confused her.

Although Virhan had tried to prepare me for my quest, many parts of the societal structure of this realm were unclear. As was my apparent error.

"My driver? I take the bus. You have to wait for its timing. And I don't call *anyone*. I can't afford a cell phone right now. I just show up at the right time to get where I need to go."

She pointed to a scrolling screen that had information streaming in red letters. The abbreviated codes made no sense and watching the moving letters threatened to give me a headache. So much of this realm was bright, loud, and flashy. I dropped the subject and observed how she handled the situation.

I'd been in plenty of places where waiting was necessary. Taking a watch on the outer wall was a requirement for all first-year military trainees. Nothing ever happened out there. The experience was an exercise in how to control one's mind more than anything else. And that I could do easily.

Once I settled into a comfortable stance, I steadied my breathing to conserve energy.

After a time, Violet shot up and spun to face me. Blinking,

I leaned away. Her energy leaked into the air, spiking it with her floral scent, and proving that she'd lied about her heritage. But it was the annoyed purse of her lips that caught my attention most. What had made her angry?

"I want you to know that despite all this," she gestured to my person, "you don't scare me. But seriously . . . why are you still here?"

"I have an important mission. The survival of my race depends on finding others of my kind among humans."

"Ha! Are you for real? I'm not asking about your life mission. Why are you standing here with *me*?" She placed a hand on her hip as she continued, "I have places to go, and I don't need you following me around. Go wherever you were heading before you got into that streetfight."

"I've decided that it's in my best interest to stay with you."

Her face hardened, and I tried a different tack.

"I realize that you don't serve my house, but since you can hear the minds of others, I request your services."

Violet thrust her hands between us and shuffled her feet backward. "Listen, I don't provide *services*. I realize that you're not from here and don't get our culture, but back off, man."

She dropped her hands but continued to edge away. "Clearly, you have a few screws loose, and I don't want to turn you in. I think you should leave."

Once again, I didn't understand her hostility or reluctance. Or this talk of screws . . . Serving the crown was a privilege. Why didn't she understand that?

"But you have skills that will help me," I pleaded. "Would you prefer my race to suffer?"

"I don't have anything you, or anyone else, needs. Whatever your mission is, it doesn't include me."

Frustration churned inside me. She didn't grasp the seriousness of my situation.

"I only have a short time to find those who can bond with the hatchlings. To disregard your mind-reading skills would be senseless. Help me, and my homeland will honor you. If you wish to part ways after that, it will be your choice."

She was silent for a moment, as if considering my offer.

"There's something I need to do first, and it's personal. How about we meet up later, and I can help you then?" She shrugged and darted a glance to the road.

A large vehicle carrying many others within it trundled up the street and screeched to a halt in front of us. Violet hurried through the opened doors.

I hesitated at first, contemplating her suggestion, until I realized I had no way of contacting her, and hastened to follow.

The vehicle shook as I stepped aboard. The man sitting in a chair behind a large wheel seemed as if he'd been cramped in that position for some time. I ignored him and followed Violet down the cramped aisle.

Violet glanced over her shoulder and stopped when she saw me. Her back slumped, and she groaned before spinning around, muttering something that sounded like 'Clearly, I'm not pulling a fast one on you.'

Human turns of phrases were so odd.

I asked her to repeat herself, but the man in the chair interrupted me.

"Hey, buddy, pay or get off," he demanded.

I faced him and let a murmur of warning echo from my chest.

He wisely leaned away from me but pointed to a screen.

The human language and that of my people were similar. Only slight differences had emerged in the time since our cultures had separated. Some terms and modern sayings were unfamiliar to me, but mostly it was the customs I didn't understand.

Why would I need to pay to ride in this awful contraption that crowded so many bodies into such tight quarters? Were there not *private* carriages?

Violet appeared at my side. "Since you insist on coming, give the man the fare."

With a glance over her head, I noticed that every patron of the bus was watching me. I pulled a few bartering papers from my pocket and arched a brow at Violet, hoping she understood that I did not know how to use them. I didn't want to admit my helplessness in such a public manner.

Wordlessly, she pulled two of the bills from my hand and slid them into a slot under the screen. Two coins fell into a tray.

"Grab those and come sit down." Violet spun and stomped away.

The seats were too narrow for my large frame, and Violet inched closer to the wall, keeping a sliver of space between us. When the bus lurched forward, I grabbed the seat in front of me, thankful it was unoccupied. A snort came from Violet, and she tried to hide her grin by staring out the window.

"Are you ashamed of your supernatural heritage?" I

asked, trying to ignore the cramped quarters and the pungent scent of onions wafting from a man across the aisle.

Violet snapped her head around and scanned the bus.

"Don't talk like that," she hissed. "There are no such things as supernaturals, or different realms, or any of that other nonsense you're spouting. Keep your mouth shut until we get where we're going."

While no one in my realm would ever speak to me as Violet did, I was beginning to find her brazen attitude a little entertaining. Though, accepting her command was a different thing altogether. As a prince, I accepted only my parent's commands.

"Where would that be?"

"I'm going to visit my mom. It's probably best you're coming, you'll fit right in there."

"I am popular among the common people."

Again, Violet snorted a laugh.

Although I didn't understand the humor, it made her eyes sparkle like the waters of Kiptara Lake. The softening in her gaze was welcome.

We settled into silence. The bus lumbered past countless city blocks that I had yet to search.

The combination of realizing how big this city was and the smallness of my seat increased my discomfort. I kept fidgeting. The longer the ride continued, the more my irritation grew. I disliked confinement, especially here, like an animal caught in a trap. The continual starting and stopping of the vehicle had my nerves on edge.

My attention snapped to Violet when her fingers tapped on my shoulder. Right away, her breath hitched, and she jerked her hand back as if I'd burned her. I hurried to my feet so that my hot skin would not affect her.

I'd need to keep better control of my emotions in this realm and take precautions against others touching me when frustrated or angry.

Exiting the bus first, I handed the driver one of the papers from my pocket for his trouble. It seemed to startle him, but he thanked me profusely as I left. The fresh air rushed into my senses, and I enjoyed the reprieve from the odorous transport.

"People don't do that here," Violet said as she moved to my side.

"Do what?"

"Tip the bus driver. Especially not with money like that."

"Money?"

Violet pointed to my pocket. "You know, *money*, bills, cash . . . there are a lot of names for it."

My eyebrows narrowed, which elicited a sigh from her.

"The paper you've been paying everyone with."

Ah, money, so that's what they called their bartering papers. I made note of that. "He didn't seem offended."

"A Benjamin—sorry, a one-hundred-dollar bill—wouldn't offend anyone. If you have money like that to throw around, why don't you have a car? Or do you have your own driver— is that what you meant before?"

"I have no personal vehicle in this realm."

It was odd how the humans placed such an importance on their system of payment—and transportation.

Suddenly, an idea struck.

"Would you help me if I paid you to do so?"

She eyed me sidelong with a look I didn't understand.

Haggling with those of a lower class was an unfamiliar custom to me, so I hoped I had enough paper in my pocket to make the deal. Then I realized that she was probably waiting to see how much I had, so she could make an informed decision. That's what I would do, and Violet seemed intelligent enough to protect herself from getting swindled.

I dug into the pocket of my satchel for a stack of papers, and held them up in plain view.

"Would this be enough?"

Her eyes widened, then a grin tugged at her cheek, suggesting we had a bargain.

5

VIOLET

"LET'S GET THIS STRAIGHT. I have the next three days off from both of my jobs. I can work for you until my next shift at The Mystic Bean, but," I held up a finger and whipped around to face Rone while I walked backward, "I won't do anything illegal. And I swear to god, if you try to grab me again, I'll knock your block off."

I balled my fist and shook it so he understood.

Rone's lips lifted in a smirk that insinuated his annoying disbelief that I might actually hurt him.

Okay . . . who was I kidding? I couldn't challenge those muscles. But kicking him in the nuts would be easy-peasy.

"I get paid the moment the job is done. Are you cool with those terms?"

The smug look vanished from his face, and his eyebrows furrowed. " 'Cool'?"

"That means three days of no stealing or any other shady stuff," I specified further. "If you cross a moral boundary that

I don't approve of, I'll tell you. Are those terms agreeable to you, My Lord?"

I stopped walking and performed an ironic curtsey that seemed to fit his out-of-touch, fancy persona.

His face lit up at the gesture, and he bowed in the middle of the street.

I made a memo-to-self never to do that again.

"I agree to your terms," Rone said as he rose. Then he lifted his hands palm-up, extended them into the space between us, and looked at me expectantly.

"Ummm."

I lifted my own hands and lowered them onto his, palm to palm. I barely had time to notice that his skin was very warm, almost hot, when Rone squeezed my hands and bounced them up and down three times.

"Our pact is sealed," he announced.

I arched an eyebrow as I reclaimed my hands. "Wonderful."

I had a job for the weekend. One that paid better than two months at my other gigs. A part of me felt a little bad about taking advantage of a foreigner who didn't understand our money, but I squashed that good samaritan and buried her deep down. A girl had to do what she had to do in desperate times.

And boy, were these desperate times.

We'd turned the corner onto the assisted living home's street when I realized that I should clue Rone in on a few things.

"So, since you're not from here—"

"Yes, Baskara is very far away," Rone interrupted me.

"Obviously," I muttered. "Anyway, you should know that the place we're about to visit is . . . different. My mom lives there, and some things you see might make you uncomfortable. If you don't want to come inside, I get it. We can meet up somewhere at a certain time."

Rone shook his head. "I wish to remain with you. Once you have accomplished your familial obligation, we can begin work right away." He patted his murse.

Oh boy, can't wait.

"Okay, stick close by me. Don't go opening doors to the rooms we pass."

Rone gave a thoughtful hum that told me I needed to keep an eye on him.

When we reached the home, I checked in with the receptionist and listed Rone as a guest. Since I was on the approved visitor list, the receptionist processed us quickly and buzzed us back.

Cracking the door open, I glanced left then right. Mom's room was at the very rear of the building. The location was nice for her, because there was less road-noise, but sucked for me, because that meant there was a huge chance that a certain someone would spot me.

I just wanted to get in, say hi to Mom so she wasn't inconsolable for the next two days, and then begin whatever ludicrous job Rone had for me. Was that too much to ask?

"Come on." I waved for him to follow.

As we made our way through the plain white hallways, we passed dozens of rooms. The doors were closed but featured large, shatter-proof windows so the staff could see inside. Those windows also ensured that we saw lots of sadness.

To live here, you had to have lost all your mental faculties. Few luxuries existed, and none in the residents' personal spaces: only a bed, a chair, and a dresser occupied the bedrooms. Some rooms were even padded for protection. And nearly all the occupants moaned, screamed, giggled, or talked to themselves as we strode by.

"Are these humans in distress?" Rone asked after passing one room in which a woman sobbed.

"A lot of them are physically fine, but mentally, yeah, they are sorta in distress. They need others to care for them, and sometimes—because they might hurt themselves—that looks a little different from what most people would expect."

I thought of Mom, who was more often than not bound to her bed. A lump rose in my throat.

"But it's for their own good," I croaked.

Rone looked like he was about to reply when the one person I'd been hoping to avoid turned the corner and pointed straight at me.

"We need to talk, Violet," Micah said, his chocolate brown eyes sparking.

The thought of running flashed through my mind, but it vanished as quickly as it came. Ditching Mom was impossible, and Micah was her primary caregiver.

"Hey, Micah," I said as nonchalantly as possible. "What's up?"

Micah crossed his arms over his muscular chest. "You

know what's up. Are you ever going to pay me? I planned on using that dough tonight."

My teeth dug into my lip. "I'm sorry, I don't have it."

I was in the wrong, but paying rent and eating had to come first.

His lips pressed together. "What happened now?"

As he spoke, he glanced over my shoulder to where Rone waited silently.

"I planned on getting what I owed you after work, but . . . stuff came up."

There was no way in hell I would tell him about the streetfight, and all Rone's crazy talk. I still thought the guy was nuts, but he'd promised to pay me a lot of money to work for him, so I needed him outside the home, not inside.

Micah rolled his eyes. I was in for it.

"Doesn't it always with you, Vi? You know I don't have a large salary either. I want to look out for you, I really do. But I need to look out for me, too."

"I understand." My cheeks burned. I hated owing anyone anything. "I'll have what I owe you next week. Promise."

Rone stepped forward and looked down at me. His eyebrows knitted together as he took in my sheepish expression.

I considered removing my mental barriers to see what was in his nutso mind but refrained. People deserved their privacy.

"Might I be of assistance?" he asked.

Micah cocked his head. "If you got money and want to pay Violet's debt, you can help."

"So this is a funding issue? Not a dough issue?"

Micah's eyes narrowed.

Of course, Micah would use the one slang word I hadn't taught Rone. I rushed to cover for my new employer's strangeness.

"He's not from here," I told Micah before turning to face Rone.

"I borrowed money to pay one of Mom's bills two weeks ago." My cheeks scalded at the admission.

"How much?" Rone held out a fistful of bills.

"Only forty." I took the wad of cash from him and extracted two twenties before handing back the rest. "It can come out of my pay for the weekend."

Rone beamed like he was Mother Teresa, eliciting a chuckle from me. He was just so . . . odd.

"Your boyfriend?" Micah asked as I handed the money over.

"A dude I met at The Mystic Bean who has odd jobs for me to do. We're going to get started right after I hang with Mom."

"He's not dangerous, right?" Micah asked, eyeing Rone with narrow eyes.

I would bet a lot of money that Micah was studying the tattoos that lined Rone's arms. Arms he had crossed tightly over his chest as he sized Micah up in return.

"Nope," I said and hoped it was true.

He seemed so under control now. Like before had been an animalistic response, and now he was back to being a gentleman.

Micah looked unsure. "Okay, I'll take your word for it. Your Mom has been asking for you for the last half an hour."

I sighed. Mom had gone off the deep end five years ago, but somehow, she always remembered my Friday visits. It didn't matter if I visited often, or not at all during the rest of the week. In her mind, Friday was our day.

"Thanks," I said before turning to Rone and gesturing for him to follow.

I inhaled deeply as we approached Mom's door, and opened it using the fob that allowed me to access her quarters at specified times.

As soon as I opened the door, tears pricked in my eyes.

"Hey, Mom," I said, trying to keep my tone calm as I took in her position.

She rocked on her bed with her eyes closed, arms wrapped around her legs. It was a way that she self-soothed, but seeing her like this always broke my heart.

Mom's eyes popped open at the sound of my voice, and she tried to hop off the bed, but the bindings around her wrists restricted her motion. Her eyes began to water, and she reached for me. After shutting the door, which automatically locked us in, I rushed to her side and loosened the bindings.

"Rone, will you press that button?" I pointed to a yellow knob on the wall that told the staff someone was with Mom and she was unrestrained. He complied while I slipped the straps off her wrists.

Not every patient needed them, but the bindings and the button were precautions the caregivers had deemed necessary after Mom had attempted to break out three times.

I didn't totally agree with them but seeing as this home

was one of the few that accepted Mom's financial assistance, allowing me to afford an apartment for myself, I wasn't in a position to argue.

Honestly, I was just happy she had a safe place to sleep, food to eat, and people who cared nearby. Emotionally, I couldn't handle being here every day, but Micah and a few others took fantastic care of Mom.

"What did you do today?" I asked as I perched on the edge of her bed.

She pointed to a box across the room that Micah put all her drawings inside. Recently, she had become obsessed with drawing, although she never drew when I was around—or let me see her masterpieces.

"You drew, huh? That's cool. How about reading? Finish any romance novels today? Or fantasy?"

Mom shook her head. She was a prodigious reader but was limited to the e-books the library could provide. Unfortunately, those were far too few.

"So, TV?"

She nodded and then, beaming, reached for the remote.

I sighed. It looked like I was in for another *Friends* rerun. I could quote at least a dozen individual episodes by now.

"You might as well get comfortable," I said to Rone, who was still standing by the door. "We're not getting out of here until I watch at least two episodes."

I pointed to the chair in the corner of the room as I snuggled next to Mom on her bed.

Rone's eyebrows furrowed, but he followed my instructions, perching on the chair on the far side of the room. His cabernet gaze latched onto Mom as if he couldn't look away. After half of the first episode, he spoke.

"I apologize, but I don't understand what I'm seeing. Is something wrong with her?"

I sighed. I shouldn't have brought him here.

"She's mentally unstable and has been since I was fourteen, although she wasn't this bad right away. When I turned sixteen, I couldn't manage her any longer and had to seek help. No one can pinpoint what's wrong, but they all agree on a few things. She can't live alone or do things most people can. There's too great a risk that she'll hurt herself."

I shot Mom a glance, expecting to see her captivated by the awkward flirting between Monica and Chandler. Instead, she was staring at Rone.

I gaped. Nothing broke the iron-clad grasp of *Friends*. Well, apparently nothing except the sound of Rone's voice.

"Mom? Are you okay?"

She raised her finger and pointed it straight at Rone.

My eyebrows knitted together. "Have you met him?"

There was no way I would believe it if she said yes, but that she acknowledged him at all was remarkable.

Rone rose. "We've never met, Madame—" he paused and turned a questioning gaze on me.

"Ayers. Sandy Ayers," I supplied.

"Madame Ayers," Rone finished smoothly.

"However, it is a pleasure to make your acquaintance now." He bowed.

For a moment, Mom stared at him, her lips opening and closing as if she wanted to speak.

Then, out of the blue, she let out a blood-curdling scream.

I leapt up, and Rone rushed toward us.

"Stay away!" I yelled, but he didn't listen.

Instead, he moved closer, and although I was trying to shield Mom from him, he rounded the opposite side of the bed and extended his hands as if to touch her.

This freaking guy.

"No!" I tried to swat his hand away. "Don't touch her. She might hit you."

I probably sounded ridiculous. Rone had gotten in a streetfight and healed from a dagger cut. Still, I didn't want Mom responsible for hitting and injuring someone. The stigma against her illness was terrible enough, she didn't need more restrictions.

But unlike most people, who wouldn't even be able to look at Mom during her *good* moments, Rone inched ever closer, as if mesmerized.

Screams kept ripping from her throat, one after the other, rebounding off the empty walls, and increasing my heart rate by the second.

Tears began to roll down my cheeks, and I wiped them away. I hated seeing Mom like this.

I was about to push Rone back and insist that he wait in the hall when he did the unthinkable.

He reached out and cupped Mom's face.

Her screaming stopped, and she lifted her hand to land on Rone's. My mouth dropped open so wide that I thought it might come unhinged.

What the actual hell?!

Then Mom spoke.

"Water is the essence of life, and fire is the essence of power. Bring them together, or all will be ash."

My hands flew to my heart as I memorized the gibberish and waited for more. It was precious—the first real sentences I'd heard her utter in months.

And as her mouth snapped shut, it seemed that was all I would get.

Realizing that Rone had pulled something out of her I couldn't, I swiveled to face him.

"What did you do?! How did you make her do that?!"

"I didn't—"

The door to the room flew open, and Micah appeared alongside three other attendants.

"Out! Both of you! Out *now*!"

"Why?" I wailed as Micah wrapped his hand around my upper arm and hauled me off Mom's bed.

"We heard Sandy screaming. You know you can't be here when she's like that, Vi. Especially not with a visitor who she doesn't know well."

"But Rone calmed her down!"

Confusion flashed across Micah's face, but he shook his head and it vanished.

"It doesn't matter. We abide by strict protocol here. Whenever a resident expresses fear, pain, or trauma, all their visitors must leave."

"Screw the rules! She *spoke*, Micah!"

"Spoke?" He sounded like he'd never said the word before.

"Yeah, like, real words."

"And they made sense?"

A pit formed in my stomach. "Well . . . kinda?"

Micah's full lips flattened into a thin line, and he maneuvered me to the door.

"Not convincing enough, Vi. Sorry, but you two need to leave."

6

RONE

TWILIGHT GRACED the skies as Violet and I walked away from her mother's home, and an image of my own mother entered my mind. The idea of anyone trapping her in a small room, alone, wrenched my heart. How could Violet allow such conditions for hers?

Though, the way she'd been so eager to accept my help once I offered to pay her debt made me wonder if she had a choice in the matter. Perhaps that was just the way the human realm treated their elders.

A shudder rolled through me, chased by an ache for Draessonia. I had power and control there. Everything made sense.

The number of times I'd been confused since meeting Violet was enough to last me the remainder of my life.

"Thank you." Violet's voice sounded small and distant in my ears.

Perplexed, I turned to her.

She'd hunched her shoulders and shoved her hands into her pockets.

"For what?" I had paid Micah, but I didn't think that's what she referred to.

"For helping to calm Mom. It usually takes drugs to bring her down when she gets riled up like that."

I had felt a connection to Sandy when I touched her. Although Violet refused to admit her supernatural ties, her mother held the same vibration that denoted magic.

"Is it common for the women of your realm to be in that state?"

Violet huffed. "No. That's part of my mom's condition. It's why she has to live there."

Her response didn't settle my mind, but it answered some questions I had about humans and their elders.

"Where do those who are well live as they age?"

"In their own homes, I suppose. Everyone does what's best for themselves."

"In my realm, we revere our elders and don't sequester them. The knowledge they possess is crucial for the following generations to thrive."

I glanced at Violet and noticed that she'd hunched even further. Clearly, her mother's illness and care were not how she'd like them to be.

"I'm glad I gave your mother some peace."

Violet nodded without looking at me.

After we walked in silence for a few more moments, she spoke again.

"What are your parents like?"

My chest filled with a warmth that spread through my middle. I missed my family and hated that I'd left them to defend the kingdom against the whisper of rebellion without my aid.

"My father is a great, benevolent leader. The cities have flourished, and peace has reigned under his rule. He is well-loved by all. My mother is strict but generous. There isn't anything she doesn't see."

A grin tugged at my mouth.

"As hatchlings, my sister and I gave her many troubles. She always handled our rambunctiousness with a steady hand and a warm heart. She cares for everyone in that manner."

I noticed the amused glance Violet sent my direction at the term 'hatchling'. I knew humans were born differently, but perhaps she wasn't as aware of my culture as I'd expected. The idea brought me back to my mission.

I shifted my bag to retrieve the shining onyx scale from the outside pocket. Before I could withdraw my enchanted locator, Violet inhaled sharply and halted. I stopped a stride later and faced her.

"Is there something wrong?"

She nodded, then pointed with her eyes to an individual approaching behind me. I spun and positioned myself between her and the well-dressed man. My hand snaked around to hold her in place behind my back. She wriggled under my palm, and I felt my lips tighten.

She'd agreed to help me find the ancient dragonbloods, and was therefore under my protection.

Though she certainly didn't seem to understand that, as she scooted from my grip to stand near my side.

"Hello there," the man said. As he grew closer, the faint scent of menthol filled my nostrils. "I'm always impressed by a man who has the self-confidence and presence to pull off carrying a bag like yours."

He had a swagger that made the back of my neck flare. The clothing he wore fit his body like a second skin. Assertiveness and otherworldly power radiated out his every pore.

Even if he had excellent taste in satchels, I didn't trust him.

"I've had many compliments on it."

I grinned when I heard Violet scoff, but kept my focus on the man. There was an air about him, as if he wished to challenge me.

Violet bumped against me, and I reached out to steady her. If she needed assistance, I hoped she could wait.

"May I see it?" The man held out his hand as if I'd allow his request.

"I'm afraid not. We have important matters to attend to, and must be going." I stepped to the right while Violet clutched my shirt and moved with me.

"*Rone,*" she poked me in the ribs as she said my name in a low, urgent tone.

The man had shifted his position so that he remained in our path.

"I don't think you understand the situation." His expression glinted with amusement.

A jerk on the strap of my bag snapped my attention to Violet. Instinctively, I let out a throaty warning that made her jerk back a bit, but she held her ground.

Then she tapped her finger on her temple. Confused, I shrugged my shoulders. Why would she distract me in such a manner? This wasn't the time for such antics. But as I turned back to the man, she grabbed the strap once more.

"Don't touch that," I hissed.

Regardless of my responsibility to her, she needed to know her place.

"I can hear him, you fool. He thinks you've arrived to disrupt the balance?" Her brows furrowed. "He wants to drink your blood—something about proving he has more power than you." She whispered just loud enough for me to hear.

Letting go of the strap, she nodded her head toward the man without breaking our gaze.

Straightening, I refocused on the man. "You wish to challenge me? That's unwise."

"We'll see about that."

In a blink, the man slammed his fist against my jaw. The force thrust me backward into Violet, and she landed on the ground with an *oof*.

Roaring, I righted myself and rushed the man, grabbing him by the throat, and hurling him through the air. I hurried back to Violet.

"Are you injured?" I crouched down at her side and tipped her chin up to make her focus. I didn't have time to waste.

"No," she squeaked. "Just scraped up, I think."

"Good. Stay back."

I hesitated for a moment but followed through with my instinct. I couldn't allow this man to risk my mission.

"Take this. Hold it safe, and guard it with your life. Do you understand?" I slipped my bag from my shoulders and shoved it in her lap.

The sound of nearing footsteps hit my ear. The man was returning.

"Answer, quickly!"

Stunned, Violet nodded.

It had to be enough.

Still in my crouch, I spun and jumped to my feet in time to meet the man in the air.

We grappled and landed on the hard earth. He was fast and strong. Nearly as strong as me. I head-butted him, and he loosened his grip on my waist. With the advantage, I punched him in the side of the head.

Dazed only for a split second, he slipped from me and jumped to his feet. I followed. While we circled each other, I never let my eyes waver from his, those dark pits of boiling rage.

With a hiss, he bared sharp, elongated teeth.

I charged, feinting left. He darted right, but only to use his own tactic, as he spun in a blurring circle, and got behind me.

I ducked fast, but not fast enough. He bit down on the back of my shoulder.

With a grunt, I clamped my lips tight. I would not give the creature the satisfaction of showing pain.

My elbow blasted into his chest at the same time I reached over my shoulder, grabbing him by the hair. I swung him through the air in front of me. Throwing all of my weight into my shoulder as I followed him to the ground, crushing his sternum.

His head lolled to the side, unconscious. The effect would only be temporary, however.

I paced back and forth, watching as his eyes fluttered open. This man belonged to an ancient supernatural race that I remembered from texts I'd studied as a hatchling, before my age of fervor—he was a vampire. Forced out of my world thousands of years before, the creatures had settled here. They were good fighters, practically indestructible, and had mental powers.

Proving my point, the vampire rose.

I rolled my shoulder, flicking the pain away as I prepared to fight again.

The vampire glowered at me. "I represent the Komisio. Your entrance into this realm reverberated among all super-naturals and you are not welcome here," he said.

Those ridiculous fangs hindered his speech so he sounded like a demented serpent.

I had no knowledge of what the Komisio was, but if I'd needed to know Virhan would have instructed me. "You won't be the one to make me leave."

I kept moving, searching for a way to tear his head off. If I was in my other form, I'd reduce him to cinders. The idea pleased me, but I wouldn't risk my flames injuring Violet.

The bloodsucker shot into the air, flipped, and tried to land behind me. But I was onto his tricks and spun in time to face him. I grabbed at him, but he blocked me. It had only been a distraction, as I snatched the back of his neck with my other hand.

His high-pitched scream echoed against the buildings as small tendrils of smoke rose where my hand met his skin. In my aggressive state, my body temperature had risen to molten levels.

I sneered. "Don't like the heat, Vamp?"

He met my gaze, and pain, sharp like a spike, pierced through my temple. My vision wavered for a heartbeat, then two. My fingers slipped from their hold. I wobbled on my feet.

Suddenly, a voice entered my thoughts. *You are not as strong as you think.*

The cretin had snuck inside my head.

I let my heat build, then flow through every pore, including my mind. The savage presence fled and his form followed suit, huddling in the shadow of a building ten paces away.

I released all control of my rage while blazing hot energy built up within me. I stalked toward the vampire, and he slid his foot backward.

A satisfaction boiled in my core. This creature would not best me. I sprinted and landed a punch to his jaw. His head snapped to the right.

Just because I should end this, didn't mean I was ready to. He'd challenged me. Threatened those important to me. He didn't deserve a quick death.

The vampire moved to race away, but not fast enough. I caught his arm and wrestled him to the ground, landing punch after punch to his midsection before he could resist.

When he finally shrieked and tried to sink his teeth into my arm, my vision flamed red, and I grabbed both sides of his head. Smoke rose from his skin as a wail emitted from his lips. Jamming my knee against his chest, I twisted his neck until it snapped.

When it was done, I leaned back and dropped my hold, letting his head smack against the pavement.

I rose to my feet and brought my temperature under control. Stretching my neck from one side to the other and rolling my shoulders, I let myself relax.

I spun, slowly scanning the area for Violet. Across the street, cowered with her back against the wall of a building where I'd left her, she stared at me with wide-eyed panic.

A spark rattled my chest as I noticed the protective way she held onto the satchel. She'd done well.

I strode over to her. All was well again. We could resume our search for the dragonbloods.

7

VIOLET

I CLUTCHED Rone's murse tight. The bag was strangely warm, but I had little time to dwell on it. At that moment, I suspected that the solid reality of the murse was the only thing keeping me from losing my shit.

Rone had killed a man.

Rone, who I'd told Micah wasn't dangerous.

Rone. The man stalking straight toward me.

My arms trembled like leaves in the wind, but as much as I wanted to sprint away, I didn't.

Obviously, I'd been wrong—Rone was lethal. Maybe one of the most dangerous men I'd ever met.

And yet, even though my nerves crackled like firecrackers, and I'd just witnessed one of the most horrific things in my life, something told me he wouldn't hurt *me*. We'd only known each other for a few hours, but a connection stretched between us—one that I kept trying to push away but couldn't.

"Are you injured?" Rone asked as he approached.

The anger that had lined his face while he'd been fighting

had vanished. Only concern remained, providing reassurance that I was right to think he wouldn't hurt me.

"I'm fine," I squeaked, rising from my crouch.

"And my bag?" he gestured to the murse.

"Safe," I assured him, although I didn't release it to him.

"That's good." Rone gestured to the right. "We should distance ourselves from the body before anyone happens across us."

I nodded, not wanting to be anywhere near the dead guy, and followed Rone. After we'd gone a few blocks, I'd calmed down a little, so I didn't shrink back when Rone turned to me and placed both hands on my shoulders.

"I realize that fight might have come as a shock to you. Judging by your physique, I doubt you've had any military training?"

He'd basically insinuated that I was a weakling, but that didn't matter. I wasn't sure why Rone was asking about military training, because I had about a million questions for him that needed answering first.

"That guy . . . he was thinking about biting you and drinking your blood. And he was so strong and fast." I bit my lip. "I've lived in shitty neighborhoods and seen plenty of street fights, but I've never seen anything like that."

"You mean like a dragon battling a vampire?"

My heart skipped a beat, and all my muscles tightened. A dragon battling a vampire?

I wanted to interrupt him, but Rone continued talking as if he hadn't said the craziest thing ever.

"To be honest, I haven't either," he shrugged.

"Vampires don't exist in my world. However, I have read of

their prowess. I suspect that one might have been the alpha of his clan. He was very powerful." His lips curled up. "But not strong enough to best a dragon."

Pride laced his tone. An undeniable ego that, as far as I could tell, was justified. Rone truly believed that he was a dragon—and crazily enough, after what I'd witnessed, I did too.

My palms became slick as adrenaline blasted through me. If dragons and vampires were real, what else was there? How much larger was the world?

And how much scarier?

"Violet? Are you okay?" Rone asked. The pride in his expression had vanished to leave furrowed brows.

"Yeah." I shook my head. "Sorry, it's just . . . you really are a dragon, aren't you? You're not just some crazy guy talking about being from a different land. This is all real. Holy shit, it's *all* real!"

I'd heard tales of vampires, and even a few about dragons. The dead guy fit the vampire stereotype. Obviously, Rone didn't look like a lizard with scales, but the stories could have gotten some details wrong. Humans didn't know everything, and in some cases, like *me*, they were totally ignorant.

Rone's eyebrows pulled so close together, he might as well have had a unibrow.

"Well, yes. Why would I make that up? Do people go about claiming false dragon lineage to garner respect?"

"What? No! No one talks about being a dragon, because they *don't exist* . . . Or at least, I thought they didn't." I gestured to him. "Why don't you have scales? Or look like a lizard?"

Rone's spine stiffened. I'd said the wrong thing, but I didn't regret it. Hell, I'd lived my whole life in ignorance. What was one dumb question when I would probably ask a million more?

"Dragons are not lizards," he said, his tone firm. "We're magical beings with both a human-like form and a dragon form. We're born as dragons—"

"Hatchlings," I breathed, recalling his earlier comment.

"Yes, and those hatchlings learn to shift into human form shortly after birth. They will continue to appear human until they reach the age of fervor around thirteen, when they make their first voluntary shift. I might choose my other aspect at any moment, but around humans, it would be inadvisable."

A nervous laugh trickled out of me as I thought about a dragon's version of puberty and the enormous beasts they became afterward.

"What else is there?"

He shook his head as if he couldn't believe that he had to explain the supernatural to me.

"In this world, there are humans learned in using magical energies known as witches. Other shifters who can take on a variety of animal forms and vampires. Those are the most common types of supernaturals. There are also some mage-bloods born with magic, fae or fae-borns, demon-touched, and dragonbloods. Although, those four races are fewer because most of their kind live in different realms."

"Holy shit."

The idea of all those creatures walking around next to me was enough to make my head explode.

I stiffened as another bout of realization washed over me.

"They're who I can hear. Aren't they?"

Rone nodded. "The man who attacked me the first time appeared to use the wind to assist him in his acrobatics. Almost certainly, he's mageblood. And the second attacker was a vampire."

I released my grip on the bag. It slid down my hip until the strap snapped taut.

"This makes so much sense! After I heard him, I felt this cold sensation come over me! Totally fits the stereotype." My chest grew tight. "They all seemed like weirdos . . . and there are so many. If I'm not careful to keep my mental barriers up, I come across at least two a week."

"A fair number, yes," Rone agreed. "I'm surprised you didn't come to that realization earlier."

Not me. I'd spent my entire life trying not to seem crazy. Gabbing about witches, vampires, shifters and a lot of other imaginary creatures would have ruined all that effort. Plus, it was tiring and freaky to hear voices. I blocked them out as often as possible.

I cocked my head. "Do you think I'm part . . . something else? And that's why I can hear them?"

Rone looked conflicted but nodded. "I knew the moment you told me you could read minds that some sort of supernatural blood ran through your veins. Perhaps while we're on our quest, we can try to figure out which species you're born of."

His eyes strayed to the bag that hung at my hip. "Speaking of the quest, we should move on."

"Oh, right." I slid the bag over my head.

Maybe it was good that I was hanging with Rone for the

weekend. I'd have plenty of time to pick his brain about this whole new world I'd discovered.

"Here you go."

He laid a gentle hand on the bag, and his eyes grew as large as saucers.

"They are growing cold."

"What does that—"

"We must get them warm!" he roared.

He grabbed me by the wrist, and we sprinted down the street once again.

8

RONE

I CARESSED the bag as we ran, and cursed beneath my breath.

The eggs had cooled. I'd wasted too much time fighting that menace.

My apartment was near the coffee shop, and I had to get to the warmers as quickly as possible.

"We need transport. How do we get it quickly?"

"To where?" Violet's voice rose.

Her emotions were still running high, which was understandable. Though, with the eggs cooling, I didn't have time to wait for her to settle herself.

"To my lodgings, near your place of employment. How do you summon the transport bus?"

"You don't. It runs on a schedule, and we need to find the right stop."

Her breathing grew heavier as we ran, but there wasn't time to waste. I wanted to carry her so that we could run faster. Although based on our other interactions, I doubted she'd allow such a thing.

"Fine. It's important for me to return to my dwelling. Point the way to this stop we need. Please."

I'd picked up on the fact that she seemed to respond better if I softened my words. I needed to remember that humans reacted differently than those at home.

"It's just up there." She pointed. "That bench."

There was no one else at the stop, which was ideal because my frustration was on display for all to see. I hated being on someone else's timeframe. Especially when the eggs were in desperate need of being warmed.

I rubbed my hand over the smooth leather of my satchel, checking each of the six eggs once again. If they became cold, they would die, and I'd have destroyed the hopes of the noble families of Draessonia. I wouldn't allow that.

"Don't worry, this is a mainline. There should be a bus in a few minutes."

I twisted toward her, slightly incredulous. "Can you listen to my thoughts like you can the others?"

Guilt washed across her face.

"Yeah. Sorry I didn't tell you that earlier. I've kept my secret for so long that divulging it doesn't come easily."

My lips parted in shock. Of course, she could. I was supernatural. The larger surprise was that I hadn't considered such a thing earlier. "All the time?"

"No, I keep my barriers in place most of the time, especially when I see someone suspicious—supernaturals, I guess. I've just listened enough to understand that your intentions with me don't seem violent or creepy. Most of the time, I try not to listen, but sometimes supernaturals show up

60

before I'm aware they're around, and I hear them." She darted a glance at me as if unsure if she should continue.

"Is there something else?"

"I'm comfortable around you for some reason. That's definitely not like me. I barely know you, and most of the time, I stay the hell away from strangers."

I nodded, lowering myself to sit on the bench next to Violet. Her admission soothed me more than I expected.

"What's in that bag? It seemed like rocks, but it's not as heavy as it should be if that's the case. I heard you say eggs, but that can't be, right? They would have cracked, with everything we've been through."

"I'll show you when we are safely inside. I can't risk exposing them out in the open, where there are so many dangers."

Her presence comforted me. The thought shocked me, and I quickly shoved it aside.

This was a mission, and it was already in danger. I reminded myself of the discipline drilled into me from my years in the military.

I darted a glance at Violet, catching her staring at me, too. She had a slight curve to her lips, and her cheeks pinked as she snapped her attention away.

Energy surged through my body, urging me to scoot slightly closer so our knees touched. Violet had proven herself to be determined and strong of mind, yet the impulse to protect her flooded through me. My gaze strayed to her slender fingers as she tucked a wisp of hair away from her face.

I jerked my eyes forward, inhaling slowly to calm my increasing pulse.

Training. Mission. Duty. Keep perspective, and stay focused.

———⊥—

THANKFULLY, the bus arrived promptly, and we exited on the corner nearest to my building. I escorted Violet through the lobby and up the elevator to the top floor. She kept glancing around, fidgeting with her hands.

Perhaps she was in need of sustenance, as I was. The sandwich I'd had earlier was not enough to make up for the energy the last fight had cost me.

"I don't have food stores," I told her apologetically. "However, after all is settled, we can arrange for an evening meal."

"I'm not hungry, actually." She gazed at a piece of artwork on the elevator wall. "This is a fancy building. How do you afford all these nice things? Are you, like, some eccentric billionaire in your world or something?"

I didn't understand what she meant. "My mentor provided me with the means to function in this realm as befitting my station, if that's what you're talking about."

"Yeah . . . your station. Well, whatever that means, just *functioning* isn't the way I'd put all this." She waved her hands as if to encompass all the building.

I furrowed my brow and considered her words. Perhaps Virhan had provided me with more than the average human.

I exited the elevator, and Violet followed behind. She

murmured a few more comments about the decor of the hall-way, but I was too eager to get to the warmers to listen.

As we approached my apartment, I noticed the latch was bent at an odd angle, and the door wasn't closed all the way.

A flash of heat blasted through me as I held out my arm to stop Violet.

"Stay behind me."

I slid closer to the door and slowly pushed it open. The place was dark, but I didn't risk turning on the lights. I sniffed, noting that the lingering scent of sage hung in the air. Holding my breath, I cocked my head to listen. Someone had entered my lodgings, yet there weren't any sounds of intruders.

Crouching down as a precaution, I crept inside and hugged the nearest wall. Prepared to jump anyone who might be hiding, I slapped at the switch on the wall, finally bringing light to the room.

"*NO!*" The scream erupted from me.

Scattered around the room were pieces of the warming devices. Broken shards of glass covered the floor. Someone had twisted the metal frames of each bed out of their rectangular shapes, the heating lamps smashed. They'd destroyed everything.

I tried to right the first box and set it back on the stand where it should rest. But the legs had broken, and it fell again. Glass cut my palms, but I didn't care.

"Stop, you're hurting yourself!" Violet called to me.

I ignored her warning as I frantically tried to restore the pieces of the devices that kept the hatchlings alive.

"You don't understand. These are vital. They'll die without them."

As hard as I tried to reshape the metal, I couldn't. Whoever had done this must have used a weapon to smash the boxes. They had even cut the cords, and a fishy smell emanated from the singed wires.

I roared and threw one of the dismantled wooden legs from a broken stand, impaling the wall. The bag weighed heavy at my side.

I'd let my kingdom down.

"You're scaring me."

I spun to face Violet. "You don't understand what this means. I've failed, and now they'll all die. How can I ever return home and face the others?"

"Who will die? What was all this stuff?"

A terrible thought occurred to me, and my fists clenched. "Tell me you had nothing to do with this—that all the traipsing around today wasn't to distract me. Twice I've needed to fend off attackers since you've been in my presence."

I moved closer to her.

She scrambled back toward the open doorway and threw her open palms into the air in front of her.

"Listen, back off. I came here with you willingly, and if I'd had anything to do with this, I'd have ditched your ass before we ever got back on the bus. I even kept that stupid murse safe. So you tell *me* what's going on!"

I clamped my mouth so hard, my squeaking teeth echoed in my head. My chest heaved, and my thoughts grew muddled. Heat rose through me, but I battled it back.

It wasn't logical that she would have come with me if she were involved. And she had helped me get here more quickly than I could have on foot. I was wrong for accusing her, but my fury and worry prevented me from saying so.

"These need repairing," I said instead, gesturing to the mess with one hand. With the other, I clutched the satchel, hoping that at least my heightened warmth would help the hatchlings.

"What are they?"

"They *were* warmers. Necessary devices to keep the eggs at an optimal temperature for their safety. I can only carry them for a few hours, and then they require more heat."

"The eggs in your bag?"

"Yes. Now help me repair the devices. Quickly!"

9

VIOLET

RONE SCRAMBLED to fix the warmers, but I allowed my gaze to travel the room. It was plush in a way I had never personally experienced. And Rone had called it a dwelling. Basically, a cottage in the woods. I sniggered at my own joke.

Rone whipped around to face me. "Why aren't you helping? Are you not my assistant?"

He had a good point, so I dropped to my knees and began trying to piece together the bits of metal, wiring, and knobs strewn about the ground.

I had never used a warmer for anything in my life, let alone fixed one. I had only a vague idea of what it would look like, and imagined it holding a reptile with a heating lamp above.

Although, judging by the pieces, it had probably been fancier than the vision in my head.

While I wasn't entirely sure what I was doing, at the very least, I had repaired things in the trailer I once shared with

Mom. Repairmen were expensive and not a luxury we could ever have afforded.

I noticed that while my skills were limited, they seemed advanced compared to Rone's.

That didn't shock me. The guy didn't even know what a bus stop was; the idea that he had ever fixed anything was almost laughable.

Still, after a few minutes, it became clear that we were the blind leading the blind. With every passing second, Rone's anger seemed to grow, and I doubted we would get the warmers fixed as quickly as he wanted.

I lifted my gaze and scanned the room for something to improvise with. There were thick, knitted blankets strewn over the couch, a high-tech thermostat on the far wall, and a jetted tub in the bathroom right off the living space. All things that provided heat, and yet Rone hadn't mentioned them.

"What about the hot tub?" I asked.

He twisted his head to look at me. "The what?"

The realization struck that he didn't know that there were heating alternatives in his apartment. I stopped rummaging among the rubble.

"How about we find a temporary solution until we can get this fixed?"

"Temporary solution?" Rone's eyes grew large. "Only if it is precise. Mage Virhan told me the eggs must remain at two hundred degrees Fahrenheit, minimum, for four hours. Once they've had that stream of energy embedded into their shell, I can pull them out of the warmers for up to four hours, but after that, the hatchlings are at risk."

The mention of such an exact temperature gave me another idea. I darted into the kitchen to find a high-end double oven in all its chrome and black glory.

I shook my head. He had no idea what *anything* was.

"You have a double oven," I said as I re-entered the living room. "If the eggs can fit in your murse, they can all fit inside two ovens."

Rone's eyebrows furrowed at the word 'oven,' and I let out an exasperated huff.

"How the hell do they cook their food in Dragonville?" I asked, blanking on the name of his country.

"Draessonia," he corrected. "And we cook by fire, of course. The best cooks in all of my world live in Baskara. They use dragon fire to cook exquisite dishes. My favorite dish is salted and bathed in our fires for days on end until a perfect crust forms on the meat." His nostrils flared as if he were smelling the meat at that very moment.

I arched an eyebrow. "While that sounds wonderful, don't you have eggs to be warming?"

Rone's eyes widened and his spine straightened as if he'd surprised himself by going off on a tangent.

"Show me this oven."

I brushed aside his commanding tone. Once he was less freaked out, we'd have a word about how to address others. I might be his assistant for the weekend, but I did not appreciate being talked to like a servant.

I punched numbers into the oven's control panel, and it started preheating. "It should be up to the correct temperature in a couple of minutes. And it can get even hotter than two hundred degrees if you like."

"How hot?"

"Probably around five hundred degrees. That's how high a lot of them get."

The one in my crappy apartment didn't go past four hundred, but a place like this wouldn't have those limitations.

"Set it at three hundred, then. They've grown too cold. We need to warm them quickly."

I upped the temperature.

"Okay, we can put them inside now. They'll warm more gradually that way, which might be nice for the . . . hatchlings." The last word tripped off my tongue, unfamiliar.

Rone moved to open the bag. Then suddenly, he stopped and glanced back up at me, suspicion clear in his gaze.

I rolled my eyes.

"You're not about to go down that 'you might be the enemy' path, again, are you?" I gestured to the oven. "Would I have mentioned this thing if I was your enemy?"

He didn't comment, only opened the bag, and exposed the eggs.

As soon as I laid eyes on them, I gasped. Six round eggs, each about the size of a small cantaloupe, were nestled in his bag. They were all a shade of emerald, but with variations of gold or silver specks, dots, and lines on the shell. Strangely, they looked as though they would be scaly to the touch. They were the most beautiful things I'd ever seen.

"Why do they all look different?" I asked, my fingers itching to caress one.

Rone lifted his gaze from the bag. He looked as dazed as I felt. Apparently, the eggs influenced him, too.

"Each one of these represents a child from a noble house

of Draessonia. Many of the houses produce a particular color dragon, depending on the mother's bloodline. Although, admittedly, sometimes there are unforeseen variations in color at birth. The eggs look different too and the patterns are usually passed down as well through families." He paused. "I assume children from different families here appear different when they're born?"

Well, when he put it that way, I felt a little dumb for asking.

"Can you tell which is which?"

I pointed to one that was bright emerald and gold-speckled in a way that reminded me of someone flicking a drenched paintbrush at the shell. It was my favorite out of the bunch.

"Is this one from the highest house? Here, a lot of gold would mean it's the most important."

Rone's lips turned up in a small smile.

"Each of the six noble families under the crown is equally prestigious. They all have different strengths that they bring to Draessonia."

He examined the egg I had pointed at.

"And yes, I can identify them. That is the egg from House Zimurra—my mother's ancestral house."

"Interesting," I said, trying to take everything in. "Well, let's get these babies in the oven."

As if he was handling precious china, Rone lifted a light emerald egg with dots of gold resembling thumbprints.

I mimicked his care, and as soon as the shell of the first egg brushed my skin, I sucked in a breath. Rone had said they were cold, but beneath my touch, they were warm—and getting hotter. Not only that, but something inside the egg had lit up. I squinted, trying to figure out what was happening, but Rone broke my concentration.

"Violet," he whispered, "if there was any doubt you were supernatural before, now I am certain that you carry magic within you."

"Because they're lighting up?"

Rone nodded, and I noticed the eggs had lit up beneath his touch, too. The effect was even brighter than when I cradled them, which I supposed made sense. He was a dragon, after all.

"Huh." The light beneath the shell seemed to follow where I placed my fingers, reminding me of those bulbs that buzzed with tendrils of electricity in science museums.

Feeling like I'd just bonded with the egg, I brought it close to my lips.

"Nice to meet you too, little guy. I hear you're cold? How does a nice hot oven sound?"

I opened the door and placed the egg inside. When I turned back around, Rone was looking at me curiously—like he didn't quite understand what he'd seen.

Join the club, man.

In just a few hours, my entire worldview had been smashed to pieces and reassembled with a lot of missing parts. The two biggest being how I fit into this new world, and what *exactly* Rone was doing here.

10

RONE

IT WAS rare that hatchlings responded to the touch of other supernaturals. I'd only seen it happen with mages before. Perhaps Violet was mageblood? I'd been taught that mages had sought asylum in the human realm when the tide of war turned against their kind. If so, I'd need to assure her that I held no grudges from that horrible time.

I rubbed my hand on the back of my neck. "Thank you for helping me with this."

I hoped she'd recognize my sincere gratitude. I'd been abrupt when I saw the destroyed warmers. Fear of failing my mission had taken over, and she didn't deserve my wrath. Placing my royalty aside, I owed her respect.

"No problem. It's a pretty standard piece of human equipment. I've been using one since I was five."

Violet didn't look at me as she spoke. Her attention seemed transfixed on the eggs. She stroked each one as they came to rest against the metal slats inside the oven.

I could feel the heat emanating from the device, and my nerves settled.

"Virhan instructed me on key points of how this realm works, but he was unable to tell me everything about it." A churning stirred in my gut. It was an unfamiliar sensation to admit a weakness to one in my service.

Violet shut the oven door gently and pushed another button, which made a light shine inside. The illumination allowed us to watch the eggs through the glass. My heart rate, which had been far too rapid, slowed a bit. It was comforting to observe the eggs as they warmed.

"How long will this temperature last? When will the heat need replenishing?"

Violet chuckled quietly.

"It stays at the temperature you set it. See how it says three hundred degrees right here?" She pointed to the white numbers above the door she'd closed.

I nodded.

"That means it will stay at that same heat level until you turn it off. You said the eggs needed to heat quickly. The oven will stay high, but would it be better to turn it down to two hundred degrees after a few minutes?"

My chest squeezed a little. The way she seemed genuinely concerned for the hatchlings touched me. "Once they're warm enough, the lower temperature would be best."

I reached for the handle to see how the eggs felt, and Violet grabbed my arm. "Don't open it. That makes the heat come out, and then the temperature inside will fluctuate."

"How will I check if it's working?" I trusted her knowledge

of this world, but for my sake, I wanted to verify the device was doing what I required.

Violet sighed.

"Fine. We can't open it too often, though. Check, then shut the door again quickly so they stay warm."

My mouth twisted into a half-grin. The lines etched across her brow gave her a sweet appearance. "I assure you, I'm aware of how to take care of the hatchlings."

I mentally shook myself back to the job at hand. Opening the door enough to snake my arm inside, I reached for the closest egg.

"Be careful! You'll burn yourself." Violet reached out to stop me, her eyes wide with panic.

"I'm impervious to burns."

She'd accepted the truth of who I was. Did she not understand what my kind was truly like? Virhan had assured me that humanity revered dragons. Though he'd also told me that I'd find dragonbloods easily, and yet, I hadn't found a single one.

When my hand rested on the nearest egg, the one from House Solaris, I could feel that some warmth had returned. But it wasn't enough to warrant a lower temperature from the device.

"Leave it at this level for a while longer. They are doing better already." I closed the door and turned to face her.

Violet's eyes raked over me as if she was in deep thought. After a few prolonged seconds, she sighed.

"You're a dragon—as weird as that is, I believe you. But don't think I'll go around asking people if they've met any dragonbloods. There's too much risk in that. I'm already sure

I'll end up like my mom, and talking about dragons and another realm would just ensure that she and I get adjoining rooms at the home."

"Your mother is not insane." My words came quickly because I believed it. "Confused, yes. If I had more time with her, perhaps I could help calm her mind. I'm positive she, too, is supernatural. It's disheartening to think of her in that condition simply because her abilities are untrained."

Violet's gaze turned watery, and I frowned. Had I upset her? Human emotions were confusing, but I wanted to clear the slight. If I could figure out what it was.

"I didn't mean to offend. Just to clarify, because her situation doesn't settle your fate."

She spun away from me and swatted at her tears. "It's a lot to take in. I'm fine."

I saw the way her back rose and fell, showing she was collecting herself, so I waited. When she turned back to me, her expression was clear and resolute.

"Tell me more about your mission. Why do you need my help, and how does it connect to your world? I want to know as much as you're willing to tell me."

"One moment."

Explaining my mission to her would take a while, and I didn't want to leave the eggs until I was confident they were at the correct temperature. There were two stools on the other side of the counter, so I fetched them. I wanted Violet to remain calm and comfortable as I spoke.

Her lips tugged upward, but she rolled her eyes as I brought in the seats, indicating the return of her spunk.

"Heaven forbid we sit in the other room on the comfortable couch, huh?"

"This will allow us to monitor the eggs."

I hoped hearing how crucial her help would be to my realm would bolster her bond further with the hatchlings and my quest.

"So, lay it on me. Why are you carrying a satchel full of dragon eggs?"

I smirked at her sassy attitude.

"Draessonia differs from the human realm. The part where I live is ruled by our monarch, King Endri. Long ago, the mages ruled, and there was a civil war. During the conflict, the tide turned against the dragons. Many fled the lands, ending up here—"

She leaned forward slightly. "Like, they used to fly around here and stuff?" Her face sparkled with interest.

I enjoyed the way she listened so eagerly, so I had to smile despite the interruption.

"I'm unaware of their behavior upon arrival. However, to hide from those in our realm, the refugees most likely maintained their human forms. Eventually, they assimilated into the culture, blending their blood with those of the humans. Truth be told, it's shocking to me that so much of this information is new to you. It's as if you haven't learned even the basics of my lands. Are dragons not studied in your schools?"

Violet leaned back, and a thoughtful expression crossed her face. "Nowadays, people consider dragons to be mythological creatures that never really existed. Whoever told you differently must not have been here in a while."

I absorbed the information. It was possible that Virhan

may have possessed old intelligence on human culture. That would also explain why I hadn't yet succeeded in locating dragonbloods.

It made it even more essential that Violet understood and connected with my quest. I hoped it would make it easier for her to locate those with the ancient blood.

"Perhaps. I shall have to ask Mage Virhan when he last ventured here," I conceded. "No matter his personal history, the tale of my land is the same. Later, the tides of war in Draessonia turned again, and my ancestors were victorious. The mages were subdued, and peace settled over our lands. The first king of Draessonia was a black dragon of House Ignatius, also known as, the Aukera. There is only one born in each generation blessed by the ancient departed souls. My father is the fourth of my line to rule since, although he is not the Aukera."

"Wait, so that means you're a *prince*?"

Violet jumped from her stool and stared at me with her mouth agape. She remained like that for so long, I worried that I'd irreversibly shocked her. I was about to check on her vitals, when she started giggling uncontrollably.

"Oh my god, a freaking prince. That makes . . . *so much* sense."

My eyebrows pulled together. "I fail to see the humor."

Violet waved her hand as she shook her head.

"No, it's not so much that it's funny." Her giggles slowed as she settled herself by inhaling deeply. "It's par for my life. I've always believed I was a nutcase headed for a ride on the crazy train. Now, in one afternoon, I learn that supernaturals exist, I can hear them because I'm one of them, and to top it off, I get a job with the prince of a different realm. Nothing in my life has ever been normal."

I stared at her and slowly curled my lips into a smile. She had a glow about her that hadn't been there earlier in the day. It lifted my spirits.

"I've never had to tell anyone my title before. It didn't occur to me that I needed to, because everyone knows me by sight in my world. What is so new to you is common to me— that's shocking to both of us, I suppose."

I needed to remember that Violet would be as confused by my world as I was with hers if the tables were reversed.

"No wonder you got all smug when I curtsied to you earlier. I did that in sarcasm, by the way. Don't expect me to do it again."

Leaning closer, I met her gaze.

"I understood what it was—didn't mean I didn't like it, though." I grinned when her cheeks tinged pink and she diverted her gaze to the oven.

"So, nothing you've told me explains why a prince would be in the human realm, carrying a murse full of his cousins. What's the deal with bringing these little guys with you?"

She flicked her finger toward the eggs.

The gesture reminded me to check the temperature again. This time, Violet said nothing as I stuck my hand into the heated box and rested it against an egg.

"They're warm enough now. How do you adjust the heat level?"

She showed me the correct order of buttons to push. Then how to start over when my larger fingers struggled to only touch one at a time.

"Now, Your Supreme Highness who can control an oven, won't you please continue telling me why you're here?"

I sighed and closed my eyes to hide the fact that I enjoyed her playful disrespect. My reaction evoked a cascade of giggles from my companion. I did my best not to show that I liked the sound.

Once she calmed down, I cleared my throat.

"Recently," I arched a brow to make sure she was ready to listen to my explanation, "there has been unrest in the kingdom. A group of mages called the Maisu claim to have accessed the ancient magic of their race, even though the treaty signed at the end of the war forbids its use. Their claims can't be true, since a library, hidden and locked since the end of the war, holds all the texts. The group seemed insignificant at first, but they've gained followers, and their attacks had grown larger before I left. The threat of a coup was a true concern. This quest is essential to ensure that all the dragon lines continue."

"The mages of your world are stronger than dragons?"

"Not physically, but with magic on their side, they are great competitors. It's obvious the rebels have gained some access to the old magic, which means their threat is serious. Ancient magic is dangerous. Its use caused the first war."

"Did they find the secret library or something? I mean, if they have access to dangerous magic, they would have used it before now, right? Or maybe that library doesn't have all the books, and they found another text somewhere?"

Violet hopped off her stool and was practically bouncing on the balls of her feet. I stared dumbfounded at the number of questions she'd asked in short order.

When I'd regained my composure, I set about answering.

"The books were inventoried, and none are missing." I reached out and took a gentle hold on her arm, guiding her back to her seat. "A mysterious leader controls the Maisu, though none have seen his face. He goes by The Emissary. He has gained many followers, and what's more than that, I fear they have an influence in this realm."

"What? How?"

"The symbol on that dagger you warned me about earlier today. It's called the opes and is an ancient mage symbol, only found on the old texts. Only one who has seen the books should know of it. The Maisu have adopted it to represent their fight. They use it on all their weapons, which they infuse with spells and magic. If the one from today had been one of theirs, we wouldn't be having this conversation."

"If they're here, I should be able to hear them, right?" She stood up again as she awaited my answer.

"I suppose that's true." I didn't understand her point, but I could see she had a plan.

"I think I know where we need to be. Let's go!"

There was no way I'd let her get near enough to a mage to hear his thoughts. We needed to take some time to form a plan that would ensure her safety and that of the hatchlings.

"I'm not leaving the eggs," I told her. "We'll stay here until they've warmed enough to carry with us."

Violet skirted around me and walked out to the other room, where large windows lined the outer wall. She scanned the sky and turned back my direction.

"You told me they needed to warm for several hours. We have two hours until it's fully dark outside. If they're able to come by then, great, but if not, we should leave them behind so they stay safe—which is probably better, anyway. I doubt that whoever did all this plans to come back. When we leave, we can notify the security guard downstairs to be extra careful who he lets in."

I frowned. It was as if she didn't care to listen. Why couldn't I have found an assistant who respected my authority?

"I'm not leaving them. And if you hear the mages, you will likely already be in danger. I don't like the idea of you putting yourself in harm's way."

"You hired me to help you find dragonbloods, right?"

I nodded, leery of where she was going with her argument.

"You *do* want to continue your quest, don't you?"

I didn't like her tactics, but she was correct.

"Fine, we'll follow your plan." A sparkle from the light hitting a shard of broken glass drew my attention.

"Besides, that will give us two hours to clean up this mess." I rubbed my hands together, ready to restore order, knowing the eggs had a safe place to rest.

Violet groaned, but shuffled closer. "Where do you keep your trash bags?"

11

VIOLET

I GAZED out the bus window, happy to no longer be cleaning —one of my least favorite things to do.

A shudder rolled through me at the memory of how disturbingly pleased Rone had been to tidy up the apartment. While we'd been picking up, he'd actually reminisced *happily* about the time he'd polished his military buttons to such a shine that it rivaled that of his dragon scales.

Forget thinking being a dragon shifter was weird. Who in their right mind *enjoyed* cleaning?

Fortunately, polishing buttons wasn't all he had talked about. I learned quite a bit more about his world, too. He'd even shown me the black dragon scale that had been doubly enchanted to help him find dragonbloods and contact High Mage Virhan back in Draessonia. The flake of skin from the dragon prince, marking him as the specially blessed Aukera, was about the size of my hand and in the shape of a guitar pick.

As impressive and unique as the object was, it was also,

apparently, defunct. Rone claimed that the scale had worked perfectly when he and Mage Virhan had tested it as a communication device in Draessonia. Unfortunately, since arriving in my world, it had been nonfunctional in the two instances he'd tried to reach his mentor.

While I thought it sounded like a bad omen that the scale was failing to find dragonbloods *and* reach Virhan, Rone was optimistic. He believed it was just a matter of time until it operated as it should.

I shook my head and twisted a little to peek at Rone. He sat next to me on the bus, lightly caressing the murse in his lap that held the dragon eggs.

It was so hard to believe. Besides his eyes, which were unique and often seemed to burn with flame, Rone looked like other muscle-bound hot guys in magazines. Nothing about him screamed magical.

"Have you been to one of these parties?" Rone asked when he caught me staring. "When they contact the other realm?"

"Nope. Most of the time I avoid parties like the plague. *Especially* ones where people claim to do weird stuff like contact other realms."

"Because you don't want to read so many minds?" His brow furrowed as he tried to work out my logic. "Even though you didn't believe in the supernatural, you thought it possible that you might hear them?"

"Not that, exactly . . ." I said, trying to put my old beliefs about my ability into words. "I didn't really know the specifics of what or who I heard, just that they were all weird people. Llewellyn is my friend and all, but her other friends are super strange. I guess I was worried that they'd figure out what I could do and I'd lose control over my life. ”

"Your friend is the one with the hair like a grandmother?"

"That's her." I snorted out a laugh. 'Hair like a grandmother' was not how she described the latest trend, but it fit.

"I believe I have seen one of her friends coming to the coffee shop. I must agree with you, he looked rather odd. A male with a shock of bright blue hair."

"Oh, you spotted Ganon. He's a total tool."

"Tool?"

I kept slipping on that. Rone wasn't from a different country where it was possible that he might've heard American slang on television. He hailed from a different freaking world. My patience would have to grow if we were going to hang out together for the next few days.

"A dummy, or someone you don't want to be around because they're fake. They're—"

I searched for another term to describe Ganon's douchebaggery.

"Foolhardy," Rone supplied.

"That about sums it up."

The bus began to slow.

I glanced outside. "We're here!"

The bus dropped us off at the stop closest to the address Llewellyn had given me, which was still a fair walk away. The home was in the outer reaches of the suburbs, where the houses were spaced far apart. Some homes even had little patches of woods or fields between them that a farmer had probably refused to sell.

Rone's long strides allowed him to travel fast, which

meant I was practically jogging to keep up. After four stupidly long blocks, a wave of exhaustion rolled over me.

I hoped the party had food. I hadn't eaten since lunch, and at this point, I'd even take vegan fake cheese.

After about ten minutes of traipsing down dark streets, the sounds of a party met my ears. I began searching the homes that we passed for the correct address. When we came across it, I wasn't surprised at all.

The home, which Ganon had inherited, was rundown and old, but in its day, I was sure it had been magnificent. The Victorian structure boasted turrets and a full wraparound front porch. Three stories climbed skyward, and mature trees dotted the lawn. I knew from Llewellyn that five twenty-somethings trying to make it in the occult circles around Portland lived in this home, and yet, no lights burned inside.

However, I did hear music featuring a banjo and drums blaring alongside voices that came from around the back. Following the sounds we opened the side gate and strode into the backyard.

As soon as we were around the house, my breath hitched. Ganon didn't have a backyard, he had *property*—and a lot more of it than I'd expected. At least four normal city lots had been squished together, and abutted a patch of woods behind the house.

"There's a lot of land back here," I said, impressed.

"Land?" Rone narrowed his eyes. "Are personal lots normally smaller than this?"

All the homes that Mom and I had lived in had dinky yards. And in my current neighborhood, people could reach out their window and touch a neighbor's home.

"Way smaller," I confirmed and tilted my head to listen. "It seems like they're actually in the woods. Come on, let's go find them."

Finding the party was easy because they were so loud. They'd been smart to host the shindig in the woods rather than the backyard. I was sure that the neighbors would have complained otherwise.

Lights burned brighter, and the familiar hum of a generator hit my ear. Soon enough, we were walking into a massive clearing. Tiny, twinkling lights draped from tree to tree, and tables of food and drink littered the open space. Tents stood everywhere, indicating that many people intended to make a night of the party.

"Holy crap."

I made sure my mental barriers were in place. There had to be fifty people at the party—about forty-eight more than I was accustomed to being around.

Briefly, I considered grabbing Rone and sprinting out of there.

"Oh my divine Goddess! It's Violet!" A familiar voice yelled over the din of people chatting, singing, and chanting.

I pivoted to find Llewellyn striding through a group of people sporting elaborate animal masks and heading straight for me. She wore a long, black velvet dress, and at least a dozen crystal necklaces hung from around her neck. A flower crown perched atop her silver tresses, and her smile stretched wide. She was totally in her element.

"Your friend is a witch?" Rone asked, skepticism rife in his tone.

"She identifies as one, yes."

"Hmm. We have no witches in my realm, but the mages are not so . . . flamboyant."

I turned to face him.

"Listen. I get that you're not from here, but how about you forget about the other realm for a bit? In fact, why don't you let me do the talking? From what I've seen so far, your conversational skills aren't what people around here are used to."

Rone looked affronted. "Where I'm from, I'm quite the celebrated speaker."

"Yeah, I bet, but we don't need any speeches, we need information. Trust me. Let me take the lead."

He was about to retort, when Llewellyn wrapped her arms around me.

"It's a miracle! Is there a new moon in Scorpio that I missed?"

"Errr," I bumbled, already thrown off.

I hated when Llewellyn spoke in New Age code.

"It lures people out of their comfort zone," my friend said. "Which obviously describes you."

Her eyes shifted to Rone, and she curtsied. "Or maybe this hunk is to blame? I'm Llewellyn, mistress of these woods."

Rone smiled wide at her curtsey, and I imagined him thinking that finally someone knew who they were dealing with.

"This is Rone," I said, not wanting him to start spewing off about being a prince or, even worse, a dragon.

"Rone. What an appealing name. Are you two together?"

My cheeks heated. Llewellyn *would* just come out and ask that so bluntly. This was the same girl who told me about all the freaky-deaky things she and Ganon did, even though I begged her not to.

"He's a . . . friend," I said, catching myself before I could tell her that Rone had hired me for the weekend. She'd never let that one go.

"Hmmm, too bad. I've seen you in the coffee shop but, it's nice to meet you for reals, Rone. Now, come on, you two. Let's grab you a beer or something to loosen you up. The first circle starts in a few minutes, and you don't want to be all stiff when you take part. It would hinder the magical energies that Ganon worked so hard to cultivate in his clearing."

Oh good grief. I should have known I wouldn't be able to show up at the party and just ask a few questions. Now that I was here, Llewellyn would make sure I joined in on the fun.

Rone and I followed her to a table, beneath which were four coolers that my friend opened. "Beer? Wine? Canned cocktail? Shots? Pick your poison."

My eyes popped open at all the booze. No wonder people were planning on sleeping here. Judging by all the crazy dancing, the elaborate masks, and traipsing through the trees, a lot of them had already been indulging for a while.

I was glad they weren't considering driving home. A drunk driver had killed my dad, and I hated when people drove irresponsibly.

"Rone? What do you want?"

Rone shot me a glance. He was honoring my request that he not speak, although personally, I thought he was taking it a touch far.

"A beer?" I pressed.

"What do they taste like?"

Good grief. I should have chosen a drink for him.

Llewellyn, understandably, appeared shocked that a man in his mid-twenties had never had a beer, but rolled with it. She explained the taste, and at Rone's request, detailed all the other types of booze. After five minutes of Q&A, Rone chose —of all things—a peach wine cooler.

I asked for a shot of vodka, because I could already tell this party was going to be a shit-show.

Llewellyn showed us around and introduced us to people. After about the fifth person, she ditched us, which suited my needs. I'd rather she not know that I was interrogating people about other realms. She'd think I was taking too much interest, and never let me hear the end of it at work.

Plus, Rone was antsy about being introduced to so many people. I didn't know why, but I suspected that he wasn't as social as he claimed. Either that, or the wine cooler was affecting his body chemistry in a weird way.

We ended up talking to Jadis, a witch who Llewellyn proclaimed would help Ganon lead the circle that would shatter the wall between the realms. Judging by her long, black robe and the dark crown atop her head, Jadis took her role as circle leader seriously.

Almost as seriously as she took staring at Rone.

"So, you're going to try to contact a different realm? Any one in particular?" I asked, hoping to keep her attention off the dragon prince and on the conversation for more than five seconds.

Maybe she'd even mention Draessonia. Even though Rone had given me a crash course while we cleaned his apartment, I still had so many questions.

My tactic seemed to work, as Jadis threw her shoulders back as if she were about to give an important speech and focused on me again.

"Ganon and I believe that the veil has thinned between our world and Faerie. So we'll try to reach them tonight. Of course, if our powers penetrate the aether further, and we reach another world, we'll happily talk to them."

Rone had mentioned that fae existed. I supposed it would make sense that they lived in Faerie.

"How will you know if you're ... umm ... Going too far?"

"To reach Faerie?"

I nodded.

Jadis closed her eyes and drew in a slow, elongated breath. "Have you ever tasted magic in the air?"

I blinked. "Umm, no."

"Well, then my description of how Ganon and I will determine when the circle should halt will not make much sense to you. All I can say is that we will *feel* it in our bones. It's almost as if you become weightless and the most grounded being in the world simultaneously."

Behind me, Rone snorted.

As much as I wanted him to keep looking pretty and staying quiet, I agreed with that snort. Jadis' methods sounded like a load of hooey.

"I guess I'll have to see for myself."

"Oh, but if you're not indoctrinated in the ways of magic, you won't see what the rest of us will. Although, if you're naturally magically inclined, you might sense it a *little*." Jadis peered at me through narrowed eyes. "Unfortunately, I'm not getting that vibe from you. Let's hope that this is one of the rare instances in which I'm wrong."

She looked at me as though my non-magical existence was the saddest thing in the world.

If only she knew about my capabilities. Or that Rone shifted into a freaking dragon. She wouldn't be giving me any pitying looks then. But whatever, I was content to let Jadis keep acting all high and mighty as long as we made progress tonight. A new question was on the tip of my tongue, when Rone broke his silence.

"Actually, if someone is physically attached to a person who opens a portal between worlds, they'd be able to peer into that realm no matter how familiar they are with magic."

I nearly groaned. Oh boy, here we go.

Jadis' spine straightened, and her expression morphed from one of benign pity for me to intense interest in Rone. "I sensed that you knew more than you let on. You're familiar with peeking beyond the veil?"

"I am experienced with stepping through portals," Rone corrected her.

Jadis' face lit up.

"Would you like to help lead the circle, then?" she asked. "We could use someone of your expertise. None of us have gotten to . . . that level yet, and we could use a formidable, *strong* leader."

Her gaze landed on Rone's huge biceps, and I could practically see the saliva beginning to form in her mouth. "Did you bring supplies to assist in our magical endeavors?"

Rone placed a hand over the bag and scowled, as if Jadis

had asked him to hand it over. "I'm no mage," he spat, and then walked away.

"Hey! Where are you going?" I called, baffled by his actions.

"To get another bottle of this delicious nectar," Rone replied, and held the now-empty wine cooler bottle over his head. "I'm going to need it."

I watched him stomp across the clearing. A few people tried to engage him, mostly women who were attempting to flirt, but Rone brushed them off. Obviously, he was not enjoying the party.

While I wasn't having a blast either, I realized this was our best chance at getting information.

"Something I said has offended your friend," Jadis remarked. She licked her lips as her eyes honed in on the dragon prince's broad back.

My lips tightened, not liking her attention on him, but I tried to play it cool. I shrugged. "He's prickly. And between you and me, he can't hold his alcohol very well."

That brought a smile to her face, and I resumed my careful questioning.

She continued to give only vague answers and glance around, obviously keeping track of Rone. I began to wonder if I would be forced to interrogate Ganon, when the blue-haired devil himself called the party to attention with the lighting of a torch and a few shrill whistles.

"Thank you, everyone, for attending tonight!"

Ganon wore a purple velvet cape dotted with stars. He gripped both sides, and brought the cape close around him, so he looked like a bat as he bowed to the group. "I'm pleased to announce that the circle is prepared, and we can now attempt to contact realms beyond the veil."

Cheers flew from the mouths of party-goers, and a few people broke out in dance.

"Is your friend joining us?" Jadis asked.

I glanced over at Rone sitting in a chair by the drinks table, watching people with narrowed eyes and frowning.

"Nah. It's for the best that he doesn't. He's low-vibe," I said, using terminology I'd heard Llewellyn use.

Jadis looked dejected, but since there was no denying the sourpuss look on Rone's face, she nodded. "How unfortunate. Well, come with me, I'll make sure you're positioned between seasoned witches so they can monitor your energy output and keep the circle safe."

I followed her, ready to see what would happen and, once there was less commotion, I'd drop my barriers to suss out real supernaturals.

Rone seemed frustrated and dubious that this would work, which I understood. I was sure most of the people here were posers. But if there was even the slightest chance that this could reveal dragonbloods, or even a supernatural who might help, then it was worth a shot.

Jadis led me to where a circle was already forming, and we stepped over a line of salt drawn on the ground. In the center, seven candles burned on an altar, and what had to be one hundred tea lights formed a pentacle around it.

I shivered. I didn't know the first thing about magic, but this sure looked like it could work.

"This will be the safest place for you," Jadis said, stopping and gesturing to a spot next to Llewellyn.

My friend beamed at me. "Perfect positioning. Ganon and I will monitor her to keep the circle safe."

"Exactly." Jadis inclined her head and left, taking up a spot on the opposite side of the circle from where Llewellyn stood.

I dared to hope they meant Ganon would protect me from afar, until he twirled out of the crowd and took up position at my side.

"Violet! So good to see you stepping into your personal power! I welcome you into our circle, and extend my prodigious protection to your person as we step forth into the unknown."

I forced myself not to roll my eyes. Ganon was so extra, even in a crowd like this.

"Thanks. So, I guess I stand here and . . . chant or something?"

Ganon reached his hand out to me, and I took it reluctantly. "We shall chant, yes, but for the circle to work best, you must focus all your inner energy—your magic or power, whichever you prefer—into the center of the circle. Everyone here knows that you're a beginner, it's conspicuous in . . ." His gaze ran over me, and he let out a soft sigh, "well, everything."

Had the obvious insult come from someone other than Ganon, I might have been offended. As it was, I shrugged. Who cared what he thought?

"But we shall take your energy and transmute it. By Llewellyn and I holding your hands, we shall bear most of that burden." Ganon's eyes shot to his girlfriend. "If you wish, I can handle most of Violet's energy."

Llewellyn batted her eyelashes like Ganon was a white

knight. "I'd love that, my Burning Star. I wanted to focus on opening the veil tonight. If you take care of my friend, I'll be more able."

"Of course, Moon Goddess." Ganon blew her a kiss. "Violet, follow my lead. I shall keep you safe."

"Sounds great," I muttered, not at all loving Ganon's 'I'll save you' attitude.

Appeased that I'd do as he wished, he called the crowd to attention. "Witches and wizards! It's time!"

The party-goers stopped chatting, and turned to face Ganon.

"Clasp the hands of your brethren, and we shall begin."

Everyone followed his orders, linking hands with those on either side of them and closing their eyes. I darted a glance to Ganon and Llewellyn. Their eyes were closed.

I wasn't about to close my eyes. For one thing, if this worked, I didn't want to miss it. Secondly, I planned to drop my barriers right as the circle ended in hopes that I'd be less bombarded and more able to discern individual voices. And, perhaps most importantly of all, I noticed that Rone was watching the circle. I needed to keep an eye on him so he didn't barge in and blow his cover.

Ganon led the chant, and a few beats later, everyone except me joined in, their eyes closed and faces screwed up in concentration.

I listened and tried to make out the words, but they spoke in Latin or some other archaic language I didn't understand. Determined not to miss anything, I switched to investigating the atmosphere—searching for anything that felt off, something that could be magic.

The chant was cyclical and picked up speed with each round. After a few minutes, Ganon lifted his arms to the sky. As we were holding hands, mine rose, too. The effect rippled out and around the circle others' arms rose. All their eyes were still closed, and many looked to be experiencing either an emotional crisis or complete ecstasy.

I was wondering what they were feeling when my hands reached their zenith, and a jolt of . . . something . . . shot through me.

A few people murmured, suggesting that perhaps they'd felt it too, but the chant didn't break. It became more fanatical.

My eyes snapped to the center of the circle. I wasn't sure how I knew, but I was positive that if anything were to happen, it would be soon.

I gasped when less than a second later, I received the shock of my life as the air in the center of the circle became light blue, shimmered, and pulsed.

Holy crap! Is this happening?! Someone here is a true blue supernatural!

The chant became so fast, I could barely tell when one word ended and the next began. People in the circle were swaying, their frenzy pervading the clearing.

The energy built, and briefly the thought that I would have to apologize to Llewellyn for being a non-believer flashed through my mind.

My eyes locked on the space above the altar. I waited with bated breath for something else to happen, a portal to pop open, or a mirage of a new world to appear. For that moment when a calm would settle over the group before victory or defeat, and I would listen in.

My attention was so intense that, when an eerie yowl ripped through the air, I jumped, and my mind barriers crumbled.

The chant fell silent, and everyone opened their eyes and scanned the area.

Instead of rebuilding my mind barriers, I listened to each person in the circle, starting with Llewellyn on one side of me, and ending with Ganon on the other.

What the hell?

A lump lodged in my throat.

Not a *single* person was audible. They were all plain humans.

But then . . . what had I seen?

As if in answer, a voice—one that sounded familiar—spoke up inside my mind.

What a waste of time.

My eyes widened. I did another sweep of the circle and my attention stopped on one guy. I recognized his tall form and how he held himself from somewhere, but I couldn't put my finger on it. What I could see of his face looked familiar too, but most of it was obstructed by a blue mask adorned with feathers. I honed in on him, trying to hear his thoughts, but heard absolutely nothing. Odd . . .

My eyebrows furrowed, and I searched for Rone. He was still over by the drinks, holding onto his bag for dear life, and looking as grumpy as ever. Rone was within my range, but I was certain it hadn't been his voice I heard.

The circle erupted into cheers that shattered me. Unable

to hold in my frustration at not being able to pinpoint the voice, I released Ganon's and Llewellyn's grasps and stepped back. Quickly, I mumbled some excuse about needing the restroom, and removed myself from the circle.

I wouldn't be able to pretend to be happy like the rest of them, but just because I was annoyed didn't mean I had to bring them down. They might not be real witches, but who cared? They deserved to have their fun.

And someone here *was* a real supernatural . . . even if I couldn't find them. As I made my way toward Rone, I took in the hardness of his jaw and the tightness of his lips.

"Let's take a walk," I said, once we stood face to face.

Any minute now, he might explode, and I didn't want it to be here.

Without speaking, Rone gave me a curt nod and stormed off into the woods.

12

RONE

WE'D STOMPED along without speaking for several minutes before I halted to confront Violet. My frustration over participating in that balderdash gathering had reached a boiling point.

"You convinced me we would search for dragonbloods. Instead, you played me for a fool, dragging me to see your friends who claim they practice magic." I clenched my fists at the thought of all the pretenders in the clearing.

"Those impersonators wouldn't know *true* magic if it singed their hides." Tension pulled at my face as I spat the words.

Violet took a step back, intimidated, but I didn't care. I'd explained the seriousness of this mission, and she'd said she understood. Yet she had lured me into the trees to watch a farce. The festivity appeared more of an excuse to dress up like children than a serious attempt at magic.

Her blue eyes widened as they took me in, searching.

But I'd said my piece. I expected an apology and reassurances that such a thing would never happen again. And so, I waited.

The seconds ticked by as Violet studied me. The air between us thickened, and flames licked at my nerves.

Violet took my clamped lips as a sign that I would not continue expressing my frustration, because her silence broke.

"It wasn't a waste of time." Her words came out in a rush, although her hands had migrated to her hips, revealing that she actually believed what she said.

"I realize that most of those people aren't what they think they are, but I thought an event like that might draw out real supernaturals."

I opened my mouth to speak, but she held up a hand, stopping me, and I snapped my mouth shut in fury.

"It was a good idea," she shouted, and my scales itched the underside of my skin. "I actually heard—"

I stepped closer to her, and her mouth snapped shut.

"It's clear to me that you still don't understand the gravity of this situation." I spoke through clenched teeth, and my jaw felt like it might crack in half.

Holy fire, Violet wasn't penitent at all. She was testing my patience. "I do not—"

"Rone," she hissed. Her spine straightened as she glanced away.

"Don't interrupt me. This is *my* responsibility. It's *my* people who will suffer if we continue with shenanigans like this. Who knows—"

"Rone!" she shouted, lifting her hands, open palms

replacing clenched fists. Her eyes darted about as if she was searching for a way to escape my wrath.

"Look at me when I speak!" I roared back.

She rose on her toes and slapped her hand over my mouth.

The action took me by such surprise that I could only stare at her, incredulous.

"I can hear someone. It's another vampire, I think." She spoke in a hushed tone.

My emotions were so charged, I was ready for another fight.

For a split second, I realized Violet hadn't pulled her hand back when she'd touched me. But my body crackled with heat. How had I not burned her?

The question would have to wait, though, because a male voice rang through the air behind me.

"What do we have here—a lover's quarrel?"

I spun, expecting to find a single vampire. Instead, I counted four. At least, until two more came around the corner.

The slight menthol aroma that I'd noticed from the earlier vampire wafted through the air, more pungent, with so many of the creatures in one area. There were too many to charge at right away. I needed to secure Violet and the eggs first.

Grabbing her hand, I rushed for a wide field positioned between two homes, where dense thickets of trees lined the edges. The dark would help keep her hidden, though if my information was correct, the vampires had night vision nearly as acute as mine. As a defenseless human, Violet was the most vulnerable, and I wouldn't leave her unprotected.

We'd only made it to the center of the field before the vampires arrived.

I grabbed Violet by the shoulders, and forced her to look at my face. "Go, hide in the trees and keep yourself and the eggs safe. I can handle these creatures if you don't distract me."

I slipped the satchel over her shoulder and helped her wrap her arms around it as she nodded. The traces of panic emanating from her made her hydrake scent spike the air.

"Go!" I urged.

She didn't hesitate, sprinting for the tree line thirty feet away.

Exhaling, I turned slowly to face the vampires walking toward me.

"That won't keep her safe," one vamp said.

Dressed in tight, dark jeans, a three-button vest, and a long duster jacket he stepped forward as the leader. The others were similarly attired, though most wore dark button-downs, sleeves rolled up. So concerned with fashion, they didn't seem to be serious adversaries, but I knew better. Vampires were worthy opponents, even if their pants were so tight that I was sure it would hinder their movement.

Still, overall, I held the advantage in this battle. I was a dragon and, as I'd learned, rare in this world. None of them would have faced my kind before.

Shifting my feet, I broadened my stance to project confidence, but also to prepare myself for an assault. "Walk away now, that is, if you wish to keep stalking these streets after tonight. Otherwise, you will die here."

Two vampires laughed, and wide grins that revealed sharp, gleaming white teeth played on the faces of the rest.

I paced back and forth while keeping watch on all of them. I needed them to stay in front of me for as long as possible.

"Don't take him down too early, boys. We want to have some fun first, don't we?" the duster-wearer spoke, cementing him in my mind as the headman.

He'd be my main target. Though I knew from experience that the attack would start from an underling.

Sure enough, one of the skinnier vampires in the back came wide and tried to flank my right side. I twisted enough to keep him in my peripheral. A blur of motion shot toward me from the left.

I spun and landed a punch to the side of the vamp's head, knocking him off balance. Then, ducking, I whipped my leg around and knocked the feet out from under the sneaky one coming from the right.

I jumped upon the sneak, grabbing a fistful of his black and silver vest, and lifted him to his feet. Before he could set his stance, I twisted his neck and ripped his head clean off.

I possessed no mercy for these beasts.

A weight landed on my back, and I roared. Yanking my attacker by the hair, I flung him over my shoulder. He landed a good twenty feet away on his back. It was only a brief setback though, as he sprang to his feet within seconds.

In the meantime, I blocked the jab of another opponent. I couldn't keep track of who was who as they darted in and out.

A blow landed here and there, but none that hindered me. Swinging punch after punch, I was able to keep them from attacking all at once.

I kicked one away before another darted in. He made the mistake of staying within arm's reach a second too long, and joined the other headless corpse on the ground.

Four left, and I wasn't even winded.

The others regrouped and spread out in a semi-circle in front of me.

"Last warning, leave now, or there will be a bigger pile of dead bodies."

Instead of smiling at my announcement this time, they let out a chilling hiss. The coordinated sound brought to mind a viper's nest.

The hair on the back of my neck rose. Warm-ups were over.

A vampire charged forward. I braced for his attack, but he didn't come at me. He ran for Violet.

A surge of panic rose in me like I'd never experienced before.

Doing the worst thing I could have done, breaking all the rules of engagement, I turned my back on the others and raced to protect my human charge.

I barely stopped the vamp before he reached her. My heart thundered as the vampire's nails raked the air inches from her face. Her scream echoed into the night as she scrambled backward.

The vamp twisted in my grip as soon as Violet was out of his reach. He hit me in the gut with a force that belied his size.

My torso crunched inward, and my breath seized. I didn't have time to gather myself before another attacker pulled my arms behind my back.

I slammed myself forward, and landed a headbutt on the man in front of me, surprising him enough to make him take a step back. Then I bent hard and fast at the waist, throwing myself and the one who held me, to the ground. Wrestling myself free, I shoved my thumbs into the beast's black eye sockets, blinding him before I jumped back to my feet. He wasn't dead, but incapacitated enough that I could ignore him.

Violet screamed again, and my head snapped in her direction. The satchel lay on the ground as she fought off the well-dressed leader.

It would take only seconds for him to overpower her.

Ignoring the two coming at me from both sides, I rushed to her aid.

"The eggs!" I shouted, but she could do nothing except protect herself.

The satchel had fallen over, and several emerald and gold eggs had rolled out onto the cold ground.

Before I could get to them myself, a sharp pain lanced my side. I stumbled as I turned my focus to the gash across my ribs.

The horrid creatures had weapons. I should have expected a race like theirs to fight dirty.

Another blade jammed into my shoulder. Roaring, I spun and wrenched the arm of a light-haired vamp. Yanking the knife from his hand, I turned it on him and sliced a deep gouge across his throat.

He crumpled to the ground, but the other one was already pounding his fist into my injured side.

I ignored the pain and sprinted toward Violet.

Held by both wrists, she stared into the leader's face.

A vein in my neck thumped so hard that it hurt. The leader was using compulsion on her, that mangy son of a conjurer. I could not allow such a thing.

Fortunately, as all of his attention was on Violet, he didn't see me coming, allowing me to slam my shoulder into his side and take him to the ground in one fell swoop.

Although it surprised him, he recovered quickly, and we traded punch after punch, until I dazed him enough to get to my feet.

With a hard kick to his jaw, I snapped his neck sideways. It wasn't enough to kill him, but it gave us time to get out of there.

I hurried back to Violet. Thankfully, she'd come to her senses and was scrambling to place all the eggs back into the satchel. As soon as she'd thrown the strap over her head, I grabbed her by the arm and swung her so that she landed on my back.

"Hold on!" I ordered.

Her arms tightened around my neck as I took off running. I needed to break from the trees before I shifted. The only way to make sure we both survived was for me to change forms.

A hand grasped for my foot seconds too late as I jumped into the air. My shift was underway, my body growing and contorting into the massive beast of my other form. Claws thrust out where my fingers had been. Two rows of spikes sprouted down my elongated spine, eliciting a scream from Violet as she settled between them like a saddle.

Smartly, her toes dug into footholds between my smooth, black scales, reassuring me that she sat securly.

When my wings snapped open, I hurled them forward with a deafening crack that resounded like lightning in the night sky.

I huffed out a breath of relief. We were airborne. That was all that mattered.

From the corner of my eye, I saw a blue flash of light. Something had flown near me. A vampire, the leader most likely, had to have used magic. The air sizzled with it.

I hadn't realized that vampires possessed such powers, but as I was learning, I hadn't come to this world as well-equipped as I thought.

Whatever the flash was, it didn't cause any damage.

I adjusted my wings, making sure that Violet was still secure and safe. Soaring higher, I curled around, and prepared to char my enemies below.

13

VIOLET

I CLUTCHED the glowing egg for dear life as we rose higher and higher in the air. Giving me the shock of my life, Micah had burst from the trees and thrown it to me after Rone launched into the air. Sweat slipped down my face, and my breathing came in thin streams. A part of me couldn't believe that I'd actually caught the damn thing. Another part was sure that I hadn't done it alone.

I'd seen the air around the egg glow light blue. It had been the same color that appeared in the center of the circle at the party. Even more intriguing, Micah had worn the same blue mask with feathers that I'd noticed on the one guy who looked familiar.

He'd been at the party. Micah had performed the magic at the party and used his power to get the egg to me. There was no other explanation.

What happened back there? A voice, Rone's, spoke in my head.

My barriers had fallen when he'd transformed into a

monstrous black dragon. He must have guessed that would happen, because this was the first time I got the sense that he was talking directly to me, instead of me overhearing him.

Thank goodness he doesn't know I almost lost an egg.

You almost lost an egg?!

I blinked. What the hell? Had *he* heard *me*?

But there wasn't time to figure it out, because at that moment, Rone performed a serpentine twist that pivoted us back toward the vampires. I clutched onto one of his spikes just in time to keep from flying off his back.

The next thing I knew, a stream of fire left Rone's mouth and encompassed a vamp who had leapt into the air to attack us. The other vampires scattered, but Rone was fury and fire embodied as he soared over the clearing, lighting up patches of the field in his wake.

Holy crap. Where was Micah?

Hoping Rone wouldn't pull any tricky maneuvers, I stuffed the last egg in the satchel. Then, reclaiming my vice-grip on his spikes and digging my feet deeper between his scales, I craned my neck to see if I could spot Mom's caregiver. Although it was difficult to see around Rone's wings, I took in bits of our surroundings here and there.

Two charred bodies littered the ground—vampires, judging by how fast they were disintegrating. And two others were running back toward the road as Rone gave chase.

Was Micah hiding in the tall grasses or trees?

I scanned the thickets but didn't spot any movement. Either he had gotten away, the vampires had killed him and thrown his body deeper into the trees, or I simply couldn't find him in the darkness below.

Tears pricked my eyes, but I couldn't wipe them away because, at that very instant, Rone dipped downward, his jaws aiming for another vamp.

Under my seat, the tremor that preceded flame intensified, and Rone's scales grew almost too hot for comfort. Another stream of flame flew through the air. It hit its target dead on, and Rone released a roar of victory.

The sound vibrated his entire body so intensely that I let out a squeak of fear.

Rone turned his massive head toward me. *Are you okay?*

Never been better.

If scared as hell and worried for my friend was 'okay,' then yup, I was dandy.

Good. Hold on—

Rone's head snapped forward, leaving his thought dangling.

I gasped when I saw why. He had swooped too low, and the final vampire had leapt up astonishingly high to stick a dagger into Rone's neck.

With a grunt, the dragon shook the dagger free. Blood oozed over his black scales, and another rumble built below me.

Oh snap.

The vampy asshat really shouldn't have tried to get the last word in the fight. He should have just taken advantage of Rone asking after me, and disappeared into the tall grasses. The bloodsucker's pride had cost him, and I watched as he exploded into a cloud of ash when Rone's stream of fire hit him.

One final roar penetrated the night air before a calmer voice infiltrated my mind.

Hold on tight.

I gripped Rone's spikes and squeezed my eyes shut as he beat his wings to lift us higher, and we soared away.

A million questions should have been running through my mind as we retreated from the field, but I found that I couldn't think of anything.

It was my first flight ever. And while I was sure that being on a plane would have been scary enough, being on the back of a dragon had to be worse.

It was damn terrifying.

And yet, it was also totally exhilarating.

My sane brain told me to keep my eyes screwed shut until we landed. My heart, however, urged me to peek, to take in the experience.

In my case, my heart almost always won.

That night, the moon shone bright. The moonlight and twinkling house lights illuminated beautiful patches of forest. But what really took my breath away was the *feel* of flying.

It felt like freedom—like the winds and the dragon beneath me could take me wherever I wanted. I could leave my worries behind, start over. Up here, with the wind ringing in my ears, I was born to soar.

With Rone's back rising and falling beneath me, and his wings beating against the air, filling my ears with the sound of rushing wind, I could take on anything.

Rone twisted to change directions, and I clutched the bag of eggs. Their warmth radiated through the leather and into my skin, much like the warmth of Rone's hide below me. If it weren't nighttime, and we weren't so high up, the sensation might have been too hot. As it was, I found that I needed the dragon's heat for comfort.

We'd traveled for less than ten minutes when Rone descended. I arched forward to glimpse past his wing, and looked below us to see a football field coming into view. There must have been a game earlier that night, or perhaps the lights used timers, because although the stadium was empty the lights glared, bright and obnoxious after my cocoon of darkness.

Are you sure this is safe? I asked Rone mentally.

Yes. I can use sound waves to detect places where there are no forms of life or abnormalities.

Oh that was nifty. And strange.

Like sonar?

I don't know what that is, but I can manipulate sound to do my bidding in a couple ways so if that's sonar, then yes.

The dragon's feet touched the ground. Carefully, I slid off Rone's back and stood before him. A part of me had expected that my legs would wobble or I might even collapse, but they didn't. Though my mind was going a mile a minute after what I'd seen and experienced, my body was strong and strangely invigorated by the flight.

My gaze traveled over Rone, taking in his dragon form properly for the first time. He was about the length of two school buses from snout to tail, with two rows of spikes that started out small near his neck, and grew as they progressed down his spine. The dragon was absolutely mesmerizing, as black as the night sky, with a pearlescent sheen. All except for his deep cabernet eyes, which were watching me carefully.

We locked gazes for a moment, before his eyes darted to the bag resting on my hip. Then, suddenly, the air warmed around us, and the space around Rone began to shimmer.

His body distorted and shrunk with surprising speed. The moment he transformed back into his human shape—clothed, thank god—he strode toward me, nostrils flaring.

I stumbled back a step as he approached.

When his hand came up, I flinched, and he jerked back before touching me.

"Are you hurt?"

I shook my head, surprised by the concern in his voice and the softness of his eyes.

Rone closed his eyes, and his shoulders lowered. But when he met my gaze again, I noticed a different glint to his hypnotic eyes.

"Now then, what did you say about almost losing an egg back there?"

My lips pressed together. Yup, I'd screwed up. But a vampire had been coming after me! So sue me.

I straightened my shoulders and matched Rone's stare.

"I dropped the bag when that vampire attacked me. Some fell out, and I tried to scoop them back in, but I must have missed one. Someone threw it to me when you were flying away. Micah, I think . . ." I trailed off, unable to connect Micah with Llewellyn's crew. They were so different. "I'm not sure why he was there."

Rone stood silent as a stone. My heart began beating faster under his glower, and just when I thought he might never speak to me again, he released a heavy exhale.

"I forgive you for nearly losing one of my charges."

I hadn't asked for forgiveness, but that wasn't the most important thing on my mind.

"Did you burn him? Micah?"

Rone's confidence faltered for a split second. "I believe I only incinerated the vampires, but to be honest, I can't be sure."

My heart plummeted. I opened my mouth to continue my questioning, but Rone cut me off.

"I must ask, does he know of your abilities?"

His tone was softer than before, and the heat that radiated from him had lessened. He was calming down.

At least one of us was.

"No way!" I said.

The idea that Micah knew about my power made my pulse race. He worked at the assisted living home. Would he make sure I got a suite next to Mom if he knew?

"No one knows that . . . except Mom and you."

"Perhaps your mother told him?"

I shook my head. "She almost never talks, remember?"

Rone screwed his lips to the right, clearly trying to piece everything together.

But Rone didn't know anymore about Micah than I did, so for the time being I pushed my worry for my mom's caregiver out of my mind and focused on another question.

"Did you hear my thoughts when we flew away?"

"I did," Rone confirmed. His eyes narrowed as he took me in, like he was trying to see into my soul.

"My kind can hear other dragons' minds when in dragon form. Although, when they hear them that strongly and in such an uninvited fashion, they are usually related or mates." His eyes strayed to the scrapes on my arms and hands.

A tingle ran up my spine at Rone's mention of mates. I mean, sure the guy was odd, but he was also gorgeous and the physical attraction was definitely there. But I didn't know if he felt the same and didn't want to be alone feeling all gooey inside, so I pushed the reaction down and stared down at my arms.

Some of the marks I'd earned scurrying away from the vampire, while others were from Rone's rough scales rubbing against my skin during the flight. Riding aback a dragon was not for the feeble. All of them hurt like the dickens.

Recalling that he'd been injured too, I glanced at where the vampire had plunged a dagger into his neck. There was no mark. All of Rone's injuries had healed already. I sighed, relieved that he was okay.

"Well, considering I don't heal like you, it's safe to say that I'm not a dragon. Once again, I'm weird—a mystery."

"At least you are a helpful mystery."

My lips quirked up. Rone had every right to be mad at me. I'd wasted hours taking him to that stupid party, and I'd almost lost one of his eggs. But it seemed like he was willing to forgive and forget.

"Thanks," I said. "You know what . . . I wonder if my powers transferred to you? I can always read minds, but maybe when you're in dragon form, you can too because your human defenses are down?"

As soon as I spoke it out loud, my theory sounded stupid.

"I suppose that is possible," Rone said, surprising me by

not laughing at my idea. "I've never met another being like you."

Something in his voice made that sound like a compliment, and my heart warmed.

"Same here," I said. "So, what do we do next?"

Rone opened his mouth to respond, but the next second, it snapped shut, and his eyes darted behind me and hardened.

"Rone? What's wron—?" I was about to spin around when an unforeseen force threw me to the ground. As I fell, a flash of light flew above me, making me yelp.

Rone darted forward. Whatever had knocked me over, hadn't affected him. Had *he* been the source? Was he manipulating sound like he'd just said? I really needed to clarify that later.

"Violet, stay low! The sound waves—"

Another flash of light caught in my periphery, and Rone stilled unnaturally and released a low groan. The light had hit him and whatever it had done was causing him pain.

"*Both* of you stay put," a bone-chilling voice cut through the night.

I lifted my neck to see a middle-aged woman with short, brown hair picking herself up off the ground. Once she was upright, she strode toward us, a sneer on her face.

If you only took in her face and clothing, she looked like a soccer mom. The rest of her, however, was a different, terrifying story. A poisonous green light shimmered and spun around her.

I blinked, and my eyes traveled down the woman. They

stopped when they reached her hands, where the light seemed to be coming from.

As if to confirm my theory, the woman extended one arm outward, and the magic leapt, crackling and pulsing through the air. The next thing I knew, a glowing, bright green dome surrounded us.

"Rone?" My arms prickled as if someone was dragging a cactus over my skin. "What's happening?"

"She's a witch," Rone growled through clenched teeth. "A real one."

"That I am," the woman sneered, and two balls of energy formed in her hands. "And if I'm not mistaken, *you're* the one causing all the magical disturbances I've felt around town."

14

RONE

THE PAIN SEARING through me subsided as soon as the witch's trap fell into place. Her magic fizzled to a dying ember that I flicked away. How did she have such power over a dragon?

I paced like a caged animal, my insides scorching hotter with each step. That I'd let a witch capture me was unbelievable, and yet, I found myself confined.

Witches didn't exist in my homeland. And if they crossed the threshold between worlds, usually their feeble powers would fizzle away to nothing. But here, it was different. Her powers were unfamiliar, surprisingly strong, and beyond my power to counteract.

Slamming my fist against the shield produced a lightning-bolt flash of pain through my arm. I stumbled backward with a roar.

"You can try all you want, dragon. You'll not break through my spell. While your kind has been setting your-selves up as supreme leaders of your realm, the supernaturals here have advanced as well. We will no longer cower before you."

She strolled around the outside of the shield. Smugness rippled across her face, and she looked like a cat stalking a caged bird.

"We fought for our right to lead," I seethed. "Those with stronger magic than yours accepted our rule. Wherever the dragons have gone in this world, I'm sure they would agree with me."

The witch threw her head back and cackled. The sound echoed into the sky like a thousand crows jabbering at once.

"There are no dragons here. We've found our way without the need for a single leader, especially an arrogant reptile."

"As if I'd believe your lies," I sneered. "How did you find us?"

"You disrupted the magical realm with your intrusion." The witch twirled her hands in the air. "Not everyone can feel it, only those who are powerful enough and learned in extinct races, but we can all agree on one thing. You're not welcome."

Extinct races . . .

"That can't be true," I replied. There was no way I'd accept the word of a witch over Mage Virhan. "The dragons must be in hiding."

Violet shook her head sadly. "I don't think so, Rone. I—"

"You are interesting, girl." The witch cut Violet off. "What are you?" She stepped closer to the barrier and peered at Violet with her head tilted.

I watched her, waiting for the slightest wobble in her magic.

That I'd allowed her to capture us sawed my guts into smaller and smaller bits. At least I was in a realm where my family couldn't witness my shame. "Leave her alone."

"Ooh, so protective." She smirked but kept her gaze trained on Violet. "Answer me, girl. Or I'll draw it out of you."

Violet gasped, and I lunged in front of her. "I said to leave her be."

"It's fine, Rone. She just startled me." Violet rested her hand on my elbow and scooted to my side.

"What I am is still a mystery," she answered the witch.

I inhaled sharply, at her insistence to expose herself. Why couldn't Violet accept my protection? My teeth ground down as I spoke to the witch.

"It makes no difference what blood runs through *her* veins. Your fight is with me, witch. What do you want?"

"I want you to leave. No, that's not correct. The entire supernatural world *demands* that you leave since the Komisio council rules as one voice. There is an order to things in this realm now, and it doesn't include dragons. None of your kind are welcome here." The witch waved her hand at the satchel, as if she'd seen the hatchlings inside it.

I darted a glance to Violet, who clutched the strap hanging over her shoulder so hard her knuckles were white. Her willingness to protect them overwhelmed and inspired me.

"Your demands mean nothing when I'm sure there are others here. Even as powerful as you seem, you'd not be able to defeat all of my kind. Especially once they've joined me."

The witch resumed her stroll around the perimeter of the shield she'd created.

"You're thickheaded, aren't you? I stand by my claim. There are *no* other dragons. They've all either fled, or met their end. And it will stay that way."

She was lying. There had to be others. I would never believe that dragons had simply died out. The ancient bloodlines were strong. It was more likely they were hiding somewhere—defeated and waiting for restoration to their rightful place. Whether the resilient dragons had lost a war I didn't know of, or had been hunted, they were alive. My kind were survivors.

"I can see your little wheels turning, but listen to me. There. Are. No. More. Dragons. In. This. Realm." Her voice rasped deeper with each word. "Was that slow and clear enough for your simple brain to understand?"

"Rone. She's telling the truth. She's positive that the dragons are gone," Violet leaned closer to me, her voice soft and quiet . . . comforting.

She believed the witch, that much was clear. And she would not do so without good reason.

Fire seared through me as my breath became tight. No, this couldn't be happening. That would mean that my quest was irrelevant. My entire mission was a failure before it had even begun. I'd risked a precious egg from every noble family of Draessonia for nothing.

What would it mean for the hatchlings, to be born in a land that hated and hunted them? I had to leave as soon as possible.

I spun to pace, and stopped short as I almost ran into Violet. She gave me a half-hearted smile that barely moved her lips. My heart clenched at the sight.

What would it mean for her if I left now? She was a supernatural, but what kind, we still hadn't unraveled. It was like she didn't fit in anywhere. Now that she'd accepted the world she belonged to, would she be able to live as she had before? The money I owed her wouldn't last forever. Worse than that, she'd spend the rest of her life running from other supernaturals.

"Stop your moping long enough to listen, dragon. This is the important part. Since you seem a little slow, I'll use simple words." The witch cackled again, and I pictured myself ripping out her throat.

I'd had enough. The sooner she rid us of her presence, the better. "Are you going to quit preening, and tell me your terms?"

"We in this realm have kept the humans ignorant of our kind. Sure, some figured out that we exist, but the numbers are negligible, and they have no valid evidence. We need it to remain that way. If all humans discover that we exist, they'll meddle in our affairs. And when humans get involved in anything, they cause problems."

The witch rolled her eyes.

"Along those lines, you flying around in full view of anyone who had the mind to look into the sky is an issue. It's all too likely that you've already blown our cover, which means the locals, namely my coven and I, will need to clean up your mess." She sneered at me, as if I had any care at all about her coven's troubles.

"Why not allow humanity to learn of us?" I said, and the witch's lips turned down at my words. "We've lived together in the past. Wouldn't it be a better world if we did so again?"

The witch shook her head. "You are such a simpleton. This world is not like your own. Word spreads like wildfire, and hysteria often follows close behind. No . . . we will never coexist ever again. In fact, my coven must now search for any human that may have seen you, and eliminate them."

Violet released a gasp. "You mean . . . kill them?"

The witch scoffed at Violet's words, but never stopped watching me.

"Of course that's what I mean," she said to Violet, then addressed me as she continued. "Let that loss of life and your little friend's fear weigh on your conscience as you flee the realm, dragon."

"I will not flee," I said, unable to stop myself. This witch had no right to command me.

She chuckled. "The council has ruled and you are to leave this realm within one week. If you do not, the supernaturals of this world will rise against you. Nowhere will be safe. Every species representative with a seat on the Komisio has agreed to hunt you down. You are strong, obviously, since the vampires now need a new clan leader to join our council. However, you won't stand against us all. Not for long."

"I will take great joy in ridding this realm of as many of you as I can," I vowed.

Her arrogance had pushed me to the breaking point. I could feel my heat rising and had to fight for control as my scales itched, ready to break free. Within the shield, shifting would be far too dangerous, particularly for Violet.

"That may be true. And I believe you're stubborn enough to try." The witch closed her eyes and mumbled a barely audible string of words I couldn't decipher.

When she met my gaze again, her countenance sparked with danger. "I've taken measures to prevent that. If you stay past the gracious time frame we've provided, the girl dies."

Violet let out a cry. She raised her arm, revealing that a simple gold band now encircled her wrist.

"It tingles," she screamed as she yanked on the bracelet. Hyperventilating, she bent over when it wouldn't budge. "I can't get it off!"

I took hold of her hand and examined the bracelet. It had the acrid scent of magic, and there wasn't a clasp or any way to open it. It slid just enough to meet the end of her palm, but even if she broke her bones, she'd not be able to free her hand of the circle.

"Each day, the band will grow tighter. If you are still here when the seven days are up, it will meld with her skin and drain her life, until only her bones remain."

Violet and I stared at each other and then down at her arm.

It wasn't only my quest at stake anymore.

I snapped my head up to negotiate with the witch, but both the witch and the shield were gone.

15

VIOLET

As soon as I was positive the witch had left, I burst into tears. The band of gold she'd spelled around my wrist didn't hurt, just tingled a little, but her words were terrible beyond belief.

Rone stood close behind me, the heat rippling off of him growing in intensity as his anger mounted.

The witch had told him that his mission was all for nothing. That dragons didn't exist in this land, and he'd wasted his time.

Had I been in a more thoughtful mood, I would have comforted him. But after hearing the witch's final promise, I didn't have time for that. I needed to pull myself together and focus on something that I could fix. Like finding the one person who I was certain had seen Rone in dragon form.

Micah.

I wiped the tears from my cheeks and spun to Rone. His face was set in hard lines, his cheeks red, and cabernet eyes blazing.

"We have to find Micah," I said. "He saw you in that field,

and we have to warn him not to go spouting off tales. Let's go to the assisted living home and ask for his address."

"Micah is not my problem."

My mouth dropped open. Although his words came out in little more than a whisper, they resonated through me as if Rone had slapped me in the face.

"Excuse me? Not your problem? Micah might die because he saw you! How is that not your problem?!"

Rone turned his back to me. "I came to secure homes for my kind in this new world. I came to save the dragons, but I have failed."

"So it's all over? We're no longer working together, and you're going to—"

"Find a way back home before the eggs hatch here and the hatchlings imprint on someone they should not. Yes. That is my plan."

A wash of anger rolled through me and threatened to overtake me, like a child being swept away by the ocean. Rone began to walk away, and a fire of fury inside me built so that at any moment, I might explode.

This was so wrong.

I looked down at my bracelet, the tie binding me to him and the rest of the supernatural world. A brand of sorts.

I lifted my arm.

"You're not going anywhere. You owe me."

Rone stopped and turned. "I apologize."

From his pocket, he pulled out a wad of cash and extended it to me.

"Not the money! You owe me for *this*." I thrust the band of gold in his direction. "And for nearly getting me killed. I told you I'd help you find the dragonbloods, I didn't sign up for any of the other stuff." I sucked in a breath, hoping my next line would work. "And because you're in my debt, I demand that you help me find Micah and warn him."

Rone's lips lifted in a snarl, but I wasn't having any of that.

"Don't tell me you're about to argue."

His snarl vanished, and he released a sigh. "I don't wish to remain here, but I shall help you find Micah. After that, I'll depart."

Something inside me rejoiced over his declaration that he'd stay, but I squashed it. He was helping me because his honor dictated it, not because he wanted to hang out with me.

"Good," I replied and glanced around the field. I didn't know where we were, but convenience stores were usually located near schools and they had bus schedules.

"Let's go down that road. We'll search for a mini-mart or something. We can figure out where a bus stop is from there."

Rone shook his head. "I will *not* step foot on another bus as long as I live."

I placed my hands on my hips.

"I'm sorry, Your Royal Highness, but how do you expect to make it to the assisted living home in a timely manner? Ganon lives on the far edges of the 'burbs. For all I know, after your little flight, we might be in the countryside right now."

Rone arched an eyebrow. "Isn't it obvious? We fly."

I shook my head. I'd enjoyed my dragon ride, and leaving the battle in one piece, but that didn't mean I was chomping at the bit to go again. Plus, it was too dangerous.

"What if someone sees us? That's putting even *more* lives at risk."

Rone's eyes grazed the sky.

"It's dark, I should blend in." His tone was calm, assuring. "As long as I soar high and do not fly in front of the moon, no one will spot us."

I crossed my arms over my chest.

"Otherwise it might take hours to get there," he added. "Micah could have spoken to someone by then. And from what I've seen, word of a dragon in this world might spread like wildfire."

He had a point. And I doubted that he even knew about the internet and how quickly it could disseminate information. The thought of a viral post had my heart leaping into my throat.

"You win," I conceded.

I inhaled a long breath as I pulled my shoulders back, readying myself for my second dragon ride.

———⊹———

I MADE Rone shift back to his human form on the top of a dark parking garage a few blocks from Mom's home. By the time we got there, all the lights were off inside, which meant it was past midnight.

"Crap," I muttered. "I was hoping we'd be able to speak to the front desk people."

My gaze landed on a phone outside the home. I'd walked past it a million times before but never used it. Apparently, today was a day for firsts.

I strode over to the emergency phone and followed the instructions to dial the operator. For a few frustrating moments, all I heard was a recording, but after pressing the appropriate numbers, a man's voice came on the line.

"Saint Francis' Assisted Living Facility emergency line. How can I be of assistance?"

He sounded annoyed, like I'd interrupted something. I imagined that he'd been watching YouTube or trying to write the next great American novel.

"Hi. My mother is Sandy Ayers, a resident at Saint Francis'. She—"

"Is Ms. Ayers in trouble, miss?" the voice interrupted me.

"Um, no. I don't think so. But I was hoping you could help me."

"This is the *emergency* line for residents, miss." The man's voice was hard. "We do not appreciate misuse of the line. What if someone with a real emergency was trying to dial in right now?"

"But this *is* an emergency! I need to know where my mom's caregiver, Micah Johnson, lives! I need to tell him something."

Silence filled the line for a few beats until the man spoke again. "It is against company policy to give out the personal information of employees. I'm going to have to decline your request and ask you to get off the line."

"But this is an emergency! He—"

I stopped. What was I going to say? Micah had seen my friend shift into a dragon? If I said that, this dude would have someone hunt me down and put me in a shared suite with my mom.

"I'm sorry, miss. I'm ending the call now. Please do not dial this number again unless there's a *real* emergency."

The dial tone rang in my ears, and I slammed the phone into the receiver.

"Dammit!"

"What happened?" Rone asked.

"That asshat won't help me! He won't give me Micah's info. But we have to let him know. This is life or death."

My eyes snapped to the windows of the home, and I rushed toward the building.

"Violet! Where are you going?"

"To break in and find Micah's employee file!" I called back.

In the building's shadow, I began to examine the windows. Of course, none were open; the residents were too high-risk for that. But I'd seen them airing out the rooms before, and knew they *could* open.

I gripped the frame with my fingers and pulled.

After a few minutes of letting me struggle, Rone sighed. "Let me help."

I stepped aside and watched the massive dragon-man wrestle with the window frame. Soon enough, it became clear that the windows were more secure than they looked—probably locked down or something.

I threw my hands in the air, frustrated. "This is such a crock! Maybe I should throw a stone through the window and just climb in."

Even as I suggested it, I knew it was the worst idea ever. The home had a security system that was sensitive to shattered glass, in case residents tried to escape. A system Mom had tested herself once or twice. The cops would be on me in minutes.

"If I shift, we could attempt to break in from the top. I noticed a door up there. Perhaps it would be less secure because of its location?"

My eyes bugged out. "No! Look all around us! Someone will see you!"

I gestured to the buildings that surrounded the home. Lights were on, and despite the late hour, figures milled about inside their apartments. Trying to break in was risky enough. If Rone transformed, and someone glanced out their window, it could put even more people in danger. I couldn't have that . . . but I didn't want Micah to die, either.

The weight on my shoulders felt heavier than ever. A lump rose in my throat and, unable to stop them, the waterworks started.

Pull yourself together, Violet, I scolded myself as yet another big, ugly sob burst out of me.

It had been one hell of a day. My body felt like it had been pummeled. I was emotionally drained. And this whole mess wasn't even over yet.

My eyes traveled to the band of gold on my wrist.

When *would* this be over? A week? Would it end with my death?

I pressed the heels of my hands into my eyes, and released another sob.

The sound of shuffling hit my ear, and I expected that Rone was scooting away, embarrassed by my hysterics. So when his hand landed on my shoulder, I jumped.

"I'm sorry this has happened to you. We'll fix it," he said, and dammit I couldn't help myself.

I flung myself at him and wrapped my arms around his muscular torso.

He stiffened.

"I need a second!" I sniffed.

For a moment, I thought he'd pull away. Then his arms wrapped around me, and his big hand began stroking my hair.

"It's fine. Take all the time you need."

Something inside me broke and, knowing I could count on him, I pressed my face into his chest and let the tears flow.

16

RONE

HAVING Violet wrapped in my arms seemed so natural that I wasn't sure what to make of it. As I stroked her hair, the tension in my shoulders lifted. I'd spoken true, I would fix this. I would help Violet, no matter if my mission was over.

The bitterness of my defeat churned like ash in my gut. I'd never failed a mission before, and throughout my training, I'd always been a leader. Once I returned home, why would anyone follow me when they learned what happened? And once I gained the crown, who would want to have Draessonia led by a failed king?

Violet had stopped crying, and her shoulders no longer shuddered. Her breathing settled into a calm, even rhythm, yet I didn't want to let her go.

"Rone?" Violet whispered.

"Yes?"

"I don't want you to go. If you leave, how am I going to find out who I really am? Maybe there's a way we can figure out how to break the spell and get this thing off me so you can stay for a bit."

I felt the same, but I didn't believe it was something either of us should dwell on.

"Even if we did, you'd have no peace. You don't want to live for the rest of your life looking over your shoulder."

I paused, not wanting to admit my next words to her but needing to. "Besides, at some point, I would have gone home anyway—once all the hatchlings bonded with their caretakers, and all were trained."

She sighed and pushed away from me.

I reluctantly let my arms slip to my sides, and the surrounding air chilled. True cold had never taken hold of me before, but somehow, it did in that moment.

"Are you just going to go, then?"

"If the scale will actually work for me to contact Virhan."

"You said something about a portal at the party. Is that how you move between realms?"

"Yes. Though I can't make one on my own. I'll need Virhan's skill. He and I will have to communicate and work together."

"Were you trying to contact Virhan this afternoon, or looking for the dragonbloods?"

Had it only been that afternoon? We'd been through so much, it seemed as if several days had gone by.

What I'd give to have more time to get to know Violet better.

"I was searching."

"You were criss-crossing the street like a crazy man. I

wasn't sure if you were lost or on drugs or something." She gave a little laugh, and I had to smile along with her.

"It's a good thing the bus hadn't come by, it would have crushed me as I waited for it to show proper respect."

I shook my head as I thought of how different this realm was from what I'd expected.

"Of course, Your Highness, all bus schedules should follow your needs." She gave another horrid interpretation of a curtsy. I nudged her shoulder.

"Where should we go? Can I escort you to your home? I think it's best to hope that Micah says nothing until you can find him in the morning. As for me, I'd like to see you settled before I leave."

I saw her face fall. It ripped at my heart, but it was better to get this over with. The witch claimed that Violet's safety would be secure when I left, so now that it was clear we would not find Micah right away, that's what I needed to do.

"Yeah, okay. It's back by the coffee shop. Do you mind if we walk awhile instead of . . . any other way of transport?"

"Did you not enjoy flying?"

"Not at first, but then it was freeing. I'd just prefer to feel grounded right now."

That both warmed and cooled my heart. I would have liked more time to soar the skies with her.

I stretched out my hand as a gesture for her to go first, and we walked down the sidewalk, neither of us saying anything more.

"Excuse me?" A voice full of apprehension spoke behind us.

I whirled around and pulled Violet behind me. "Who are you?"

Violet wriggled out of my hold and moved to my side. "Stop doing that! I can take care of myself."

I resisted the urge to disagree, and stared at the woman standing in front of us. She was shorter than Violet, but had ridiculously high shoes on her feet. The attire she wore barely covered her body. Though she didn't give off a familiar supernatural scent, her presence could have been a decoy for someone else.

"State your business," I commanded. "Now is not the time to test my patience."

The woman shrank back and clasped her hands, wringing them in a circle. "This was a bad idea, nevermind." She spun and hurried in the other direction.

"Wait," Violet called, and before I could stop her, she ran after the woman.

"Violet!" I ran my hands through my hair before I followed. If she was going to take care of herself without me, she'd need to be more cautious.

"Did you need something?" Violet stopped within an arm's length of the woman.

I huffed. Clearly, I couldn't leave until I taught her some common sense battle tactics. Staying out of reach of a potential enemy would be lesson number one.

"I don't know why, but this spot drew me. Like something inside pulled me here."

The hair on my arms rose, and Violet met my gaze.

"Has this ever happened before?" I asked.

"No. Weird things happen sometimes, but nothing like

this." She played with her hands again. "It's like a part of me that's always been out of place told me I'd find peace here."

"Do you hear voices in your mind?" Violet blurted out.

I dropped my head and sighed. Let the enemy do the talking—lesson two.

"No!" The woman darted her wild stare between us, and then looked over her shoulder. She appeared ready to retreat, but before she bolted, Violet reached out and grabbed her by the arm.

"I'm sorry," she said to the woman, her voice calm. "I didn't mean to scare you. It's just that we've been searching for someone. And, well, the reason might sound strange."

"Violet, say nothing more. I need to speak to you in private."

"I let my barriers drop." She looked at me pointedly.

"This is too much, coming here was a mistake." The woman pulled against Violet, but she refused to release her hold.

"That only proves she's part of the *other* realm," I said, not wanting to mention supernaturals around the skittish woman. "But we can't tell *which* part."

"Yes, I can. She has the same resonance as you."

I tilted my head, not understanding.

Violet bit her lip. "I've just started to figure it out. After I isolate a person's thoughts in my head, I can actually *feel* what they are, or at least, I think I can. The vampires were all icy, like snowflakes that travel from my temples downward. The witch was prickly, like someone had thrown me up against a cactus."

"And me?"

Her cheeks flushed with pink. "You give off a vibration, a warm one, that blooms through me."

A grin spread from the comment, despite my efforts to stop it.

"Not like that." Her cheeks grew redder.

The woman snorted. "Vampires!? You two are nuts, I'm out of here."

"Please, wait." Violet met my gaze, her features serious. "You hired me to do a job because I have a talent that you need—one that you trusted before, and should now. I *swear* she's like you."

I took several cleansing breaths while I stared at the woman. If she was a dragonblood, that would mean not only had I not failed my quest, but the witch was wrong.

Relief and determination burned through me.

I turned to Violet.

"It looks like I'm not leaving."

17

VIOLET

My mind worked frantically. I had to convince this woman, the *one* person in the whole city who had been mysteriously drawn to Rone's dragon resonance, that she was a dragonblood. And that Rone and I weren't crazy. Considering her stiff stance and darting eyes, it would be harder to convince her of the latter.

Difficult but not impossible.

Just hours ago, I'd been in the dark, too. And that had been when Rone was bossing me around, spouting off details of Draessonia, and expecting me to acquiesce to his every whim.

Geez, when I thought about it like that, why *had* I stayed?

My eyes darted to Rone, and a whisper of an answer flitted through me as my heart skipped a beat.

A pretty face and a mountain of muscles can make a person do silly things. Especially when he offered you easy money that you could use to pay the rent and fill the fridge.

"*Ahem?*" the woman coughed. She placed her hands on her scantily clad hips.

I got the sense that she wouldn't stick around for long; I needed to work fast. I stuck out my hand.

"We got off on the wrong foot. I'm Violet, and this is Rone."

"Actually, it's Rone Egan Moray Ignatius of Baskara. But as Violet says, you may call me Rone." The dragon prince performed a shallow bow.

The woman's eyebrows furrowed at the strange gesture, but a second later, she took my hand and shook.

"Candy."

"As in the food?" Rone asked.

I had to work not to roll my eyes. He thought *I* was being too forward, but couldn't the guy keep his otherworldly quirks to himself for two seconds?

"I suppose so. I didn't choose it, but my mama always did have a sweet tooth. She coulda been dreaming about sugar when she named me."

I placed a hand on Rone's arm. "Let me talk to her, okay?"

His lips pressed together, but he nodded, so I went for it while he was still being quiet.

"Anyway—Candy—thanks for sticking around. You said a weird sensation led you here tonight?"

She nodded. "A pull. Almost like a vibration brought me to you two."

That was interesting. Candy's experience was similar to mine. I'd felt her closeness as a warm resonance. When I was really paying attention to Rone, I noticed that the hairs on my arms vibrated a little.

"Well, thanks for approaching us." I gave her a warm smile. "Obviously, you did it for a reason, and we might have a clue as to what that reason could be."

Candy's spine straightened as she leaned in closer. Already, this was a major improvement over her trying to run away.

"You might suspect this already, since you are in-tune enough to feel and follow vibrations, but we can tell you with surety that you're not entirely from this world," I said, careful to keep my voice as level as possible. "You actually have a lot in common with this guy here."

Candy shot a glance to Rone, and a look of disbelief that I totally understood crossed her face.

There was no familial resemblance. Nor were there resemblances in how they chose to present themselves. She dressed like a stripper, and Rone looked like a soldier on a day off.

"It's hard to see, but you're both part of the same . . . errr, family tree." I sidestepped calling her a different species because I wasn't sure that was true, and even if it was, it sounded rude.

"Family tree?" Her eyebrows knitted together. "I know my family, and we don't have anyone in there that looks like him."

"That's because—"

"Why is this taking so long?" Rone interrupted. "It should please her to be of the dragonblood."

Candy tilted her head, clearly confused as to what the hell he was talking about. I opened my mouth to interject, but Rone kept right on talking.

"And as the crowned prince of Draessonia, I require that you help your kind. I've been sent to save the future of our race by distributing hatchlings to dragonbloods in this realm. How many eggs would you like to care for? One or two? Do you have a mate to assist you? If not, I believe acquiring one is a wise choice. If you have a partner, I request to meet him before I entrust you with two hatchlings."

The blood in Candy's face had drained away, and although I'd stayed out of her head until that point, I couldn't any longer. Not if I wanted her to help.

I dropped my barriers and listened.

It was as I suspected, Candy's brain was abuzz with fear. Thoughts flitted through her mind, of men who had demanded demeaning, scary, and strange things from her.

My stomach knotted up in sympathy.

I gotta get away from these two. Shit, I should already be three blocks away. They're talking crazy.

I twisted to face Rone. "Stop it! She—"

Candy bolted.

I threw up my hands in frustration.

"Where's she going?" Rone asked, his muscles as taut as a bowstring.

"She's freaked out. Your talk about eggs and entrusting offspring to her was the straw that broke the camel's back."

"But . . . why?"

"Rone, this is a different world," I shook my head.

As many times as I'd tried to plant that in his beautiful skull, he still didn't seem to get it. I understood that he was from elsewhere, but still, it was frustrating.

"You can't expect everyone will want to do your bidding

here."

Rone's face reddened, and his fists tightened into balls. "I'm a prince. That's exactly what I expect from those of my blood." He darted a terse glance at me. "More likely, I shouldn't have let you deal with dragon business. I will talk to her."

Before I could even respond, he was running away, following Candy.

Oh, hell in a handbasket.

I dashed after him.

"I demand that you wait!" Rone yelled.

Candy threw a frantic glance over her shoulder.

"Go away!" she screamed, and flipped him the bird.

Even though I was sure he didn't know what the gesture meant, it clearly came across as rude, because Rone picked up the pace.

Sweat dripped down my face, and my lungs heaved as I chased after him and shouted for him to stop. Thankfully, a long semi crossed the street in front of him, allowing me to catch up.

I grabbed his arm milliseconds before he could take off again. "Rone! Chill! We can still get her help—she's curious —but you can't *demand* it of her. She's dealt with too many men doing that sort of thing. Even if what you're asking is totally different from what they wanted, she won't respond well to orders."

Tears pricked in my eyes as I tried to push away the thoughts that had run through Candy's mind.

"We have to *ask* and maybe see what we can do for her in return. Which makes me wonder, are you planning on paying these people who take the eggs? Or setting them up with any kind of help, monetary or training-wise? You realize that people here don't know how to train dragons, right?"

"Of course, I have plans to train them. You don't think I'd leave the eggs and never check on them again, do you?"

"And the money?"

Rone pulled a wad of cash from his pocket. At least three Benjamins waved up at me, alongside a bunch of fifties and twenties. "They can have it all. It means nothing to me."

It almost made me sick how little he cared about money. For someone who had been living on the razor's edge of homelessness for years, it was unfathomable.

But at the moment, that wasn't important. What was important was getting the eggs to good homes, and doing so in a way that wouldn't scare people. Or prompt the police to search for a crazy dragon man.

"Okay, good." I pressed the money down. "Now put that away. We don't want to be mugged or something because you're flinging bills around."

He stuffed the cash into his pocket.

"Thank you. Unfortunately, I can't hear Candy any longer, she's out of my range. We'll have to scour the streets to find her."

"Or I can follow her scent."

I cocked my head. "Excuse me?"

"Dragons possess an excellent sense of smell. Now that I know what Candy smells like, I can find her," Rone explained, as if he were teaching me how to add two plus two.

He lifted his nose into the air, ready to get on with it.

I blinked, unsure what to make of the idea that Rone

could sniff out someone like a bloodhound.

As discreetly as possible, I lifted my arm and took a whiff. Thank goodness. I hadn't forgotten to put on deodorant that day.

"I've caught her trail. Follow me," Rone said.

I stopped him by placing a hand on his chest. Surprisingly, a jolt of electricity shot up my arm, and my breath hitched.

I glanced up at Rone. His eyes were wide, questioning. Had he felt whatever that was too? Or was he shocked that I was trying to stop him?

He shuffled a little to the right. I was making him uncomfortable.

"Okay." I tried to keep my voice calm and natural despite my squirming insides. "You can lead. But when we find her, please don't go all, 'I'm a prince and you must listen' on her. Be *gentle*. Let her ask questions. And maybe let me talk more than you?"

He looked like he wanted to argue, but after a few seconds of intense, almost smoldering eye contact that made my mouth go dry, he nodded.

"Fine, we'll do it your way."

My lips curled up in a smile and, trying to dissipate the confusing mix of strong attraction and lingering frustration swirling through me, I punched him playfully on the shoulder.

"Look at us! Such a team. Now lead the way, teammate!"

Rone's stern expression broke, and for a second, he seemed like he wanted to say something else. Instead, he turned and stalked down the street to find Candy.

18

RONE

Violet rattled me for a split second with her talk of mates. That was not a light conversation, and would have to wait. First, we needed to find this woman, Candy.

Her scent lingered, allowing me to trail her, though oddly, I couldn't place the house of her bloodline.

When I glanced back, the purple streak in Violet's hair flashed as we crossed beneath each street lamp. She was muscular, however, I could tell my pace quickly tired her. If I shifted, it would be more convenient and allow her to ride on my shoulders.

The memory of her holding my scales, unafraid as we soared the skies, flashed through my mind. My insides warmed, and a shiver dashed down my spine.

We needed to discuss the nature of our relationship soon. For now, the focus was on finding Candy.

It was obvious I didn't understand the differences in our cultures, but it grated on my nerves that I'd been in the realm a week and a half already. Then the first dragonblood I'd come in contact with ran away.

It equally bothered me that Violet would defend someone else, and wanted me to hide my royal status. Sticking up for her kind made sense. However, I was running out of time to save the eggs.

Nothing in the realm was what I expected. Virhan must not have known about all the changes, since he hadn't traveled here in so long. An urge to contact him struck me, yet he would be as disappointed in my failure as I was. It would be better to wait and seek his advice when I could share better news.

"Perhaps we should rest a moment." I slowed in my pursuit of Candy, though it was mostly to clear my own thoughts.

Violet immediately stopped. She had her hands on her knees, and was sucking in heavy gasps.

"How many hours per day do you spend in training?" I asked her.

"Do you know how much a gym membership costs?"

I didn't understand her question, and suspected she meant it to avoid giving an answer. "This mission may require more physical exertion than you are capable of. Once we secure this egg, we'll begin a training regimen."

"You can shove your regimen, I'm fine. Let's go before she gets away."

Once again, I'd offended Violet by stating the facts. Even so, the air in my chest swirled into a tight ball over how her annoyance caused her eyes to sparkle in the low light.

I clamped my lips together and inhaled, slow and deep.

My mission was the priority. She was a distraction. I had to keep moving and trust that she'd stay with me.

Avoiding eye contact, I spun the other direction and caught Candy's scent once more. I charged ahead and nearly passed her because she'd hidden in a dark alley behind a large green container.

With considerable effort, I masked a calm expression before I strode in her direction.

"Madame, I'm sorry if I've frightened you. Violet tells me that you may have misinterpreted my earlier offer."

Candy whimpered but didn't exit her hiding place.

Violet was supposed to speak to the woman, so I twisted to ask why she remained silent.

She was missing. Apparently, she hadn't been able to match my speed.

"Do *not* leave, I will only track you down again. I'll return momentarily." I hoped that Candy understood that I meant her no harm, so she'd stay. But I had to find Violet.

Rushing to the main street, I looked back, and Violet was nowhere in sight.

Heat surged through my chest as fear gripped me.

I increased my speed and pushed myself harder. Two blocks later, I found her.

When she saw me, she balled her fists at her sides and stomped my direction.

"Why didn't you keep up? I found Candy."

"You effin' left me behind! And now, what—you left her too? You are something else. You tell me that I need to work out, but you need *human* lessons!"

I rubbed my neck. Nothing with this woman was easy.

Staring into the sky, I tried to figure out what to say. Nothing came to mind that might not offend her further. It was best to deal with Candy first, and our other issues later.

"She's this way." I spun and strode back to Candy at a slower pace. The slap of Violet's shoes on the concrete ensured that she kept up this time.

Thankfully, Candy had stayed hidden as I'd instructed. It was a good sign that she'd care for the egg properly.

I twisted out of Violet's way and gestured for her to take the lead. She glared at me as she stepped around the odiferous box.

"Candy, it's Violet," she said in a low, gentle tone that made me pause. Perhaps I had been too forceful earlier. "Can you come out of there so we can talk?"

"You seem like a decent person, but I'm not up for whatever kinky roleplay he was spouting. It was a mistake for me to find you. Just leave, and let's forget we ever met." Candy still didn't exit.

"Are you stuck behind there? Do you need assistance?" My question only induced Violet to shove her hands against my chest.

"You agreed to let me speak to her. Go stand over there," Violet threw her arm to the side and pointed at the main street.

I opened my mouth to protest, but she sliced her arm through the air again, her lips so tight they formed a white line.

It wasn't in my nature, or experience, to heed such an order, but the situation was dire. There was more at stake than protocol or damaged pride.

I moved away, crossed my arms over my chest, and waited.

Violet rolled her eyes at me, but turned back to the hiding woman.

"I'm sorry about that. He's not from around here, and doesn't always know how to behave."

I bristled at being forced to accept another comment against my character, but didn't move from my spot or speak out.

"I don't deal with foreigners anymore—too many bad experiences," Candy said in a low voice I almost couldn't hear.

"This is different. We don't want to hire you for what you might be thinking. We have something we'd like to give you. It's important, and we believe you're the right person for it. That's why you felt drawn to us. Can we please speak face to face?"

Violet was so comforting, she even relaxed me. I let my arms fall to my sides, and softened my stance. Her voice must have had the same effect on Candy, because she scooted out of her hiding spot and rose to her feet.

"You don't want some weird threesome? Because if you do, I'm out of here."

"I promise it's nothing like that. Though you will think what I'm about to say is strange. In fact, it might be easier if we sit down to talk. There was a diner a couple blocks back, how about we go there and have a cup of tea and maybe a slice of pie or something while we chat?"

Candy glanced at me, then back to Violet. "You promise that's all?"

"Yes. Then after we share our story, you can decide what to do."

"Fine."

I recognized how the woman's shoulders lowered in the same manner as Violet's had when she'd first trusted me. The offer of a warm drink and some food seemed to have changed her demeanor.

From what I'd observed, the human realm was not poverty-stricken, yet both women I'd interacted with had seemed to lack the same necessities. It was another question I would save for Violet when we spoke later.

———✦———

VIOLET WRAPPED the egg in a blanket salvaged from one of the broken warmers, so that it resembled a human infant. Candy entered the elevator with the egg cradled against her chest. I'd written out detailed instructions on where and when to meet in Wyoming, and what to do if the hatchling arrived early. With the money Violet chose as compensation, Candy was well prepared to care for the egg until I could secure an account with funds for maintenance. Violet promised to help me with that and would contact Candy at the number she provided when the information became available.

When the elevator door closed, I heard Violet sigh. Relief and excitement flooded through me. We'd found the first dragonblood, and I was ready to find the next.

"I'm exhausted." Violet rolled her neck and stretched as

she mumbled. I heard a few cracks before she finished. "It's time for me to go home."

Apparently, she wasn't as ready as I was to continue our search.

"Perhaps you should stay here? It's late."

She arched an eyebrow.

"I have an extra room," I hurried to add, so she wouldn't confuse my offer with the type Candy received. Such a proposal would be a shock in my realm as well.

"I think it's better that I go," Violet said, interrupting my thoughts.

"You're very safe here. Besides, I'd rather we not part until all the eggs are with their proper caretakers. What if you hear someone on your way home?"

She kept darting looks between the elevator and the floor in front of her.

"Or, if you prefer, I can stay at your place. I can sleep anywhere you designate."

"No! That's not a good idea." She didn't elaborate, and I got the impression she wouldn't tell me her reasons even if I pried.

"Then here it is." I smiled and opened the door wider so she could pass into the apartment.

She hesitated for a moment, then entered. "You have a second bedroom?"

"Yes, with an attached bathing chamber. I hope that meets your needs?"

Violet glanced at me with a smirk. "That'll do. Point me toward the servant's wing, oh Prince. I need sleep."

I snorted, unsure if she was intending her comment for

humor or not. I hardly had a full wing for her in this small domicile.

We crossed through the shared living area, and Violet paused at the wall of windows on the far side of the room. The lights of the city twinkled in the distance below. Her shoulders lowered an inch as she stood there, enjoying the skyline.

"Does the view soothe you?"

"It's beautiful. I don't get to see the city like this from where I live."

"Then it will please you to see the same view from your quarters. It's right this way." I headed down the hall and figured she'd follow when she was ready.

"I don't suppose you have an extra toothbrush lying around, do you? I can feel the fuzz on my teeth."

Her comment made me halt between the room I used and the one where Violet would stay. "Is that normal?"

"It's an expression, big guy. I just want to brush my teeth. If you have some toothpaste, I can use my finger."

"I have extra supplies in my quarters. It's through that door."

Violet twisted around and crossed the threshold of my chambers.

A surge of adrenaline rippled through me to have her in my domain. I shoved it aside and found the drawer where I kept my teeth-cleaning supplies.

"Your room is huge. I think it's as big as my—whoa, dude! Why do you have so many toothbrushes?" She gaped at the open drawer as she entered the bathing room. Turning to me with a wide grin, she continued her commentary.

"I mean, I don't mind a metrosexual man or anything, but your sexy smile can't require this much care."

I fought the urge to grin at her description of my appearance. "I didn't want to repeat the market experience for more supplies. Without knowing how long I'll be here, I got what I deemed I would need until I expect to return home at the Summer Solstice. Is that not what you do?"

"There are, like, twenty toothbrushes here. That will last you for years. What do you do, just use a new one every day or something?"

"Is that not correct?"

Violet erupted into a hearty laugh. While I enjoyed the way it lit up her face, it went on longer than I found entertaining.

I leaned against the counter and folded my arms over my chest as I waited.

"I'm sorry, I shouldn't laugh. Most people—humans—use one of these for about three months. Thankfully, that means you've got one to spare for me." She grabbed a toothbrush and searched the other drawers. Snickers kept coming from her as she gathered other supplies.

Apparently, I'd also misunderstood the use of several other hygiene products.

"It's a good thing I have so many things for you to use." I shook my head and let her continue searching for her needs while I went to the other room.

When she emerged, I escorted her down the hall.

"I'll leave you to settle in. Will you join me in the morning to break our fast?"

Violet didn't pull away from the tall windows, absorbed once more by the view. "Mmhmm."

"Thank you for helping me today. You've done a wonderful thing for my people." I didn't wait for her to answer or turn toward me. A lump formed in my throat as I spoke, and I didn't want to embarrass myself further.

Hopefully, I'd be able to keep myself better composed by the next sunrise.

19

VIOLET

My eyes cracked open, and I stiffened. An unfamiliar comforter was wrapped around me, and a work of art that I couldn't place stared back at me from the opposite wall. Sounds of cabinets opening and closing somewhere close by hit my ear, and I jolted up, my heart pounding.

Then a voice swore, and the recognition of where I was clicked.

Rone's apartment. Thank goodness.

My heart rate slowed.

Of course, it was still strange that I was relieved to wake up in the home of someone who I'd only known for a day. A guy who was a little volatile, bossy as hell, and a freaking *dragon*.

But at this point, waking up in Rone's house was the least of my worries. Images of the soccer-mom witch hunting Micah had haunted my dreams all night long, and they threatened to take me over again. Micah was still out there, a danger to himself—all because of me.

We had to find him.

Gingerly, I hauled myself out of bed. My muscles ached, and the scratches on my arms itched a little. My poor body had been through hell, trying to keep up with a dragon. Not only that, but I was starving. Before we did anything, I needed food and coffee. Lots and lots of coffee.

I sighed and pulled on the same clothes that I'd worn yesterday. When I entered the kitchen, Rone was bent at the waist and slamming another cabinet shut.

"Whatcha lookin' for? Can I help?"

The dragon prince rose, his face scrunched up in a way that made me giggle.

His face screwed up even tighter. "I'm searching for suitable food so we may break our fast and get moving. I've gone through the rations I carried with me from Draessonia already, and hoped to find something here. This is all I came across."

He held up a bag of coffee beans and a box of saltines.

"One smells like your place of employment, but looks nothing like the beverage you've served me."

"When did you last go to the grocery store?"

"Grocery store?"

"The place where you buy food."

His confusion cleared.

"Ah! A market! Not since I arrived here. Once I went through my rations, I began eating at your place of employment."

Oh, boy. I cringed at the thought of Rone living off the horrendous sandwiches he ordered.

"It looks like we need to make a few stops today," I said,

making a mental note to find the nearest grocery store and get the basics. But right now I couldn't wait that long to eat. Plus, I had an idea that might kill two birds with one stone.

"I wanted to talk to you about our plans. Want to go to the café for breakfast?"

"Splendid idea," Rone said, dropping the bag of beans and saltines on the counter.

I thought so, too. We'd skipped dinner, so not only did I need food, but I thought Llewellyn might have information about Micah.

As the café was only twenty minutes away, we opted to walk. Along the way, Rone insisted that I listen for supernaturals in case one was a dragonblood.

Unfortunately, I didn't come across a single one, which I could tell frustrated him, but what could I do? It had taken us an entire day to find Candy, and technically, she'd found us.

The idea that I wasn't earning my keep flitted through my mind, but I pushed it away. I *could* sense the dragonbloods, dammit. Just because none seemed to stray across our paths didn't mean my ability had disappeared. Maybe there weren't a lot in the Portland area or something.

The idea made some sense. Rone seemed to like spicy things, and if the infernal temperature that he kept his rental at was any indication, he loved the heat. The Pacific Northwest wasn't known for spicy food or blazing sun. Why would dragons choose to live here?

Questions were still buzzing in my mind when I pushed open the door to the Mystic Bean. Behind the register, Llewellyn shot up from where she'd been resting her elbows on the counter.

"Did I catch you napping?" I teased.

In answer, she released a yowling yawn. "It's been so dead in here today. Everyone's downtown. There's a parade or something." She paused, her eyes traveling over me. "Are you wearing the same clothes as yesterday?"

Her eyebrows wagged as she shot Rone a sly glance.

"It's the Rose Parade," I said, grateful that a customer had mentioned it the day before, and I could use my knowledge to try to deflect her insinuations.

"Right." She gave me a look that told me I was in for some grilling later. "Whatever it's called, I'm happy it's going on and that we're slow. I'm so wiped."

"Should I make my own coffee?"

She gestured to the espresso machine. "Be my guest."

Her eyes sought Rone, barely flitting to his murse. "And I suppose you want that disgusting sandwich you always order?"

I stifled a laugh as Rone's mouth fell open wide.

"It is not disgusting," he retorted. "It's hearty and deli- cious—the perfect fuel for a quest."

"And so much meat. I feel bad for your arteries," Llewellyn said before puffing her cheeks up. "You got that too, Vi?"

I rolled my eyes. Good grief, she was a mess.

"I've got our stuff, but if a real customer comes in, they're all you."

My friend nodded and leaned against the counter again.

I began to make our drinks. Once I'd served up Rone's coffee and downed half of mine, I started on the food.

"So, Llewellyn," I said, placing the tenth piece of roast beef on Rone's sandwich. "How do you know Micah?"

"Mi—who?"

"Micah Johnson. Tall, dark skin, enormous brown eyes with lashes you would kill for, and a body like Michael Phelps."

At the mention of Micah's eyes, Rone grunted. Apparently, in Draessonia, long eyelashes weren't that impressive. Too bad, 'cause Rone's lashes easily rivaled Micah's.

Llewellyn shook her head. "No idea who that is, and if I met him last night, I don't remember him."

Interesting. Micah was memorable. Not only was he attractive, but he was personable and charming—as long as you were following the rules.

"You said that party was for your coven, though, right?"

Llewellyn, who had placed a damp cloth over her eyes, nodded. "You two were the only non-members. Which reminds me . . . are you interested in joining? Ganon agrees that you have the spark. You probably just need our help to hone it."

"Errr, we'll see," I said as I handed Rone his sandwich.

Without so much as a thank you, the dragon prince accepted it, took a massive bite, and stomped off to the corner table.

What was up his butt?

"Well, let me know. Summer solstice is coming up, and we're always looking for magic virgins to sacrifice."

I choked on my coffee.

My friend's lips quirked up at the corners, clearly hearing my shock, even if her eyes were still covered.

"Joking, Vi. But it would be cool if you joined."

"I'll consider it," I said even though the sacrifice remark had already made up my mind.

Hell to the no. Witches be crazy.

A few customers trickled in, and thankful for the out, I grabbed my scone and left Llewellyn to her own devices. When I joined Rone at the table, he looked pointedly out the window.

"Hey, what's up?" I asked.

"I didn't realize this would take so long."

So long? We'd been at The Mystic Bean for less than ten minutes.

"Sorry, making food takes time, and I wanted to see if Llewellyn knew anything about Micah. I don't want him getting himself killed because he told the wrong person he saw a dragon."

"Right." Rone stood. "Should we continue searching for dragonbloods? You know, the assistance I am paying you for?"

I considered telling him I didn't appreciate his tone, but decided against it. Maybe he wasn't a morning person. Mom had always been a grump until noon. And while that wasn't an excuse, he had a point. He'd hired me for a job, so I should get on it.

After I made one more stop to look for Micah . . .

WE MADE it all the way to the assisted living home before Rone recognized where we were.

His expression grew stony. "Why are we here?"

I gulped. I wanted to help him, I really did, but I couldn't throw Micah to the wolves.

"Candy found us here. Did you ever stop to think she wasn't drawn to us, but to this place?"

Rone looked doubtful, and I couldn't blame him. I was pulling excuses out of thin air, and I knew it.

"The home has . . . strange energies, don't you think?" I added, channeling Llewellyn.

His expression cleared, but the clarity lasted only a moment before he grunted. "Fine. As you were intent on speaking to your mother yesterday, I assume you weren't on the lookout for other dragonbloods in the vicinity. And I didn't have my scale out when we arrived."

He pulled the shiny, black scale that alerted him if a dragonblood was nearby out of his murse. "Today, I'm better prepared."

"Sounds good," I said, relieved my excuse had worked.

We entered Saint Francis' Assisted Living Home, and a cheerful receptionist began to check us in.

"Has Micah Johnson been in today?" I asked as she scanned my fob.

At my side, Rone stiffened.

The receptionist shook her head. "Nope. Sometimes he comes in the side entrance, though."

My shoulders slumped. Dammit. If Micah wasn't here, then I would have to be on the lookout for one of the other caregivers I recognized. Hopefully they knew where he lived and would remember that we were friends.

After a few more minutes of checking us in, the receptionist buzzed us through the door leading to the residents' rooms.

I was a little surprised it had been so easy. I'd half-expected Micah to have put Rone on the banned list. Of course, I didn't mind investigating the home by myself, but leaving him alone in public was nerve-wracking. I never knew what he would do or say.

As if to emphasize that point, Rone pulled out the scale that resembled a black guitar pick about the size of my palm, and began watching it.

"What is it supposed to do?" I asked.

"Virhan said that the tip should point to a dragonblood. But he also claimed there would be many of those in this realm. As we've found only one, I'm beginning to wonder if he was mistaken. Or perhaps the device got damaged as I moved between realms."

"Was that journey hard?"

"No, merely disorienting."

I nodded as if everything he said made total sense, and he resumed staring at his scale.

A few minutes later, we stood outside Mom's room.

I released a sigh. My plan was not going as I wished. I hadn't seen a single caregiver who I recognized, and I couldn't risk asking just anyone about Micah. The caregivers were kind, but also strict and diligent about maintaining privacy.

Oh well, while I was here, I might as well see Mom. I would feel shitty if I came all this way and didn't at least say hi.

I peeked in her window and was relieved to find her reading.

"You should wait in the hall. We don't need another scene like yesterday."

Rone's eyebrows furrowed.

"And that way, you can be on the lookout for any dragonbloods who might walk by."

That did the trick. His annoyance cleared, and he nodded. "I'll wait right here, but please be quick. I wish to find a dragonblood before the eggs grow cold again."

I nodded and let myself in using my fob.

"Hey, Mom."

My mom looked up from her book and her eyes lit up. She patted her bed, and I went to sit next to her.

"I can't stay long, but I wanted to see you. Whatcha reading?"

Mom held up the book. I recognized it right away as a sci-fi adventure that Micah had loaned her. That sparked an idea.

"Looks awesome. Hey, Mom, has Micah been by today?"

She shook her head.

Apparently, he really hadn't been in, but that didn't mean that Mom didn't know more about him.

"Bummer. I've been looking for him. You wouldn't happen to know where he lives, would you? Or how to get hold of him?"

Mom's spine straightened, and she flipped to the front of the book. Inside the front cover, Micah had scrawled his name and phone number.

I sucked in a breath, thankful that Micah was the type of nerd who put his name and phone number in a cheap paperback novel.

"Can I see that for a sec?"

She handed it over. I went to the stack of paper that the caregivers allowed her to keep in her room and, using a blunt crayon, scribbled down the number. After we left, I'd have to find a phone and try to call him.

"Thanks, Mom. You really helped me out."

She beamed, pressed one hand to her heart, and held the other arm out for a hug.

Bits of my heart broke as I slipped into my mom's embrace. The world might be chaotic, and moments like these were rare, but at least I still had them. She was the only parent I had left, and even if our relationship wasn't everything a daughter dreamed of, I loved her so much.

I CLOSED Mom's door and turned to find Rone glaring at me. My eyebrows knitted together. "Is something wrong?"

His arms crossed his chest. "Yes. There seems to be something very wrong, don't you think, Violet?"

Oh boy, now I had a vague dragon on my hands. I did not have the patience for this. Then again, it was best that Rone didn't blow up inside the assisted living home. So instead of trying to pry whatever was bugging him out, I grabbed him by the hand and marched down the hall. We made it to the lawn before he ripped his arm away and growled.

"Dude! I'm sorry I grabbed you, but I could tell that you were about to explode. What's up with you?"

His eyes widened incredulously.

"*Dude*? Is that how you speak to your employer?"

My lips parted in surprise.

"I'll take that as a no." His face became even stonier. "Then why would you find it permissible to speak to me that way? For that matter, why do you believe that I wish to waste my valuable time in this world looking for Micah, rather than completing my quest?"

The way he spat Micah's name like it was a dirty word got my attention. I cocked my head to the side.

"Do you hate him or something? Because I don't understand why you wouldn't want to make sure he's okay. Or that he won't tell people he saw a dragon." I shook my head. "Micah is my Mom's favorite caregiver, Rone. I don't want to see him hurt."

"Is that all he is?" he growled before turning on his heel and storming off.

I blinked. What the hell had happened? He was acting so weird and moody. Sure, I'd spent time searching for Micah, but someone's life was on the line.

Because Rone's legs were stupid long and the guy walked as fast as a freaking cheetah, he'd already covered three blocks by the time I caught up.

"Rone! Hold up! Don't you understand? Micah could die!" I held up my wrist to remind him of the witch.

Rone's cabernet eyes latched on to the gold bracelet. For a moment, I thought I saw regret flash across his face before the scowl returned.

"I understand completely." He put on another burst of speed. "While my quest isn't as important to you as it is to me, it too will result in death. An entire magical race will be lost if I don't succeed."

I stopped in my tracks.

"You're right." When he put it that way, there was no excuse. "I wasn't thinking about those eggs and how you've risked so much to bring them here. I'm sorry."

The dragon prince halted and slowly turned around. His eyes had softened, and once again his gaze went to the enchanted bracelet.

"I accept your apology," he said, and then, looking as if it cost him the world, he continued. "And I apologize, too. Perhaps I overreacted back there."

He gestured in the direction of the assisted living home.

A small smile graced my face. "I accept your apology. Now, what do you say we look for dragonbloods?"

"I'd like that," Rone replied.

"Then let's get this party started!"

I threw my hands up in the air and wiggled my fingers, trying to lighten the mood.

Once again, Rone's gaze followed my enchanted bracelet. His lips twisted, and guilt for throwing the bracelet in his face earlier overcame me. He wasn't responsible for it.

I dropped my hands to my side. "Hey. I want you to know that I don't blame—"

Rone thrust a hand as if to shush me.

I reared back. "What the—"

"Violet . . . look." Rone's finger pointed over my head.

20

RONE

"THAT'S THE SYMBOL! THE OPES!" I pointed to the building, but Violet didn't even turn. She gaped at me with a confused expression.

"This must be where the Maisu conclave is in this realm."

I splayed my hands in excitement as I waited for her response. The partially overlaid triangles, one inverted and one sitting on a wide base, both sprouted arrows from the points at the top and bottom. The emblem, complex and filled with symbology from my world, was unmistakable.

Violet finally twisted to view where I pointed. "That's a bank or investment company or something. I don't know, but using the opes is just a coincidence, I'm sure. That's just their logo."

"It's more than that." I hurried toward the building, but she jumped in front of me.

"No! That's just a regular human business that won't understand all of your Draessonia talk. Let's keep going, we're sure to find another dragonblood—that way." She pointed in the direction we had been walking.

But I knew better. Whoever owned that establishment could answer my questions.

I dodged around Violet and continued my pursuit of information.

I heard her mumble one of her favorite curses before she stomped after me. "Rone!"

Obviously, she didn't understand the importance of the task, but she would once we spoke to those inside.

I grabbed the handle of the tall entry door on which another opes was etched in the glass, further convincing me I was correct. Violet reached my side and followed me in.

We entered a large, open hall—indicative of the high position the group held in the realm. It stung my heart, as it reminded me of the grand entry to my home in Baskara.

The chilled air inside pebbled my skin. Clearly, whoever ran the place intended to resist dragons. The openly hostile environment irritated me, but it also confirmed that not all humans in the realm were ignorant of my kind.

My growing frustration helped increase my temperature. I didn't rein myself in, as I hoped my warmth would seep through the satchel and keep the eggs warm.

"We need to go. We shouldn't be here." Violet grabbed my arm and sucked in a hiss when she felt my heat, but didn't take away her hand.

Her potential as an advocate for the dragons was stronger than I had perceived earlier.

"This place holds information. It's connected to the man who attacked me in the street with the athame, I'm positive.

They know of the ancient symbol, and I'll not leave until they explain themselves."

"Why does this matter? Your mission is finding drag-onbloods, remember?" Violet kept her voice barely above a whisper appropriate for a place of worship. She had to know it was the right place for answers.

"It's not a coincidence that the symbol for an ancient race in Baskara is on this building, the doors we walked through, and on the floor under our feet."

She scanned the floor, finding a large opes symbol within the tiles as I crossed the room to a woman who sat behind a short wall.

It was an odd place to station a hostarius, but I didn't have a handle on the customs of the realm—as Violet had pointed out more than once.

The woman glanced right and left as I approached, and I did the same. There were glass-walled rooms on either side of the large entrance, filled with desks and chairs inhabited by men or women in suits. For such a sizable building, there were very few individuals in view.

"Inform your leader that I demand his presence."

The woman's eyes widened at my command, then a wobbly curl formed on her lips.

"I'm sorry, sir, do you have an appointment?"

Ah, it made sense there would be regulations for seeking an audience.

I tried a different strategy.

"You must set aside the customs for today. I'm sure all will be well once the man and I can speak."

Because I needed to make it appear that I was an ally, I smiled and rested my arm on the top of the wall between us.

"I'm sorry, I'll get him out of here. He's foreign and gets confused sometimes." Violet grabbed my arm, attempting to pull me away. "Come on, Rone, it's time to take your medicine."

Her eyes narrowed as if she was angry.

Whatever irritation she had could wait. I would get some answers.

"I'm in perfect health. Until I've spoken with the leader of this faction, I'm not going anywhere." I ignored Violet's tugging and returned my gaze to the woman.

She regarded me through a pair of teal-colored glasses that were in stark contrast to her alabaster skin and dark hair.

I leaned closer and peered at her station. It consisted of only a table and two devices. There were no papers or any other indications that she had a list of supplicants for the day.

Movement caught my attention as others entered an inner sanctum to the right of the woman.

The door-keeper was no longer necessary—I'd find the one I sought on my own.

"Sir, you can't go back there! Stop, or I'll call security," the woman called out.

I heard Violet speak with her, apologizing for me. It was irritating, but I ignored them and continued my search.

Two men and one woman scrambled away from me as I strode down the hallway, proving they were not my target. About halfway down the passage, a man leaned against the wall as if he didn't notice my approach, though his musky scent told of his eagerness to do battle. Dressed in the same style as all the rest, it didn't hide his larger, more muscular build.

The corner of my mouth tipped up in amusement. His actions were like the posturing some guards would use with me when we trained, the nonchalance an attempt to lure into a surprise attack.

I'd found the right place.

"You there," I called, so he knew I'd recognized his tactics.

Instead of acknowledging me, he ducked around the corner.

My nostrils flared. I loathed a coward.

Violet called to me again, concern clear in her voice. Quickly, I glanced over my shoulder and saw her in a struggle with the dark-haired woman over a device from her table. She didn't appear in danger, so she'd have to handle that issue herself.

I rounded the corner where the man had disappeared, and a fist landed against my jaw that sent me stumbling, momentarily stunned. I recovered quickly, charging and slamming him into a wall, enjoying the grunt it forced from him.

"What is this place? How do you know of the opes symbol?"

I had the man pinned under my forearm. From years of training, I knew that he could still breathe, which meant he could answer me.

"Rone, leave him alone!" Violet yelled from behind my shoulder.

I felt the man tense, then determination flared in his

features as he tried to escape my grasp. He growled and thrust his knee into my groin—a more craven act didn't exist.

Unfortunately, it proved effective, and I released my hold on him while the sudden pain passed. When I righted myself, Violet and the door-keeper woman had shoved themselves between us.

In Draessonia, every child learned to fight. Everyone, regardless of gender, was charged with protecting themselves and the kingdom. From what I'd seen of the human realm, that was not their way. I could crush both of the women, yet that would accomplish nothing. Why were they putting themselves in such a position?

"Violet, move out of the way." I snarled to fortify my point. This man would not escape.

"We need to go. This isn't worth the trouble." She forced her words through gritted teeth as she shoved her hands against my chest.

"Yohan, we don't need this kind of publicity. If the boss gets wind of what's happening, we're all in trouble. Let him go." The woman used her shoulder to shove the man back out of my reach.

"He needs to be taught a lesson," Yohan answered.

I thought the same of him.

"We're leaving." Violet fisted my shirt in her hand before twisting to address the dark-haired woman. "How about I get him out of here, and we all agree this never happened?"

"Done," the woman nodded and braced her hand against Yohan.

He grumbled, but didn't move.

"Let's go, *now!*" Outrage, aimed at me, radiated off Violet's face.

How could she dare to ask me to walk away when I'd been challenged in such a manner? And I had gotten no information yet.

"*Move!*" Violet grunted while she held my shirt and tried to push me.

When the coward, Yohan, agreed to the woman's demand for retreat, I sank to my heels. I'd have to return another time to finish the search on my own.

I spun and marched down the hall, forcing Violet to release me so she could keep up.

When we exited the building, the warmer outdoor air washed over me. My anger still boiled within, but the change in atmosphere soothed my nerves. Enough that I decided to speak with Violet about some of the issues between us.

She'd misjudged her position too many times. I would not have her make me out to be a fool any longer. It was time I took full control of the mission.

An area of grass shaded by trees appeared ahead and I strode for it determined to explain to Violet how wrong she was. There weren't many people around, so I halted and faced her, watching as she narrowed her eyes in a glare meant to slice me in two. She started ranting before I could get a word out.

"You need to knock that shit off! What would have happened if they'd called the cops? Huh? Did you even think it through before you went charging down that hall, ready to pummel some guy? No, of course you didn't, because you're the great Rone of Ignatius, first of your house, or whatever crapload of titles you need. This is the human realm, and you need to figure out that things work differently here."

"You're angry with *me*? They have an ancient mage symbol all over that building, and we need to know why. That man, Yohan, basically admitted he was Maisu when he attacked me. For this mission, you need to learn your place."

"My *place*?!" Violet threw her hands in the air before clenching them at her sides. "How dare you? Without me, the eggs would have grown too cold in your apartment because you didn't know how to use an oven. If I hadn't convinced Candy who she was, *none* of the hatchlings would be secure. This is *my* realm, Rone. You need to respect me and believe I know how to function here better than you."

That she was right warred within me. She had over-stepped—more than once—but it was only through her efforts that the eggs were still safe.

It didn't change the fact that she needed to follow my orders. Especially when there were dangers involved.

"Are you even listening to me? With your arms crossed over your chest, as if you're some hulking bodybuilder. You're not royalty here."

Without warning, she slammed her fist into my arm. It almost ricocheted back in her own face.

Twice more, she attempted to punch me, though with little effect. Whatever else we still needed to discuss, Violet had no fighting form. No wonder she was so fearful; she had no ability to defend herself.

I grabbed her hand when she swung it at me again. She tried to wiggle out of my hold while I released a long breath. The feel of her soft skin calmed me.

"We may come against more dangerous situations. You were winded as we searched for Candy when she ran, and now, this attempted challenge is feeble at best."

She slumped and averted her gaze as I shifted my hand so her fingers rested in my palm.

"You must be a better warrior," I told her firmly.

It would be best to remove the satchel, but I'd have to show her what I could with it still over my shoulder. Her skills were such that it would take several lessons before I needed to concern myself with the eggs' safety anyhow.

"We'll start training immediately." I positioned myself in a basic fighting stance. "Adjust your feet to match mine, one slightly in front of the other, equal distance apart as your shoulders."

Violet sneered and made a noise of disgust as she ripped her hand free.

"You're impossible."

She marched away, ignoring my lesson.

Where was she going? This was not productive at all.

For a split second, I considered letting her walk away. Perhaps it would be best if we parted company, and I searched for more dragonbloods on my own.

My gut churned at the thought. Differences aside, Violet was important to me—to the mission.

I dropped my chin with a huff, then stomped after her.

21

VIOLET

I WASN'T sure how Rone managed to zip his lips about fighting while he followed me, but I liked to think my scathing glares intimidated him into submission.

Unfortunately, I couldn't stay angry for long—I never had been able to. Anger was too hot and uncontrollable, like a fire burning inside me. It was easier to let it go rather than stay mad.

Plus, I had questions I wanted answered.

We were in the middle of a park when the last of my fury washed out of me, leaving me wrung out. It wasn't even lunchtime, but my energy was waning. Catching sight of a park bench up ahead, I walked over and collapsed onto it.

I tilted my chin to the sky and closed my eyes. "What a day."

"It has been full of events, hasn't it?"

The bench shifted beneath Rone's weight as he sat next to me.

My eyes cracked open, and I twisted my neck toward him.

"Don't talk unless you're ready to answer some questions, Rambo."

His eyebrows knitted together at the cultural reference, but at the moment, I didn't care to explain. As far as I was concerned, he was the one who had explaining to do.

"Tell me about these mages. You've mentioned them a few times, but why would they run a bank—a place that deals with money? Is that what they do where you're from?"

Rone pressed his lips together for a moment before releasing a sigh. "Where I'm from, mages are powerful, but they don't handle money. They're servants, of a sort. In Draessonia, they can't hold land for themselves, although in other countries, they can."

"That sucks."

Rone nodded. "It's not fair, but it's how society has been for a long time. Seeing as the war between mages and dragons was centuries ago, my father has been considering reversing that stipulation, but it hasn't happened yet. One would never see a mage symbol on any building in Baskara, save for their temple."

"Hmm."

I let silence hang between us while I considered Rone's words.

"Violet?"

"Yeah?"

"I truly believe that you must learn how to fight. I understand I was abrupt in revealing my wishes that you learn, but if we're to undertake this quest together, I'd prefer that you're safe."

My heart clenched. I needed to cut Rone some slack. He

was a guy from a different place. One with dangers around every corner, and creatures I'd only heard of in fairytales, some of which were dangerous and scary. Of course he considered it important that I learned to fight. It should please me that he was thinking about my well-being, but I had to admit the idea of actually fighting was off-putting.

"Thanks, but that's not the way we do things here."

"Your exchanges may look different. Perhaps they're verbal or more subtle than aggressive, physical combat, but it's still fighting."

I couldn't argue with him there. And I supposed it wouldn't be the worst thing in the world to know how to throw a punch.

"Okay, you can give me lessons. But nothing too crazy."

His face lit up, and I'll be damned if my stomach didn't squirm with delight.

"Only the basics," he agreed.

"We'll find a good location to practice. But first. . ." he paused, and his eyes grew wide as they tracked something in the park. "What luck!" He sprang up off the bench, took me by the hand, and dashed down the trail.

I almost tripped over my own feet, we were running so fast. "Oh my god, slow down!"

But the prince didn't slow until he'd run up to a man covered in tattoos who looked like he spent twenty hours a day in the gym, and only ate chicken and broccoli.

"Greetings, fellow warrior!" Rone's voice boomed with pleasure that made my heart drop.

Fellow warrior? Oh my hell.

The guy's eyebrows pulled together, but as Rone didn't appear intimidating, he gave a single nod the way guys do.

"What's up, man?"

"I'd like to get your professional opinion, if I may?"

The man shot me a glance.

Knowing that the next thing out of Rone's mouth would be batshit crazy, I gave up and dropped my eyes to the dirt.

"Uh, sure. What can I help you with?"

"Where might one purchase a dagger in this city?"

My spine straightened as my gaze shot up to Rone, who looked entirely too pleased with himself. A dagger!? Was this what he meant by "the basics"?

Unsurprisingly, the tattooed guy took a half step back. "I'm not sure, man."

"Surely, a warrior of your stature has purchased a weapon before?"

"Errr, no, bro. That's not my jam, but I guess you could try the pawn shop down the street." The guy pointed left and took another step in the opposite direction.

"A pawn shop. Splendid! Thank you." Rone gave a half bow, whipped around, and pulled me down the trail in the direction the man had pointed.

I argued and pulled back as Rone made his way to the pawn shop, but he ignored my protests that I wouldn't carry a dagger.

When we arrived at the store, I gave it one more shot.

"I'll look absurd toting around a dagger! I might even get arrested! How about you show me how to punch? Or better yet, how to defend myself from an attack? Only cops and gang members need weapons."

For the first time since talking to his "warrior" bro, the excitement left Rone's face, and he turned to me.

"Didn't you agree to learn the basics of fighting?"

Ugh.

"Yes, but—"

"Swordsmanship is a basic skill." He lifted my arm, and squeezed my tiny bicep muscle. "However, I don't believe you can lift a broadsword."

"Hey, now! I have to lift huge bags of coffee beans at work! I'm strong . . . ish."

Rone's lips quirked up as he arched an eyebrow. The expression looked much too debonair, and despite the fact that I was annoyed, the feminine part of me melted a little.

"You have strength, yes, but not enough to fend off serious foes." He patted me on the shoulder.

"We'll work on it," he assured me as he pushed open the door.

With a dramatic sigh that didn't seem to register with Rone, I walked into the shop.

The scent of top ramen and one of those little tree car fresheners, which did nothing to cover the stale stench of cigarette smoke, permeated the air. My gaze went to the main counter, and my eyes bulged.

Weapons lined the wall behind an old woman with poofy gray hair, red-framed glasses, and a smile that was missing a boatload of teeth.

"Come on in, you two!" the woman croaked. "What can I help you with?"

"Good day to you, my lady."

The woman's gappy smile grew wider.

"I would like to purchase a weapon for my friend." In what I assumed was an effort to appear disarming, Rone wrapped his arm around my shoulder.

The woman's eyebrows shot up, and her smile got even larger. "Well, you've come to the right place! The name's Lynn, but my coworkers like to call me the weapon master."

She winked, and I got the feeling that she used that line on everyone who waltzed in for a gun, or in this case, a dagger.

"My friend is a beginner," Rone said.

"Ah! Then I know just the thing for her! Come right over here. We'll find her a perfect little pistol to—"

"Not a gun!" I yelled.

Lord only knew what Rone would do if he learned that there were guns in this world. Firearms would appeal way too much to his dragon side.

"A knife," I added. "A small one."

"Like this?" Lynn pulled a pocket knife out of the case.

I beamed. "Yes!"

"No," Rone boomed over me and stepped closer to the counter.

"It must be larger. Do you have any daggers in your . . ." He looked around, clearly having forgotten what the pawn shop was called. "Varied market?"

"I see now that you're looking for more of a statement piece," Lynn gestured a tattooed arm to the right. "Move on down to the end of the desk."

I wrapped my arms around my torso, but did as she said. As long as we got in and out of here with the smallest blade possible—preferably in a bag, so no one would know what it was—everything would be fine.

"How about this?" Lynn presented me with something that looked like a ceremonial dagger I imagined would be used by a shaman in Africa.

I eyed the feathers hanging off the blade, and shook my head. "I don't think that's right."

"Not at all," Rone agreed. "What about that?"

He pointed to a blade that had to be ten-inches long. The handle was a mix of gold and steel, and decorated with, what else, two dragons twining themselves together.

"That's a little flashy, don't you think?"

I mean hell, the dragons even had gemstones for eyes. One set was red—rubies, probably—while the other was the color of sapphires.

"Why not the plain one over there?" I pointed to a knife at least half the size of the dragon blade.

"Now, now, honey. Take it from me. When a man wants to spring for the best, you let him." Lynn's pale blue eyes ran over Rone appreciatively before straying to my left hand.

"In fact, if I were you, I'd also work on getting this hunk of muscle on lockdown. You know, put a ring on it, or whatever the kids are saying nowadays. The real good men like to keep their women protected. And this one ain't so shabby to look at either." She winked at him.

My cheeks burned, and against my better judgment, I darted a glance up at Rone. He was grinning like an idiot, although I doubted he'd understood half of what Lynn had said.

At least, I hoped he didn't.

Before I knew it, I held the dragon blade, and Rone was instructing me on how to swing and jab it around inside the shop. I performed all the motions as quickly as possible. The faster this was done, the faster we could leave, and I'd no longer have to hear Lynn cooing about how cute and protective Rone was being.

In the end, he announced that the dragon dagger was perfect, even if my form was much less so, and purchased it. Lynn placed it in a box—thank god no one expected me to walk out with it on my hip—and handed the bag to Rone. He took it and then, probably giving Lynn the shock of her life, grasped her hand and kissed it.

"Thank you, my lady Lynn, for all your resourceful knowledge and assistance. We will be forever in your debt."

I stifled a groan as she lit up.

"You two youngins' come back anytime." Her adoring gaze traveled from Rone to me. She lifted her left hand and wiggled her fingers. "I'm telling you, girl. Lock. Him. Down."

"All right, thank you!"

I grabbed Rone's hand, pulling him out of the pawn shop.

Rone insisted that we practice self-defense right away, and nearly pulled the dagger out in the middle of the park. Luckily, I convinced him the park was too open, and quickly found a dingy alley near the university to practice in instead. The alley still wasn't the most private place, but it was a *massive* improvement over the park or the sidewalk. I counted that as a win.

Half an hour later, I was wishing I hadn't agreed to training at all.

"You're still holding it wrong," Rone said for the fifth time as he adjusted my grip. "This is the best way to leverage a dagger. Now, show me how you would attack that stack of wood."

My gaze traveled up the tower of pallets that sat at the entrance to the alley. I gulped.

"Is it stable?"

"If it falls, I will be at your side. I'll halt it."

I stared at him. Of course Rone was buff, but there had to be at least twenty pallets on this thing. Was he saying that he could catch all of them?

I shook my head. Like it mattered. I wouldn't hit it hard enough to make anything fall.

Doing as he'd instructed, I pulled my arm back and attacked the pallet. The moment the dagger plunged into the wood, I released a satisfied grunt.

As much as I would rather be doing almost anything else, I had to admit that attacking something was a great stress reliever.

"You're lucky to still have both your eyes," Rone said a second later, shattering my calm. "Let me demonstrate once more."

I stepped back, watched, and then tried again. And again. And again.

After what felt like the millionth occurence of Rone micromanaging my tiniest arm movements, I couldn't take it any longer.

"This is so annoying! I wasn't joking before when I said people here don't fight like this. No one gets in street brawls . . . or office brawls. At least no one who's reputable."

Rone's face hardened.

"Are you saying that, in this land, men don't fight for what they believe in?" he countered. "That they lay down and allow their enemies to pummel them?"

I scoffed. "They fight differently. More sophisticated ways."

"Unmanly methods," Rone muttered, and my mouth dropped open.

"Excuse me? What did you say?"

He frowned and turned away.

"Don't you turn your back on me! I hate that!"

He spun around to face me.

"It seems to me that you only befriend men who aren't real protectors. Those who would hide and lurk in the trees rather than face dangerous enemies."

I blinked.

What the hell . . .

Then I remembered Micah running out of the dark woods to throw me the egg. Was Rone talking about him? Was Rone, dragon prince and elite warrior, jealous of Micah Johnson?!

Oh my god. Although I wasn't sure why he'd be jealous of Micah, that would explain so many of his sour moods.

I took a step toward him. "Rone, I—"

My mouth snapped shut as a nearby voice, one that didn't belong to Rone, entered my head, and a familiar, warm vibration resonated deep inside of me.

A dragonblood was nearby.

22

RONE

I NEEDED to get myself under control. It was important that Violet learn to fight properly, though I hoped she'd never have to fight alone. The idea of her getting hurt ripped at my gut, but she was offended.

Sighing, I readied to apologize so she wouldn't give up on her training.

"Listen, Violet—"

My heart squeezed, and my words disappeared when she placed one hand on my chest and the fingers of her other hand against my mouth.

I stared into her eyes, pools of blue swirled with excitement.

"There's a dragonblood nearby. I can hear and feel them."

She removed her fingers from my lips and touched her chest.

The gesture was innocent on her part, trying to accentuate what was happening to her. Though I couldn't stop the image from searing into my heart, knowing how it was used in Draessonia.

"Did you hear me?" she asked as I continued to stare like a bewildered hatchling.

"Uh, yeah . . . dragonblood."

I mentally shook myself and shoved all thoughts of home, mates, and ceremonies aside, and forced myself to concentrate on the mission. "Let's find them."

"I don't know exactly where it's coming from." She made a slow circle and scanned the alley.

We stood trapped between two buildings in a relatively remote area, so we made our way to the main sidewalk. Violet still refused to place the dagger properly on her hip, prompting me to slide it carefully into my satchel alongside the eggs.

In the time we'd spent practicing, more pedestrians had begun to mill around the sidewalks.

Discreetly, I slipped out the scale Virhan had given me to track the dragonbloods. It pointed to the left, but before I could suggest that course, it swung the other way, then started spinning in full circles.

I gripped the tool harder in frustration. "Perhaps we should just pick a direction?"

"That's as good an idea as any, I suppose. I can't tell who I'm hearing, with all these people everywhere."

Violet took her time, studying each face we passed. I sniffed the air to help search. If I wasn't mistaken, she kept darting glances in my direction to ensure we stayed together. Several times, I had to bite my cheek to keep from grinning.

It was a serious task, and I needed to concentrate.

"The feeling is weaker, let's turn around." Violet grabbed hold of my wrist and turned us in the opposite direction. Her slender fingers soft against my skin even as her nails dug in to navigate through the crowd.

Preoccupied as I was, I'd stopped participating in the search. But the scale still rested in my free hand, and brought me back to reality when it bounced to life.

I snapped to attention. The pointer hovered one person's direction, then spun to point at someone else. I moved closer to each individual in an attempt to isolate their scent.

My efforts drew tugs from Violet when our bodies shuffled further apart.

"Watch it!" a man yelled, and pushed her out of his way when he nearly barged through our joined hands.

Losing my connection to Violet, I grabbed the back of his neck as he squirmed by us, causing him to squeal.

"Do *not* touch her."

"Rone! Let him go." Violet patted the man on the arm. "I'm so sorry."

I released the vermin, but sneered, giving him the sense to run without a challenge.

Violet maneuvered us out of the stream of people, pressing her back against a building.

"You need to chill. I can't find who we're looking for if you start fighting with everyone who bumps into us."

"We didn't *bump into* that one, he shoved you aside. I'll not tolerate that. Besides, it's hard to pick up on a distinct scent unless I'm close to the person, nor is my scale working in these conditions."

Violet closed her eyes for a second, and I watched her

inhale and exhale—to center herself, I supposed. A strand of her hair fell over her face, and I resisted the urge to brush it away.

I needed to control those impulses.

"Have you continued to pick up on the dragonblood's resonance?"

I pulled my shoulders back and recalled my military training. Calm, objective, rational analysis would get me through this momentary struggle.

"You're a dog with a bone," she muttered as she twisted her neck to scan the sidewalk one way and then the other. "It's coming from this way."

She strode away in the same direction we'd been searching, but without reaching for my hand. I rubbed my chest as I took in the space between us, and kept walking.

Ahead, items dangled from the extended eaves over the entrance of a store, emitting obnoxious twinkling sounds. Powerful scents wafted out of the door, clogging my senses as we passed.

Violet halted abruptly, causing me to dodge sideways to avoid her, only then to knock into a man standing near the entrance to the offending store.

"My apologies," I mumbled, darting a quick glance to ensure I hadn't hurt the individual.

Violet would probably classify the scrawny male as a warrior from this culture, and be angry if I'd injured him.

"Let's go in here," she said, not seeming to have noticed what happened.

I hesitated as I peered into the dark interior, unsure if I wanted to follow her or wait outside. Rolling my neck, I relieved some of the tension, and stepped forward.

Violet was in my service, and I couldn't ignore my responsibility.

Opposite the man I jostled, who was speaking with another as if nothing happened, was a woman who looked vaguely familiar. I didn't give her more than a passing glance before she shoved a paper in front of my chest.

Involuntarily, I grabbed the intrusive item, which she took as a sign of my interest.

"Tell all your friends, it's going to be a great festival. I'll be there, and I'd definitely love to see you."

The sultry tones of her voice hurried me through the door to find Violet.

Without reading the propaganda, I folded the paper and shoved it into the back pocket of my trousers while my eyes adjusted to the dim light inside. My height gave me the advantage of seeing the entire establishment at once.

For a small store, it was crammed with odds and ends in a way that wasn't nearly as orderly as Lynn's pawn shop had been. Tendrils of smoke slithered into the air from a censer near the front, explaining the pungent sage aroma, and crowded glass shelves displayed fragile-looking items that didn't appear to have a purpose.

I spotted Violet loitering in an aisle near the middle, forcing me deeper into the store. The quarters were tight, and I had to navigate carefully to avoid breaking any of the delicate wares. When I reached her, I leaned down and whispered into her ear for fear I would startle the one we sought —as I'd done with Candy.

"Have you determined if the individual is in here?"

She raised her shoulder, and flashed a grin at me.

"I don't know yet. There's definitely a supernatural in here, but I can't tell if they're dragonblood or not. The resonance isn't as strong, so my guess would be no."

While Violet occupied herself with a box of various colored crystals to appear nonchalant, I marked the rest of the patrons.

Two women giggled over something in the back corner, oblivious to everything else. An older woman spoke in a loud voice to no one I could see, except possibly the device she held to her ear. A juvenile male wandered back and forth near the door, presumably gathering the courage to run out of the store with the item he clearly had under his jacket.

For a second, I considered approaching the youth, but I didn't want to draw attention to myself. Getting into a pointless altercation, even if it prevented theft, would likely only irritate Violet.

That's when I saw how the man behind the counter kept covertly darting looks toward us.

The next time he stared, I caught his attention.

He immediately twisted and busied himself with a stack of cards featuring various images and witch symbols, giving the boy freedom to escape, and me the information I needed.

"The man you hear is the one behind the counter." I feigned interest in a carved statue while Violet peeked at him.

"And he doesn't have the same resonance as you. I think he's a witch, but not strong . . . we're wasting time. We should go." She dropped a crystal back into the box on the shelf and hurried away.

"Violet? Are you sure you're finished looking around? He seemed interested in—"

She was out the door before I completed my sentence.

Why she was leaving when we'd found the dragonblood baffled me, but I rushed after her. The man wasn't pale or well-dressed, if she was worried about another vampire.

Whatever her reasons, it didn't matter. She was gone, and I needed to catch up.

I arrived at the doorway just as she smacked into the woman handing out papers, forcing her arms to swing into the hanging chimes.

Violet slammed her back into me with a squeal and jumped to the side. With the wide-eyed panic of a frightened deer, she was about to bolt before I latched onto her elbow.

That seemed to settle her, but she yanked her arm from my grip and stared at the woman as if she recognized her.

23

VIOLET

"JADIS . . . ?"

My eyebrows pulled together as I tried to place the person in front of me.

"In the flesh," Jadis said with a huff as she straightened her outfit, which had gone askew when I'd careened into her.

Even though she'd confirmed her identity, I struggled to believe she was the same girl I'd met at Llewellyn's party. She'd replaced the long, black robe and crown with cutoff jean shorts, a flowy kimono top, and long, feathered earrings.

"You're Violet, right? Llewellyn's friend?" Jadis asked as she tidied a stack of fliers in her hand. "I saw you rush inside."

I nodded, and her attention shifted to Rone. "You looked familiar too, and now that you're with Violet, it's clicking. You're the guy who knew about peeking into other worlds, right?"

"Correct," he replied.

"Hmmm," Jadis' eyes raked over his muscular body. "I

apologize, but I'm blanking on your name. My mind was in an . . . altered state the night of the party. Obviously more so than I thought, if I forgot anything about you."

"Rone of House Ignatius." He gave Jadis a shallow bow.

I closed my eyes so she couldn't see them rolling behind my eyelids. I wished he'd stop it with the House Ignatius thing. Would it kill him to be plain old Rone?

However, instead of being weirded out like a normal person, Jadis looked delighted.

"Well, Rone of House Ignatius, did you have time to look over the flier? The Fire Festival should be amazing." Her green eyes sparkled as she looked up at him.

"A fire festival? I would be interested in such an event." He patted the bag at his hip.

I would bet the world that Rone thought he'd find a million dragon descendants prancing around. And maybe he was right, I wasn't sure. But right now, there was a dragonblood somewhere close by, and the longer we hung around with Jadis, the greater the chance we had at losing that person. Already, the voice that had once been strong in my mind was fading.

I opened my mouth to clue Rone in, but Jadis stepped closer to him, boxing me out.

"Wonderful," she said, her tone lower and more husky. "It's called the Fire and *Love* Festival. And it actually takes place in Arizona in a few days. I realize that's a jaunt, but believe me, it's worth it."

She batted her eyelashes.

Suddenly, I remembered she had been very taken by Rone the night of the party. Apparently, she still was.

I groaned internally. We didn't have time for flirting—I needed to get us out of here pronto.

"I've always enjoyed fire festivals." Rone's tone was wistful, like he was thinking about home.

"Well, I'd love to see *you* there. In fact . . ." Jadis laid a hand on his bicep and pulled a pen out of her shorts pocket.

How it fit in those teensy things was anyone's guess.

I watched, my annoyance growing, as she scrawled something across another flier.

"See this number?" She leaned into Rone so that her chest brushed up against him. "That's my personal cell. I'll be shuttling a few *select* people to the festival. Call me if you want a ride."

"That would speed things up nicely."

"I aim to please." She gave him a dazzling smile.

Oh my hell.

"*Rone!*"

I tried not to yell, but my voice came out louder than I intended, and heat dashed across my cheeks as the other two turned their full attention to me.

"Don't we have somewhere to be?"

The dragonblood's voice in my head was gone, but if we hurried, maybe we could catch it. At the very least, it would get us away from Jadis, which in that moment, I really wanted.

"Yes, of course," he glanced at me, clearly not understanding why I wasn't jumping for joy at the idea of a fire festival. "When and where should we meet you to go to the festival?"

196

"Oopsie!" Jadis sang out. Her eyes widened as they darted from Rone to me. "I didn't realize that Violet would come."

She shifted her gaze to me, and a sly smile spread across her face. "Unfortunately, I only have room in my car for one. But to hear Llewellyn talk, you don't like parties anyway, right? No worries if you don't want to come. Rone will be in good hands."

Confusion flashed across Rone's face. His eyes darted between Jadis and me.

"But I wish for Violet to join me. She's in my employ."

Jadis' eyes widened. "Employ . . .? So you guys aren't a couple?" She twisted to face him. "I guess I should have figured that out myself. You're in two *very* different leagues."

My fists balled up at her implication.

Jadis didn't believe that I was good enough for him, but I was positive that she saw herself as Rone's equal. Showed what she knew. She didn't even know about proper portals for Pete's sake!

"A couple?" Rone's voice came out more high-pitched than normal. His gaze darted to me.

My heart skipped a beat. He looked . . . hopeful?

My cheeks warmed even more, and unable to handle his attention, I looked away.

He cleared his throat. "We're not together, but I appreciate Violet."

Jadis' smile grew. She looked like the cat who ate the canary.

"Appreciate. Isn't that sweet, Violet? Such a *friendly* thing to do." She twisted toward Rone again. "Maybe *we* can work on getting to be close friends at the festival?"

That was the limit.

My jaw clenched, and something deep inside me roared with displeasure. Without thinking, I pushed Jadis out of the way and grabbed Rone by the front of his shirt.

"Vio—" Rone's words died on his lips when I pulled him down and kissed him.

For a moment, I thought he'd push me away. He was a prince, after all, and my boss to boot. Jadis had been right when she said he was out of my league. But even if I recognized that in my mind, I didn't care.

I *hated* seeing her pressed up against him. Despised that she was trying to come between Rone and me. Even if Rone rejected me—which, judging by the firm set of his lips, was seconds away—at least it got Jadis away from him.

His hand landed on my arm, and I prepared for him to pull away—to claim that this wasn't right. That I wasn't worthy.

But then Rone, the formidable dragon prince, softened. The next thing I knew, his hand dropped to caress the small of my back.

My blood lit on fire as he pulled me close, and the surrounding air crackled with electricity. I pushed up onto my tiptoes and pressed my torso into his, hungry for more. His kiss felt so familiar, so right, it was almost like I'd been dying of thirst in a vast desert, and he was water.

Nearby, someone fake coughed. "Ummm, hello? This is a public place!"

Jadis' voice was hard, upset, but I barely noticed her presence. Only Rone mattered. His lips, his hands, and ...

I froze as a distant voice entered my mind, and a familiar warmth filled me. It was the dragonblood from earlier.

I pulled away from Rone, my nerve endings tingling like they never had before. His eyes fluttered open. When they caught mine, he was still for a moment, his gaze studying me as if for the first time.

I hated to break the spell between us, this magical haze, whatever it was, but I had to. Rone's mission was important.

"The person we're looking for," I whispered.

"Are they near?" he asked.

I nodded.

He cleared his throat. The sound came out strangled and strange. Was he feeling as conflicted as I was?

"Then we must go," he said. "Lead the way."

24

RONE

DESPITE MY BEST efforts to keep my growing attachment to Violet under control, she'd just torn away my resolve. The warmth of her lips against mine lingered. When I pulled her close, the current that flowed between us was too intense to ignore.

There was no doubt in my mind that we'd formed a bond. But, could I take a human mate? The kingdom would surely not accept a human princess. Even though I wished to return to Draessonia soon, when I did my duty to the realm would require me to seek a true mate.

The thought roiled my stomach. When mates found each other, did they forget all others before? What if someone didn't want to forget? There were too many possibilities to consider.

Perhaps if I told myself such things a few more times, I'd believe it.

Violet's hair swung across her shoulders as she hurried

down the street in front of me. Her long strides cut through the crowd, propelling us toward our mission.

The mission. Yes, that's what would keep my mind clear.

I shifted my attention to those around us. Violet's steps slowed at the same time that I picked up a scent. It was similar to Candy's, but more coarse, like warm soil. The dragonblood was near.

"That's him." Violet's voice floated over her shoulder so only I could hear.

Like most in the area, the male she pointed out had a black pack slung on his back, and wore some style of hooded cloak. He was not my first choice for a hatchling caretaker, yet since he was dragonblood, he would have to do.

I gestured for Violet to continue in the lead. Too many thoughts clouded my mind, and I knew my words would come out in the harsh commanding tone that she didn't appreciate.

"Hey, buddy, I think you dropped something," she called to the man, though he seemed to ignore her.

My lips curled into a half-grin at her deception.

"I really think this is yours." She scoffed when the man scowled back at her. "Wait, we need to talk to you!"

Violet rushed forward as the man picked up his pace, bumping others out of his way.

A growl escaped my throat as she pursued with a tunnel vision. All around her, others glared and made comments as she followed the man's path through the crowd. Once more, she ignored her surroundings and put herself at risk.

Increasing my speed so I was only a step behind, I kept anyone at bay who might want to confront her. I clamped my lips tight, and people smartly moved out of our way when they noticed me.

Violet caught up and grabbed the sleeve of the man we chased, which finally made him acknowledge our pursuit.

"Get away from me," he shouted, drawing surrounding stares. "Keep your weirdo shit to yourself."

I eyed the man with confusion. Violet had called to him, nothing more. What had made him so hostile? Sure, she was touching him, but he couldn't feel anything in that . . . could he? Did she give off sparks to everyone, and I just hadn't realized it?

My thoughts were dangerously jumbled, and I murmured at myself to concentrate before getting the man's attention. "You need to listen to what the lady has to say."

"You're both nuts. There's plenty of your kind around this campus, go find someone else to bother." He lifted his hands in front of his body and backed up two steps, preparing to dash away.

He was slightly shorter than Violet, and his baggy jacket and loose jeans around his narrow hips belied his weak muscle tone. Nothing about this individual read *dragon*, yet I trusted Violet's abilities.

Before he could run, I reached around Violet and took hold of his collar.

His eyes popped wide enough to see the whites around the brown irises.

"Listen to what we have to say without resistance or running. If you do that, I'll think about letting you go," I hissed through clenched teeth.

My patience would not last much longer.

"What he means is we would like to speak with you about an important offer." Violet placed her hand on my arm, and narrowed her eyes at me.

"Let him go."

I slid her an annoyed glance and reluctantly abided. Her tone sounded similar to when we found Candy.

Humans were so sensitive and stubborn. Why couldn't they just comply?

"My friend is so excited we found you. There's something classified we'd like to speak with you about, but it would be better to do so somewhere less . . . public. Can we go over to that bench under the trees and chat with you for a moment?"

I crossed my arms over my chest to keep them from grabbing the man again when he shook his head. She was being far too kind, and it still didn't seem to be working.

"Listen, I don't want whatever you're selling, and I'm not that stupid. If you want money, fine." He reached into his front pocket and pulled out a crumpled wad of money, shoving it at Violet. "Here, it's all I have. Just go."

"We don't want any money." Violet pushed the man's hand away.

That gave me a thought. Violet hadn't agreed to help me until I'd offered her pay. And Candy had seemed relieved when I gave her funds to care for the egg. Perhaps funding, not duty, was part of the order of this realm.

"We can pay you handsomely."

Violet snapped her gaze to mine and pursed her lips.

"I'll be late to class. Really, I don't want what you're selling or worse, buying!"

"This is a legitimate offer. Even though it seems odd,

please give us a minute of your time. My friend is blunt, but that's because our offer is important." Violet kept her voice calm and kind. "Please, just hear us out before you decide. Can we go sit?"

The man lowered his shoulders and glanced at the ground. After releasing a sigh, he returned his gaze to Violet.

"Fine, but that guy keeps his distance." He thrust his hand out and pointed to me.

I grinned.

"Understood." Violet nodded and gestured to the bench she'd mentioned earlier. "After you."

We followed the sapling of a man to a small, green space with two trees towering overhead, shading us from the overcast sky. Tromping through the damp leaves added to the earthy smell of the air. The climate's constant moisture did nothing to help my disposition.

"I really do have a class soon, so whatever you need to say, do it quickly," the man said as soon as he and Violet sat down.

She twisted toward him and tucked one leg underneath her. I guessed to assume a less threatening pose.

I kept two steps back as the man requested, but stayed on the balls of my feet in case he lunged for Violet.

"I understand. First, my name is Violet, and the hulk back there is Rone. What's yours?"

"Jason."

"It's nice to meet you, Jason. Have you ever wondered why it seems like you don't fit in with everyone else? Like maybe there's something more in the world you're supposed to belong to, but don't know what it is?"

"Nope, I'm comfortable with who I am, thanks."

Jason slipped his free arm through the unused strap of his pack.

It was a good move. He was preparing to have the use of both hands, keeping his options open in a potentially dangerous situation. It was the first sign that made me believe he was a dragonblood after all, and would be a good match for an egg.

"I'm going to let you in on a secret, Jason. I know that's not true, because you were just thinking how your craziness has finally caught up to you. You're wondering how I know exactly what you were thinking, and I'm freaking you out." Violet gave a calm smile. "I know I'm right, because I can hear your thoughts."

I inched closer.

"Like I'm supposed to believe you're some kind of psychic or something? I don't go for any of that crap." Jason rubbed his hands on his thighs.

"I'm not a psychic," Violet rushed out, and glanced over her shoulder at me. "But I can hear people, people we'd think of as supernaturals, in my mind. I know this is shocking, believe me, it was for me too, but the supernatural world is a real thing. And you're part of it."

Jason rose to his feet. "Okay, I'm out of here."

Violet slid both feet to the ground, but she didn't make any move to get up.

"Then why did you just tell yourself that you 'knew it'? You've been suspicious for a long time. Admit it. We're only confirming it for you."

Her eyes narrowed as if she was listening intently. "And

yes, we know what you are. If you want to know too, please sit back down."

I inhaled a deep breath to keep myself from reaching over and shoving him back onto the bench. Violet stayed relaxed. We were a good team.

Jason's mouth twitched. He darted a look in the direction he'd go if he ran, then lowered himself back down. "I'll listen, but I still don't believe you."

"That's fine, I don't blame you. I didn't understand or believe at first either. But I want to show you something." Violet twisted to me and held out her hand.

"I think we should confirm that he'll help before we show him." I gripped the strap of my satchel.

"He needs to see them first. Some people don't believe without evidence, Rone."

I swallowed hard, unsure what to do. Trust was a dual affair, and this man had done nothing to assure me he was worthy of my kind. The ancients of my realm were commended for their faith, even when they didn't always see the future clearly. Would Jason take his vow seriously?

I released a huff, and slipped the bag over my head. I'd follow my own realm's doctrines but trust Violet's judgment.

She took the satchel carefully and rested it in her lap. Opening the top, she leaned the main compartment toward Jason, who stretched his neck to peer inside.

"What are those?"

Forgetting his reticence, he scooted closer to Violet. Which prompted me to step closer to the bench, but he didn't even notice. His attention was on the eggs.

"These are dragon eggs, and they're calling to you

because you carry the DNA of an ancient line of dragons. This is what we want to offer you. The chance to care for one of these precious babies."

While we were all concentrating on the satchel, a voice boomed in our direction.

Jason jerked back and searched for who called his name.

He jutted his chin toward another man standing with two others fifty feet away. "Hey, Chase."

I stepped in their direction so my body would be between the bench and the others.

"Are you coming to class?" Chase asked.

"Yeah, save me a seat. I'll meet you there," Jason answered.

I didn't relax or move back to the side of the bench until the three walked away.

Jason stared at Violet once again.

"I really have to go. This is a nice act, and I almost bought it. Wherever you got these made is top-notch . . . they're very convincing. Are you theater majors? Set designers?"

"I assure you, these are real, and we need your help."

"We'll pay you for your time in caring for the egg and the hatchling." I no longer cared if I intimidated him. We needed him to agree. There were four more dragonbloods to find. I pulled out some money I had remaining in my pocket.

I could see his hesitation in the set of his posture.

He tensed his legs in order to stand. "You two are serious, aren't you?"

"Very. Will you help us?" Violet asked.

I released a breath when he leaned back and settled somewhat.

"How much are you offering?"

I started to reach into my pocket again, but Violet threw her hand up and snagged my arm. "Dude, no."

She faced Jason again.

"Five hundred dollars now, and two thousand more when we meet next—as long as you agree to every one of our conditions, and execute them perfectly."

Jason's eyes widened as a smile spread across his face. "Deal."

"You're positive you will fulfill your duties?"

He met and held my gaze for the first time since we'd met him. "What do you want me to do?"

"You must keep the egg warm in an oven, and check on it regularly to ensure it never gets cold. You can't ignore it. When it begins to hatch, you must stay with it at all times from that moment forward. However, hopefully you'll arrive on my ranch before the hatching takes place."

"Ranch?"

"Yes, it's in Wyoming. We'll write down the directions for you to get there. Do you have a car?" Violet asked.

"Yeah, but how am I supposed to take off school and pay for gas to some remote place like that?"

"That's what the compensation is for. In addition to the money you receive before the birth, there will be a financial account set up for maintenance of the young hatchling until it's ready to return home to my realm," I added, tiring of his whining. "Even if you must set aside other duties, you're accepting an obligation that's of the utmost importance. The survival of an entire race is at stake."

"Sure." Jason stared at me for an extra second. "I can do all that. In fact, I can take a couple for you, if you want?"

He shrugged and settled his gaze on Violet.

"Do you live in an apartment near here?" She seemed to sense something I didn't, and unease tugged at my gut.

"It's near Hawthorne, in Southeast. I'm just here for class. Is that a problem?"

"No, but I think caring for just one is best. We really need you to understand that this is important. These eggs represent different families of dragons, and they must be protected."

"I understand. I'll care for it as if it were my own child."

A smile bloomed on my face as relief flooded through me. Nodding, I nudged Violet's shoulder for her to choose an egg for him.

She twisted her neck, cutely making eye contact with me while her head tipped backward. "Do you still have that festival paper?"

"It's in the satchel's front pocket."

After a quick search, she retrieved the paper and handed it to Jason.

"Write your address and phone number on the back of this so we can contact you later."

"Sure," Jason snaked his hand behind him and retrieved a writing device from his bag, then made the proper notations on the page where Violet showed him.

At first, she seemed to hesitate, then pulled out the egg from House Zimurra.

I bit back a gasp as Jason eagerly reached for the descendant of my mother's house.

Violet pulled the egg back.

"Open your backpack and make a comfortable space for it first. Remember, it needs to stay warm. You need to go home right after class, and put it in the oven, heated at two hundred degrees. If you let it sit in there for at least four hours at a time, and keep it covered other times, it should stay comfortable."

Jason slipped his pack off his shoulders and rummaged through it until he'd made a space she approved of. Then he carefully took the egg from her and placed it protectively in the spot.

The egg stayed dark, not reacting the same as it had for Violet, but I assured myself that wasn't a problem. After all, Candy's egg hadn't responded to her touch, either.

"Thank you. This is a grand responsibility, and we'll honor your name in my homeland for your assistance."

"Cool, that's great, but isn't there something else one of you needs to hand me?"

Violet jumped to her feet and stood in front of me.

"Yes, Rone will you hand Jason five hundred dollars?"

Her implication toward my deficiency with human money grated on me. Mostly because she was correct. I needed her to give me a lesson so it wouldn't be a problem anymore.

I counted out several bills, keeping them from Jason's view. When I'd gathered what I believed to be correct, she smiled.

Handing the bills to her, I returned the rest to my pocket, as she spun back to Jason.

"Here you go. Remember, keep it warm, and we'll contact you about when to meet."

"Got it." Jason stuffed the money into his pocket, and carefully returned the pack to its place on his back. "I'll see you soon."

Without waiting for either of us to respond, he hurried away into the crowd in the direction he'd been going when we found him.

Another egg was in the care of a dragonblood.

25

VIOLET

I WAS BUZZING with excitement as we walked back to Rone's place. We'd found another dragonblood. I'd sensed him, and we found him! It was a little harder than I expected, but still.

Finally, we'd made progress.

I turned to Rone, excited to share my happiness now that we were out of the crowd, but his expression stopped me.

A frown lined his face, and his eyes were hard.

How could he be upset when we'd just found a dragonblood?

Then a horrible thought came to me. Was he mad about the kiss? I had kind of forced it on him. Oh my hell . . . why did I do that?

My stomach dropped, and I glanced covertly at him once more. Yup, he looked pissed.

I shot my gaze to the ground, unsure how to handle this. With every step I took, my breath tightened.

When I couldn't take it a moment longer, I cleared my throat.

"Rone? Are you okay?"

He didn't answer, and my surety that he was upset about the kiss amplified.

"I think I might have overstepped my boundaries. I'm sorry about the ki—"

"That man . . . something was off about him."

My mouth snapped shut, and I swallowed my embarrassing apology as Rone cut me off.

"The more I think about it, the more I believe he doesn't understand how serious taking on an egg is," he continued with a huff. "Don't you agree that it was too difficult to get him to take it? Why doesn't he respect the ancient blood?"

Oh boy. Here we go again with the ancient blood and all that.

"It's not that he doesn't respect your kind," I said carefully. "It's more that it's very hard to believe. Remember, he didn't even know about supernaturals. That's a lot to process."

His jaw worked from side to side.

"But we got him to take it," I added, hoping to alleviate some of his stress. He'd seemed pleased just minutes ago. This change of heart was abrupt, and a little disheartening for me.

"And he said he'd meet you at that ranch you rented. I mean, for a guy you met on the street, that's pretty good. You have to keep your expectations realistic."

Rone sighed and his shoulders loosened slightly.

"I don't like it, but I understand. However, I'll admit, part of my worry is that I didn't believe it would be *this* difficult to find dragonbloods." He shook his head. "In truth, *we* have only found one. Candy found us."

I'd had the same thought, but coming from him, it felt more personal. Was he telling me that I needed to work harder? In case he was, I fell silent and began scanning the area for dragonbloods.

Apparently understanding what I was doing, Rone pulled out the dragon-finder scale.

"Has it started working yet?" I asked.

"Unfortunately, it hasn't performed how Virhan promised." The pointiest end of the scale began to spin in a circle, eliciting a scowl from Rone.

"Tell me about this mage. I know he works for your family, but what does he do? And why did *he* send you here, and not your dad? If you're a prince, your dad is the king, right? Shouldn't he be sending people on missions?"

His shoulders stiffened.

"Sorry," I blurted. "You don't have to talk about that, if it's crossing a line. I—"

"You're not crossing a line. I simply miss home, and feel badly that I left it in a time of need. As I said before, I'm here to ensure the continuation of my kind because, rumor has it, a rebellion is brewing. Mage Virhan saw the bigger picture, and sent me here in case we failed in squashing the rebels." He shoved the scale into his murse. "More than anything, I hope to finish this mission and return home to aid my father."

"Tell me about him," I said, sensing that his family was a safe topic.

Rone continued to talk while I searched aggressively for dragonbloods. We were nearing his apartment when he said that the egg we'd given Jason was distantly related to him, and he couldn't wait to meet the hatchling.

I stopped in my tracks. "Rone . . . when *are* these eggs supposed to hatch?"

"Not long. I expect they will be born in less than two weeks."

Less than two weeks. He didn't know the actual day.

"Can they fly when they hatch? How big are they? Are they dangerous?"

Good grief, why hadn't I thought of these questions earlier? I mean, between fighting vampires and witches, we'd been busy, but still . . . I might be present for one of these births. I needed to know everything about dragon births—and I needed to know *now*.

"They can't fly right away. That will take a couple of days. And they're not dangerous, they're babies looking for a dragonblood, usually their parent of course, to imprint upon. Usually that's their parent, but here it will be the caregiver until I retrieve the hatchlings before their age of fervor."

I gulped, my brain locked on one word.

"Imprint?"

"It is the dragon way of bonding with their clan."

Oh hell. I could *not* have a little baby dragon cracking open on me. What would I do with it? I wasn't dragonblood, so it couldn't imprint on me, which meant that I'd have zero control over it.

My stomach flip-flopped.

"Well we can't have them opening without the proper caregiver around." I doubled down on my search for dragonbloods, my gut churning with anxiety.

Unfortunately, I didn't have any luck. So by the time we reached his building, both Rone and I were in a sour mood. We were silent the entire elevator ride up, all the way to the apartment. Right away Rone turned on the oven like a pro and we began settling the eggs inside it. Still tucked into his murse, the glint of my new dagger caught my eye and I shook my head, unable to believe everything that had happened today.

"Do you want to practice with it?" Rone asked, though his tone was half-hearted.

I suspected that he was still thinking about how hard it had been to find dragonbloods. Or maybe considering Jason's worthiness as a caregiver again.

"Not right now. Just leave it in there for safekeeping."

My stomach growled loud enough for us both to hear. "Actually, I'm starving. How about lunch first?" Recalling that all he had was crackers and coffee, I corrected myself. "Or . . . something to snack on?"

Rone shrugged, trudged over to the couch, and began sharpening his dagger with a frown on his lips.

I huffed out a breath. I mean, we were both in a funk. Why did he feel he could just walk away from me? It was a frustrating habit, although I knew right now wasn't the time to bring it up.

Instead, I stood at the edge of the room, watching him. The silence sinking into my bones magnified my worry over the baby dragons being born, and the millions of other things that could go wrong.

Unable to take my own thoughts anymore, I walked to the TV and turned on a reality show. I needed something to distract me from the idea of hatchlings zooming around Portland and lighting everything on fire. Plus, it would do Rone some good to learn a little about modern culture.

Maybe if he learned etiquette, I wouldn't have to go around getting him out of streetfights or correcting his overly formal vocabulary. A girl could dream.

Feeling better now that the TV had provided a distraction, I returned to the kitchen and poured the entire box of saltines onto a plate. I didn't know if Rone would eat them, but I sure as heck would. Even if they were stale, I was determined to comfort-eat myself out of this funk.

After grabbing a couple bottles of water, and balancing the plate on my forearm, I made my way carefully back into the living room. Rone was still sharpening one of his daggers, but he'd changed the channel from the reality show to the mid-day news.

A smile bloomed on my face, because that meant he knew how to use the remote, and for some reason, I found that a little funny.

"Hey, how long did it take you to figure out the ..."

I trailed off as Jason appeared on the screen.

26

RONE

VIOLET STARTLED me when she rushed in front of me, a plate of food balancing on her arm.

I dropped the whetstone I held to snatch a water bottle from the air as it fell in her haste. "Is there something wrong?"

Setting the other bottle on the small table, she rocked on her feet to block me from standing. I reached for the plate, but she quickly set it down next to the water and grabbed the control device for the TV.

"I apologize if changing the program has upset you. Those people were too foolish for my liking."

She cleared her throat and appeared distraught. "Rone, I need you to stay calm."

Leaning back, I studied her countenance for clues as to what had her upset. It couldn't be over the silly entertainment, could it? Or perhaps, she wanted to discuss our kiss from earlier. It would be wise to agree to keep our distance, lest it happened again.

"Um . . . Violet, about what happened. I'm not complaining, it was nice, but, . . ."

I rubbed the back of my neck and tried to decide what I could say that would—

A statement from the TV stopped my thought at the same time that Violet gasped. Neither of us moved as we stared at the screen.

"Yeah, it even has a name, House Zimmerah or something, but I figured if they were willing to part with their cash, I was willing to hold onto a prop for a while."

Violet must have heard what I did, because she threw both arms in front of her as I rose to my feet.

"Can we put that down somewhere out of reach? Please?"

She used her eyes to point to the dagger still in my hand.

"Why is that man on the screen?" I stared at Jason tossing the egg like a ball from one hand to the other as he grinned. A growl escaped me as my grip tightened on the dagger.

Violet placed her hand on my forearm. "Please, let me have this," she begged.

I allowed her steady gaze to persuade me to relinquish the weapon, in the hopes it would hurry her to explain what was happening.

After setting my dagger on the table, she rushed back to my side. "Let's sit, so we can better listen to what he's saying."

I lowered myself onto my seat as she turned up the volume and then joined me.

"Were they trying to sell you drugs, then?" a woman's voice asked from somewhere out of sight.

"At first, that's what I thought. The drug problem around here is really bad, but that wasn't it. I was minding my own business trying to get to class when I heard them calling to me. I ignored them at first."

"What made you speak to them, then?"

"Well, they had this outrageous story. I figured they must have been tweaking, and I didn't want to upset them. So I just listened. They had this huge tale about dragons returning to our world—they must have been on something wild. Then they offered me money to keep one of these."

He held up the egg with a laugh, and the picture zoomed in close.

I could see the drab emerald color, proof the egg was chilled.

Violet gasped next to me and jumped to her feet.

I understood her sentiment. Displaying such ignorant disrespect was one thing, but holding the egg in the cool air and risking the life of the hatchling inside fueled the heat within my core.

"At least you have a nice souvenir for your shelf," the unseen woman voiced with mirth.

"Yeah, and who knows, maybe I'll be the first one to own a brand new pet dragon one day!"

A crowd had gathered around the man, and it laughed along with him.

"But seriously, everyone should watch out for them, especially the big dude. He seemed like he could hurt someone."

The screen changed to show two people sitting behind a long table, and Violet clicked off the picture before facing me.

"You need to calm down. You're getting so hot, I can feel it from here. The couch will probably combust, at this rate."

"We need to get that egg back."

"Yes, we do, but there's another problem here."

Latching onto Violet's gaze I stood and stepped closer, waiting for her to explain herself.

"What's worse than letting a hatchling die?"

"Okay, you really need to chill a little before we can make a plan." A bead of sweat rolled down the side of her face.

"I don't believe I'm capable of that at the moment."

"Fine, but listen. I'm positive that man's a dragonblood. But, obviously he isn't the right one to care for an egg. We'll figure out a better way to pass judgment next time."

I snorted, and a rattle banged against my chest as my dragon fought to erupt through my skin. My mission seemed doomed to fail, no matter what progress we made.

"Perhaps it's time for me to talk with the dragonbloods instead," I suggested.

Violet narrowed her eyes and put her hands on her hips.

"Let's not argue over if I have been convincing enough. The problem is there's a witch out there who warned us not to let the human realm know about dragons. And that idiot just went public in a big way. She's going to hear about this, and I'm concerned that Micah is in more danger now. He was at the party and helped toss the egg to me when I sat on your back after you shifted. If the witch knows about him too, she'll go after him first."

A burst of anger ignited in me at the mention of Violet's friend. Her continued fear for him proved she held him in a higher esteem than she wanted to admit, but I shoved those thoughts aside.

"The first thing we must do is retrieve the egg. It's from my mother's house, Violet! Then we can find your friend, and protect him from the witch. There's no discussion about this."

She stared at me while seeming to contemplate my words.

With or without her, I'd be finding the dreg who I'd foolishly trusted.

"You're right, that's what we'll do. But let's eat first. That'll give us time to talk, and ensure that we can think straight when we find him."

Without dropping her gaze, I grabbed a handful of the dry wafers she'd provided, and shoved them into my mouth.

Violet gaped as I swallowed the dry substance and chugged a full bottle of water.

"Let's go."

I didn't wait for a response before I strode into the hallway.

27

VIOLET

MY HEART THUNDERED SO hard as I sprinted to keep up with Rone that I feared it would crack my ribs. He was racing toward the university to find Jason, and then . . .

Actually, I didn't want to finish that thought.

Rone was a new kind of pissed off that I'd never seen before. I wouldn't be surprised if smoke began to pour from his nostrils.

In the elevator, I'd had to *beg* him not to shift into dragon form and take to the skies to find homeboy. Only my explanation that helicopters would probably shoot him down had made him see sense. But hold him back from strangling Jason? I wasn't sure I was *that* persuasive. The guy had disrespected dragons, put one of Rone's kind, and kin, at risk. Now the dragon prince was out for blood.

"Hold up!" I yelled as he neared the street that bled into campus.

Now that it was afternoon, there were more people

around. If he charged in there, I might not be able to find him.

And maybe that was exactly what he wanted, because the stubborn-ass dragon completely ignored my cries, and turned the corner without looking back.

I swore and put on another burst of speed. When I reached the turn, I sucked in a breath.

Two young men wearing hoodies were on the ground, their backpacks tossed to the side. People were helping them up, and both men pointed in the same direction, angry looks on their faces.

My eyes closed. No, no, no, Rone! You can't barge in here and accost anyone with a hoodie! Dammit!

A scream cut through the air.

"Someone call the cops!" a woman's voice rang out, and my eyes popped back open.

I needed to find Rone and get him the hell out of there fast.

I dove into the crowd. It seemed like classes had just gotten out or something, because more people than usual were meandering from building to building. Every few feet or so, I would catch sight of someone on the ground, looking dazed or fearful.

Each downed person increased my panic and anger. Who did Rone think he was? Could he act like this in Draessonia and get away with it? If so, the prince needed to learn some damn manners.

"What the hell is wrong with that guy?" someone cried out.

"He's crazy! I heard him mumbling about dragon eggs. I hope the cops get here soon," a blonde girl said loudly as I approached.

I skidded to a stop, because past the blonde, I couldn't spot any people on the ground. "Which way did he go?"

She gestured left. "He was going that way, but something caught his attention, because he turned on a dime and rampaged toward the psych building."

"Which building is that?"

She pointed. "The stone one with the banner over the front door. There's a statue of a man in front, too. You can't miss it."

"Thanks," I said, launching myself toward the psych building.

Blondie had steered me right, because a minute later, I caught sight of Rone's massive form.

And he was holding Jason up by the neck.

"*Shit!*" I whisper-screamed. "Rone! Stop! Let him go!"

Now that I was closer, it would be easy enough to get to him. Most people were scurrying away.

"Hold up." A hand reached out and stopped me when I was only twenty feet away. "He's unstable. Don't go near him."

I yanked my arm back. "He's my . . ."

What, employer? Friend? The kiss flashed in my mind. Something else?

"Friend," I settled on. "I have to help him."

I pushed the man's arm away and sprinted for the statue.

When I reached Rone, his face was fire-engine red, and his knuckles white. Jason was in his grasp, having a difficult time breathing, and his skin where Rone touched him was redder than it should be, like it was burning.

"Answer me!" Rone rumbled, not even noticing that I'd arrived.

The guy gasped and shook his head.

"Rone," I said, my tone quiet so no one in the watching crowd would overhear. "Let him down. You don't have to release him, but he can't answer you if he can't breathe."

I glanced around and gulped. People were pointing and staring. "You're drawing too much attention."

"I don't care who sees me. They should know about this swine." He pressed Jason harder into the base of the statue.

The young man wheezed again and kicked his legs weakly. I was sure he'd pass out at any moment.

"You *should* care what others think, because they're going to call the cops."

"So? I will handle them."

"No, you won't. They're armed and—oh my god."

My arm hairs rose. At that exact moment, I saw the boys in blue themselves rushing through the crowd.

I leapt up, grabbed Rone's hands, and tried with all my might to pull them down so the guy could breathe. "Let him go! They're here! We've got to run!"

"Release him!" a man's voice boomed behind me, and panic took over.

I doubled down, pressing myself up against Rone as I tried to get him to let go of the guy.

"I said let him go!" the man commanded. "Last warning!"

"I'm trying—"

A zing of electricity ran over my back, making me swallow my words, and scream in pain. I heard a grunt, and Jason slid down the statue base and onto the ground.

My eyes fluttered closed, and I joined him on the cement.

28

RONE

IF VIOLET HADN'T RISEN to her feet on her own, I wasn't sure if I could have stopped myself from shifting.

The moment those wands hit, their powerful energy flowed through my body, igniting my dragon's will to fight. But watching Violet and knowing she was safe allowed me to keep a clear head.

She'd be furious with me if I alerted so many humans to my dragon form.

If shackles and chains didn't bind my wrists and ankles, I could have easily overpowered the two larger men who hauled me into a vehicle. The restraints were already the second attempt to hold me, after the flimsy plastic ties didn't work.

"We're taking you to County until the drugs leave your system. Then whatever charges are filed will determine where you end up after that," the driver said.

He and another man sat in the front, wearing military-style uniforms. They must be the cops Violet tried to warn me about.

I huffed at the insult that I'd taint my body with mind-altering substances—if they knew of dragons, they'd understand.

———

A FOOT SNAKED between my leg chains to trip me, and I fell to my knees as I was deposited into a cell reeking of urine and sweat.

It was similar to those we had in Draessonia with a few stark differences. Familiar iron bars formed the front wall with a bolted door, but instead of being hewn out of the stone mountain, the walls were a smooth, stark gray, unmarred by claws. It also lacked a straw floor, only boasting hard, cold benches along two sides, and an infernal light that buzzed like a thousand insects.

Given some time and effort, I could no doubt free myself, even with my hands secured behind me as they were. If anything, I could increase my body temperature enough to heat the metal bands to a snapping point.

Four other males rose from the benches as I made my clumsy entrance. I ignored them, and twisted to the guard at the door.

"Tell me my companion is safe and being treated better than I, and you'll have no trouble from me."

He narrowed his eyes, and a slight curl formed at the corner of his mouth.

"I don't know what happened to your girlfriend, but have

fun with your new friends." He nodded to those behind me. "Make sure he can still talk during booking later, boys."

The guard left, and I faced the men.

They stepped closer and took up positions surrounding me. All seemed like worthy opponents. They shared a similarly muscular build, but the hardness of their expressions told me they had no concern for leaving my speech intact.

"Even chained, I can damage all of you. I'd suggest leaving me alone for your own safety."

Considering I sat on my knees at their feet, their snorts and wry grins were understandable.

Their cloying pheromones filled the dank air as they readied for battle. I rose to my feet. At least two of them darted glances to each other when my height towered theirs.

As expected, it was the one behind me who struck first. It always was, in such circumstances.

A blow landed to my kidneys, and I flinched. The action allowed the thug to my right to suckerpunch me in the jaw. My head snapped to the left, and I stumbled from the chains between my ankles.

I felt the movement of air as another arm headed for my midsection, and I dropped to the ground. Rolling over my shoulder, I landed on my backside and swung both legs at the knee of one attacker. He fell with a thud, and I rammed an elbow into his face to knock him unconscious.

Another man kicked me in the gut, and I lost my breath long enough for him to punch me in the face three times. With a roar, I sat up and headbutted the man in the nose. Blood spurted over both of us.

I awkwardly scrambled to my feet, only to have an arm

wrap around my throat. As I was held from behind by his companion, the last man of the group stepped into his punch to my ribs. I grunted.

Twice more, he slammed his fist into my side, and I felt at least one bone give way. It sent shooting pains through me as I gritted my teeth and tried to keep myself from overheating.

This would be so much easier if I could use my fire.

Even though the others seemed to have worked themselves into a fury, I was doing my best to remain level-headed and appear human.

"Is that all you men have?" I taunted.

I wanted to draw out more of their energy and tire them to shorten the altercation. They were all large, but none seemed to have warrior training.

Using my weight, I leaned into the man behind me and shuffled my feet until his back hit the wall, hard. His arm left my neck, and I ducked in time to avoid the next blow from the man in front. His punch grazed my ear, but also found purchase on the man behind me.

In order to regain his control, the man against the wall shoved his hands under my arms and locked his fingers against the back of my neck. I used this to my advantage, trapping him against the wall to swing my legs up and into the front attacker.

The force of my kick sent him stumbling across the cell. Though, the restricting hands on my neck distracted me from my commitment to staying calm.

I ground out a guttural sound, feeling my heat rise. The man wedged behind me screamed and shoved me away. I barely kept my balance as I staggered, but the little I maintained was only temporary, as an uppercut connected with my jaw.

Catapulted the opposite direction, I landed on the ground not far from the first man, who remained knocked out. Broken-nose rejoined the other two, and all three alternated between kicking and punching my body.

There was only one option left for me to win the battle, and I was unable to utilize it; not without irreparable damage to many.

Resigned to allow the men to finish their punishment, I stayed curled on the ground.

I lost track of time, until finally, in the distance, I heard the rattle of keys, and the bolt released on the door.

"That's enough!"

Multiple bodies scrambled into the room, and everyone was separated into different areas.

A guard leaned over me.

"Are you able to stand?"

I groaned and rolled to my back. He wasn't one of the men who brought me in. I nodded, though I'd have been happy to rest for a minute to catch my breath.

The injuries to my ribs would need more time to heal, meaning I had to accept help from the cop to rise onto my knees, then to my feet. I was shuffled out of the cell and down a long corridor. The movement sent nausea rolling through me.

It had been a long time since I'd been bested in a fight. If I'd have shifted, I would have won, but it wouldn't have been fair. Those men held the advantage because I was in chains, and they reveled in it.

The witch said my kind had been hunted and destroyed. From what I'd just experienced, I believed it could happen again. Humanity was not ready for knowledge of my kind.

The truth hit me harder than the punches, and the effort of moving my feet became like dragging boulders. I forced myself to concentrate on more important issues.

"Do you have information about the woman who was brought to this facility with me? Has she been harmed?"

"I wasn't on duty when you arrived, but I can check into it for you. I'm taking you to the infirmary before you see the sergeant."

Allowing human doctors to examine me wasn't a good idea. I'd already noticed the glances I got as we traversed the hallways, and I was sure it was because of the odd mix of blood splattered on me.

Besides, my injuries were already healing, and that would also cause problems as well as raise questions.

"I'm not in need of a physician's care. I'd rather speak with your sergeant right away."

"You were involved in a prisoner altercation. I'm obligated to take you in for examination."

I sighed.

"Is there a way to waive that? I have important matters to attend to outside of this facility."

We slowed, and the guard stared at me.

"I believe you can ask for that since you haven't been booked yet. There's a room up ahead where I'll have you wait while I go verify things. How does that sound?"

"I'm grateful for your assistance, especially with my companion. Her name is Violet Ayers."

"Okay, I'll look into it."

We stopped at a door with a small window in it, and the guard escorted me through it, to a room with a table and two chairs.

"If you'll sit here." The cop gestured to one of the chairs, and I perched on it, as my arms were still behind me. "I'm going to have to keep you contained until we find out what to do. It'll only take me a few minutes."

I huffed a laugh and shook my head. It wasn't like I had much of a choice, but at least the man was being kind.

The same irritating buzzing came from the light in the new room. I was sure the sound was used as a torture mechanism in this realm, because it burrowed into my skull and increased my headache.

After longer than the guard had promised, the door clicked open, and a different man entered. His uniform designated him to be of higher rank than anyone I'd dealt with to that point.

"Hello, I'm Sergeant Macklin. I understand you'd like to waive your rights to an examination and just get down to business, is that right?"

"That would be preferable, yes."

The man had a wide set of whiskers covering his lips and curling upward at the ends that I found amusing. His dark hair peppered with white gave away his elder status and set me at ease, hoping he'd be reasonable.

I wanted to test that instinct.

"Since I'd like to clear up this misunderstanding as quickly as possible, what can I do to help you decide that I'm not a threat?"

The sergeant seemed contemplative as he studied me.

"Well, for starters, let's make sure we're able to have this conversation. You arrived in a suspected drug-addled state, and were involved in a fight against four others, yet you seem barely scathed—that makes me wonder if you've come down from your high yet. How about you tell me your name and where we are?"

The sergeant settled into the chair opposite me and waited for my answer.

"My name is Rone of House Ignatius, and I mean you no harm, so you're free to release me at any time without fear of repercussions. I was told by the first set of cops that I'm in the county detention center."

Sergeant Macklin smiled when I finished.

"That's all good information, however, at what point your restraints will be removed is still to be determined. Do you know why you're here?"

"That's less clear to me. I believe it might have to do with my questioning of a man named Jason, though I don't know his house name, to retrieve my property."

Before the sergeant could ask another question, there was a knock on the door at the same time it opened.

"There's some new information you should know." A woman of short stature and a formidable air stood in the opening.

The sergeant stepped out of the room, and I once again waited alone. Macklin's face was red when he returned, and he shoved his unused chair under the table with extra force.

"Against reason, in my opinion anyway, you're going to go

over to booking now, then you'll be released. Will you stay rational if I remove your shackles?"

"Of course."

While he didn't hide his skeptical expression, he unlocked the shackles on my ankles, and removed the chains.

"And these?" I twisted my neck to gesture over my shoulder at my hand restraints.

"Those will have to wait until we're at the desk where we can finish up."

An agonizing hour later, I was led through the halls and into a holding area that smelled like the bus I'd ridden with Violet.

Violet jumped up from a chair against the wall and rushed over, and I sighed with relief. "Are you alright? I was worried."

She slipped her arms around my waist for a hug.

Her warmth against me ignited a spark in my chest that made it too difficult to speak for a few seconds. I rested my hands on her shoulders as we drew apart, and scanned for injuries.

"Are you well? I saw you fall when everything went awry."

"I'm fine. I was only tazed once, and the pain was over quickly—"

"Mr. Ignatius?" a woman called from behind a glass wall where she'd opened a window to the waiting area.

"Mr. Ignatius." Violet chuckled as she followed me to the counter.

"It seems to have satisfied the requirements for naming rituals you have here."

"If you'll sign here," the woman slid a paper toward me with a large X next to a line.

"Do you know how to write?" Violet whispered.

I twisted my neck and stared at her. "I'm highly educated, thank you."

She shrugged with a grin. "Just checking."

"I'm grateful after all of this nonsense, that we left the eggs safely in the oven. Were you able to gather any information about the one we gave to Jason?"

The woman stared at me and then at Violet as she waited for my signature.

Violet's eyes widened. "Hurry and sign that so we can talk outside."

The plastic bag with my belongings was pushed through the window in full view of everyone, before the woman slid the glass closed with a shake of her head.

I opened the bag and started to retrieve my things, but Violet stopped me.

"Let's do that outside, we need to go."

Quickly, I returned my Draessonian dagger to my boot, where I always hid it, then brought the rest of my effects as I strode to the door, eager to leave the confining space.

I stopped short when I saw Micah waiting for us.

"What's he doing here?"

I knew Violet was worried about the witch finding him, but had she left while I was held inside to find him herself? If so, that was unwise and dangerous.

"They let me make a call. I was able to kill two birds with one stone—check to make sure he was safe, and get help."

"You had to kill birds as payment to leave this place?"

"Oh man, some of the things you don't get surprises the hell out of me. I'll explain later. Let's go."

Micah stood with his arms crossed over his chest as he watched me interact with Violet. I didn't care for his appraisal.

When we reached the door, he turned and walked through it first then held it open for Violet. She claimed they were not together romantically, yet he seemed to think otherwise.

"We have things we need to discuss, Violet. You can see that your friend is safe, so we should go . . . alone," I said pointedly.

"Vi made me wait for you because she wouldn't leave until she knew *you* were safe," Micah said. "I have some information that I couldn't tell her inside. Now that you're out, you're the one who's welcome to go on your way."

He stopped in the middle of the walkway and faced me.

His tone made my lip curl, but before I could respond, Violet jumped between us.

"Knock it off, you two. Micah has a car and can take us home without the need for a bus. Besides, with *everything else*," she opened her eyes wide, probably to make sure I understood she was referring to the eggs and the witch, "Micah should stay with us."

"He seems like he can take care of himself, and I wish to stretch my legs. We can walk to my place."

"Come on." She grabbed my arm and tugged me toward her friend. "Micah, we need to talk, it's already five o'clock. Where's your car?"

"He's not safe, Vi," Micah said. "You know I've seen things."

"I know what you saw, which is why we need to get away from here and have a conversation."

"This is really a task for those more prepared. If you're afraid, you can find a place to hide until I make sure everything is safe."

I stepped closer to Violet's back. Her hair tickled my chin, and her hydrake scent played havoc with my nerves, requiring a great deal of control not to wrap my arm around her waist.

Micah moved closer, nearly pinning Violet between us.

"No, no, no! Both of you stop acting ridiculous." She ducked out of reach. "Micah—your car?"

With Violet no longer between us, I didn't wish to hurt her friend, but I would not back down from his challenge.

I matched his glower until he finally broke eye contact to dart a glance at Violet.

"Fine. It's this way."

He glared again at me while only partially turning his shoulders.

Violet grabbed his arm, twisted him away, and shoved him in the direction he indicated.

"I'm leaving. Come or don't, Rone, but if you do—no more fighting."

She stomped after Micah and didn't turn back.

29

VIOLET

THE HOUR-LONG TRIP from the police station to Micah's apartment was the tensest ride of my life. The dudes barely wanted to breathe the same air, let alone speak to each other. But even though that sucked, I spotted one silver lining.

Despite how much I could tell he didn't want to, Rone had decided to come with me.

Of course, he'd spent most of the time brooding handsomely in the backseat, but whatever. He was here, with me.

We hadn't known each other long, and we'd *definitely* had our differences, but his presence brought me a lot of relief.

"So, why didn't Jason press charges?" I asked Micah as he twisted a key into his building's front door and let us in.

"You'll see." His tone was tight and growly as he glared at Rone.

I exhaled. It seemed like the men were destined to despise each other. Instead of interrogating each of them and receiving no answer, I should probably just be happy I was no longer in a jail cell.

Keeping that in mind, we followed Micah up a narrow, creaking flight of stairs. We reached the top floor, and a distinct aroma of boiled cabbage filled my nose.

"Always pierogies and cabbage for dinner," Micah muttered, and threw a death glare to a door on the right.

He walked a few more paces, stopped before door number 35, and turned. His eyes found Rone's.

"I'm letting you into my home, not for you, but for Violet. That being said, I'd appreciate it if you showed my space respect."

I cocked my head, sensing a subtext I didn't understand.

"Fine," Rone grunted.

The agreement clearly wasn't exactly what Micah had in mind, because he paused for a second too long before finally opening the door.

A stream of curse words flew from Micah's lips.

"What happened—oh shit!" My hands covered my mouth as Micah rushed into his apartment, giving me a clear view of the room.

Chairs and a small dining table were turned over. Pieces of fruit littered the floor. Whoever had broken into Micah's apartment had also clearly gone to town on the sofa, as foamy innards poked out of the microfiber in many places. But most menacing of all were the dinner-plate-sized scorch marks dotting the walls, and the burnt scent that hung in the air.

"What happened?" My voice came out in a terrified whisper, which Micah didn't hear because he'd darted into a side room.

I was about to step into the apartment, when Rone laid

his massive hand on my shoulder. Gently maneuvering me to the side, he entered the room in front of me and scanned the area. His nose was twitching—catching the scent.

A second later, Micah burst back into the main room, his dark brown eyes frantic.

"He's gone! Dammit all to hell, he's gone! They took him!"

"Who took who?"

I watched as Micah darted to the sofa and flipped one couch cushion after the other, looking for something.

"Jason! He's missing!"

My spine straightened. "Jason? As in the kid that we . . ."

"Yes!" he roared and spun in place, as if somehow, Jason would materialize out of thin air.

"But, why was he here?"

Micah twisted to stare at me, and then with a massive huff, he threw his hands up and collapsed on the couch. Once situated, he flung his head into his hands.

"He was here because I needed to get to you quickly. I told him going on television with a dragon egg was a stupid move, and people were sure to be looking for him. I insisted that he and the egg would be safe here."

Micah lifted his gaze, and in his eyes I saw pure remorse. He'd really believed what he told the dragonblood, and now Jason was in trouble.

At the mention of the egg, Rone stiffened, and his nose went into overdrive as he prowled the room.

Micah groaned. "I thought that when I got you two out of jail, you could help me figure out what to do with him. But now—"

"There's magic in the air," Rone spoke, cutting Micah off.

For the first time, my mom's caregiver didn't look offended. Instead, he cocked his head and his eyes narrowed as if in thought.

"Yeah, I can feel it. But I don't recognize it."

"Well, you're mageblood." Rone turned to Micah, and crossed his arms over his barrel chest. "Are you not?"

My mouth dropped open. Of course I knew that Micah had magic. I'd seen it the night of Llewellyn's party, but a *mage*?! That sounded so powerful.

I scanned Micah as if I'd never seen him before, my eyes taking in his lean, muscular form, strong jaw, and intelligent eyes. When he stood to face Rone, his stance was determined —not at all cowed.

I leaned back, impressed and feeling a little dumb.

How had I never noticed that Micah was powerful before?

What was more, why had I never heard him?

"*Of course* I'm a mage," Micah said, crossing his arms, too.

"Are you able to do a time regression?" Rone asked. "Or is that beyond your scope of magic?

Micah shook his head. "Hell no, it's not. I'm the strongest mage I know."

"Really?" Rone darted a glance at the mess in the room with a smirk. "Then what are we doing standing around?"

I was about to ask what the hell a time regression was, when Micah lifted his hands, and blue, shimmering light flew out of them to swirl in the center of the living space. He mumbled a few words in a language I didn't recognize, and the light intensified. A moment later, it coalesced to form ghostly figures.

I gasped. The soccer mom witch materialized, the one who'd enchanted the band onto my wrist.

Magic soared from her hands as another figure, a man who alternated between using magic and sharpened steel, charged Jason. The poor kid darted around the room and hurled chairs and the fruit bowl at them before a blast of magic slammed into his head.

My hand flew to my mouth as he dropped lifelessly to the floor.

"Is he dead?" I croaked.

Neither guy answered. They were too busy watching the time regression.

When the male witch plucked Jason's backpack off the ground and peered inside to find the green and gold dragon egg, Rone let loose a terrifying growl. The entire room warmed as heat rolled off the dragon, and Micah took a few steps back.

"Rone. Calm down, it's a vision," I said as the witches carried Jason out of the room.

"They have my charge." His tone was gravelly, as if he was trying to rein in his anger.

"I know. They have Jason, too. We have to save them."

"I care nothing for that dragonblood defector," he spat.

My mouth flattened into a line, and my hands flew to my hips. "Rone Ignatius! You stop that right now!"

The dragon prince jumped at my tone, and Micah arched an eyebrow as he took another three steps away.

"How could you speak to me like—"

I held up a hand.

"Nuh uh, stop right there. I get it. You don't like the kid.

Hell, I don't like him much either. But I will *not* have you flat out saying you'll throw his life away. We'll get the egg *and* Jason. And if you don't agree, I won't help you find dragonbloods anymore."

Rone's face fell.

"You can't mean that. Violet, we must find the dragonbloods, and your powers are necessary to accomplish that mission. You and me, we're—" he faltered, and his cheeks took on a pinkish tone. "A team."

I cocked my head, wondering if that was what he'd really been about to say.

"Yeah, we are a *team*," I agreed. "Which means you need to care not just about the egg, but about the guy, too. I may not know what I am, but until very recently, I thought that I was human. And I would have thought the same about him. Do you get that?"

Rone stood silent for a moment, studying me, before nodding. "I understand."

"Thank you." A knot of tension I hadn't realized had formed in my chest unraveled.

"You're welcome." Rone gave me a sheepish smile. "And I fear I have not said it enough, but thank you for sticking with me through this."

My breath hitched, and dammit, I couldn't help it. I covered the few steps between us and wrapped my arms around his waist.

A low rumbling hit my ear as Rone reciprocated, pulling me tight. I buried my face in the heat of his chest, and his scent of cinnamon and faint smoke enveloped me, grounding me in this time of tension and doubt.

"*Ahem*, sorry to interrupt this . . . moment, but I have a few questions."

I jolted a little because I'd almost forgotten that Micah was in the room. Rone gave me one more tight squeeze before we broke apart.

Micah's gaze darted between me and the dragon prince, one eyebrow raised. "I know who those witches are and the location of their headquarters, but I need answers first. I'll start with Violet. What's this about you having powers?"

Oh, crap.

My stomach spasmed violently. I had to tell him but the desire to keep my secret, to protect myself, ran deep within me. And yet, if I was honest, I no longer had a choice. We needed to find the egg and Jason fast and apparently, Micah knew where they were.

"I—I . . ." A stammer flew out of me, the anxiety of what I was about to do turning my tongue to cement.

Rone's hand landed on my shoulder, and he moved to stand right at my side, shoulder-to-shoulder.

Knowing he had my back gave me strength. I lifted my chin.

"I can read minds."

The words rushed out of me, and as soon as they were gone, my lips clamped shut. The hairs on my arms rose as Micah stared at me for at least ten solid seconds.

Then he heaved a sigh, moved back to the couch, and fell onto the dilapidated cushions. "I thought as much."

My spine straightened. "Excuse me? What?"

Micah patted the spot next to him, and I went to join him.

When I sat down, Rone's soft expression hardened once more.

This guy and his mood swings. I would never get used to them.

"Your mom has a similar sort of power. Or at least, she did when she first moved into the home. Not lately."

He paused, as if making sure that he could trust me.

"I've just told you my biggest secret," I whispered as my heart rate kicked up at the discovery that Micah had known about Mom's mind reading.

It had been so long since I'd heard her voice in my head, since we'd talked like that. Did he know more about her power?

"I've always been sure my ability would land me in the loony bin. If you know more, *please*, tell me."

Something in his expression softened.

"I'm sorry, Violet. You should know that I too can hear minds. I can even manipulate people to a degree using the power. But at St. Francis, I've learned to keep a wall around my mind." He eyed me. "I wish I would have asked about it sooner. For a while now, I thought maybe you had mental powers too, but I never found the right moment to bring it up."

Excitement rose inside me. Other than Mom, I'd never met anyone else like me.

"I have mental barriers too! Sometimes they slip, but rarely. At least, not until lately." I darted a glance at Rone and then back to Micah. "Rone and I were thinking that maybe I'm mageblood? Since you're a mage, would you be able to tell?"

Micah shook his head. "I'll be honest, your mom and you are unlike any other supernatural I've come across. I don't know what you are."

My chest fell as my hope shattered. For one shining moment, I'd thought that maybe I'd get some answers as to why I was this way. But Micah didn't know. Rone didn't know. And I certainly didn't know.

"That sucks," I muttered.

Rone moved to stand by me. "Don't be distressed, Violet. We'll figure out what you are. In fact, I'll not return to Draessonia until we remove the bracelet and discover your heritage."

I sat up straighter. "Serious?"

"I promise."

Something in me brightened, and my heart began to beat quickly.

"Well, then, we'd better find caretakers for the rest of those eggs, so we can move on to more pleasant tasks." I scooted over for him, and he lowered to sit on my other side. I turned back to Micah. "Rone and I have already met that witch."

He arched an eyebrow. "Did you know she's the high priestess of the Coven of Fortuna, the most powerful coven in the Portland Metro area? And she's incredibly dangerous."

I lifted my wrist.

"Tell me about it. She branded me with a death bracelet. If Rone isn't out of here in a week, I'm a goner."

Micah's eyes grew wide. "You've got to be kidding me."

"Nope. But maybe this is an opportunity. Maybe we can get Jason, the egg, *and* have this removed. Mages are typically stronger than witches, right?" I tried to recall what Rone had told me about the different races. "Because mages are born with magic, and don't have to learn from scratch?"

"Usually, although Linda, that's the high priestess, is very strong. The guy in the time regression was her husband, he's powerful, too. And they're bound to have others with them when they do ... whatever it is they plan on doing to Jason."

His tone dropped, and I recalled Linda's threat from when we'd met her on the football field.

"They're going to kill him, aren't they?"

Micah nodded. "I think so."

"Well, then, we have to hurry. You said you knew where their headquarters is located?"

Micah stood and went to a desk on the opposite side of the room. He pulled open a drawer, extracted a map, and unfurled it. Then he pointed to a strip of forest outside of Hillsboro.

"They have a headquarters here, sort of like a warehouse-slash-office-building. To the public, they're a tech company, but the coven needs the warehouse because they deal with a lot of supernatural trading. It's why they're so influential and rich." His dark eyes lifted to meet mine. "I bet they took Jason there."

"We have to infiltrate it," Rone piped up gruffly.

"Yup, which is going to be super difficult with only three of us," Micah replied. "Particularly if the whole coven is there. Actually, if that's the case, it might be impossible."

My lips broke into a small smile. *Three* of us. Micah was going to help us.

"No, not impossible," I assured him. "Rone's an expert in

military strategy. All we need to do is get there, assess the facility, and come up with a plan."

"Uhhh, I don't know." Micah's brows furrowed. "Obviously he's strong, but he doesn't know crap about our world. He—"

I stood, stopping him. "Trust me. He'll figure it out. He has a lot at stake, and I believe in him."

I twisted to extend my hand to Rone, and found him beaming at me. "Ready to infiltrate a coven headquarters, teammate?"

"As ready as fire burns bright," he said, and took my hand.

30

RONE

EVEN THOUGH VIOLET sat in front with Micah, it wasn't a bother after how she'd supported me. She'd inspired me even more to make sure our mission succeeded.

While the scenery whizzed by on our drive to the coven headquarters, I recalled previous missions when I'd utilized my training.

Most notably, a hatchling youth had been captured by a manticore while trying to complete a dare. Four boys on a quest to build their reputation for bravery went looking for a manticore claw in Sadura. The reticent beasts shed their claws regularly, so they were easily found. Throughout the years, the challenge had become a harmless, adolescent rite of passage—I'd done it twice with friends.

However, those boys had chosen to search near the home of a beast known for his ferocious need for privacy. He'd captured one youth and trapped him in a cave filled with steaming vents of poisonous gases. Even if the boy managed to escape, he'd have had to traverse lands rife with life-threatening wildlife in order to find his way home.

Negotiations had proven ineffective, so I'd led a rescue team. Five of us, all military-trained dragons, found the boy, but not before he'd become delirious and riddled with sores over most of his body.

This time, I hoped to avoid injury to innocents. Particularly to Violet and Micah.

I glanced to the front and watched how the light coming through the windows brightened the purple streak in Violet's hair. She seemed relaxed as she propped her chin on her palm, silently waiting for us to arrive at our destination.

The woman I met in the coffee shop two days before would never be so tranquil heading to a secret location to battle supernatural enemies. She continued to amaze me, and I couldn't deny the bond between us.

I would do everything I could to make sure she stayed safe.

"The building is about two miles away," Micah broke the silence. "It's used as a front for their coven, but the business is real."

"What services does their company provide? And most importantly, will there be civilians loitering about?" I needed to formulate a solid plan before we arrived.

"I've never been there, so my information is secondhand, but I only know they work with technology of some sort. There's a trading aspect to it too, among the members of the supernatural council called the Komisio, but I don't think there are customers coming and going. Not at eight at night, anyway."

The information wasn't complete enough to warrant further questions. We'd have to find out more once we arrived.

Violet turned her attention to Micah. "Didn't you say it was a large building?"

"That's what I've heard."

A larger area would be best if I needed to shift, however until we arrived I wouldn't know if it was possible.

"Why would they need so much space?" Violet asked.

"There's no use speculating," I answered. "Any knowledge gained from hearsay has to be discounted. We'll need to make a full reconnaissance of the situation when we get there."

Violet darted a confused glance over her shoulder. She'd explained that I was the most qualified for this situation, and I hoped she hadn't forgotten.

Not much time later, we drove down a long, tree-lined lane. Micah slowed the vehicle so we could gather intel.

Between each of the large trees that created a near-complete canopy over the road were tall light posts. If we had to wait for dark to make a move, we'd need to keep those in mind. Hopefully, we'd be driving back out this road rather than running.

"There it is." Violet pointed ahead.

"You should find a place to stop where we won't be seen getting in or out of the car."

Micah scowled at my directions, but said nothing. He maneuvered the car behind a large tree so we could exit unseen and continue on foot.

The man had some skills in clandestine operations, but he'd have to earn my respect in battle if he wanted my trust.

We left the car and hurried to a wooded area for better cover.

"How are we going to get through the gate?" Violet asked.

I smirked as I scanned the area. "We aren't going through the front. This way."

I crouched and jogged deeper into the woods, angling our path toward the fence line surrounding the building. It appeared feeble, made only of meshed metal, yet the rolled barbed wire on top spoke a different tale.

Military operations were silent and precise, yet behind me, I heard the crash of both my teammates, as Violet called us, leaving a trail of cracked branches that even a scent-deprived hatchling could follow.

I held up a fist, hoping they understood the halt signal. Violet crashed into my back, but I twisted fast enough to catch her before she fell. Micah stopped with an arched brow, daring me to doubt his abilities. I sucked in a breath and concentrated on Violet.

"You have to stay low and quiet," I whispered. "We don't know what security they have, and with their powerful magic, we have to expect anything—even sound triggers."

"How am I supposed to run quietly through bushes?" She huffed and narrowed her eyes. "It's my first time breaking and entering."

I wrapped her hand inside my palm, and let my thumb caress the soft back of her knuckles. She snapped her gaze to mine, but didn't pull away.

"You're doing fine. I'll make sure you're safe, just stay alert."

She nodded silently. "I wish that we had time to go back to your place for my dagger."

"As do I."

I also had wanted to check on the eggs, still warming in the oven, but time was not on our side. Now that the witches had the egg from my mother's house and the boy, we would have to move quickly.

"Remain calm and keep your eyes open for something to improvise with. In battle one must learn to be resourceful. Remember your training so you're ready for anything."

"Maybe Violet should stay here," Micah interrupted. "She'll only get hurt in a confrontation. Since you're such a military expert, let's you and I go in, and leave her to keep watch."

"Like hell. I'm not waiting out here by myself."

Jerking her hand from mine, she spun to face her friend.

I rose to my full height and balled my fists. "I'm confident in my ability to keep her safe at my side. Out here, she's vulnerable."

Violet let out a muffled groan.

"You two need to drop this . . . whatever it is."

She waved her hands then settled them on her hips. "There are witches inside this building who want me dead." She lifted her wrist, and the gold band glimmered, reminding both Micah and me what was at stake beyond just the dragon egg.

The danger had never left my mind. Her limited skills

might not be enough, but I had no intention of leaving her alone.

"That's why it might not be good for you to be around them. That's all I'm trying to say." Micah blew out a deep breath and rubbed the back of his neck. "Let's just figure out a way inside, and hope we can find Jason without a fight."

While I disagreed with his suggestion, I couldn't discount his reasons.

"We need to move," I said, then met Violet's gaze. "And from now on, speak only if necessary, and as quietly as possible."

Violet saluted me with a mocking grin.

While it stoked the flames inside my chest, I kept a stoic exterior.

I led us closer to the perimeter fencing. From the tree-line, Micah pointed out security apparatuses approximately every ten feet. There also appeared to be several locks on the solid metal doors at every entry point.

"Besides the cameras, there's also a barrier wall of magic on the other side of the fence," Micah whispered.

That explained the faint sizzle to the air I couldn't place.

"I can feel it on my skin. It's like how the air feels before a storm." Violet wasn't as careful with her voice, and startled when I grumbled low with a glare in her direction.

"Sorry," she whispered.

Micah took hold of her hand, and every impulse in me wanted to step between them.

I needed to control the absurd thoughts making me treat her as a mate. Only a dragon could be my mate. One with enough dragonblood to shift, and by Violet's age she would have done so already or gone mad. Besides the fact that her scent would be strong enough to detect without question. She couldn't be, never would be, mine. Still, my need to protect her threatened my rational behavior.

"Maybe if we concentrate, we can see what spells they've used," Micah suggested.

Violet nodded. "Worth a shot."

"And if it works, I'll understand your power better. Maybe together, we can get this over with faster."

She smiled at him, and I had to turn away briefly.

It was a good idea. My being unfamiliar with witch magic was one more reason to get this mission completed as soon as possible. We had to recover the egg and find more worthy dragonbloods before the hatchlings were born.

Micah and Violet held hands with their eyes closed. At first, nothing seemed to happen, then the air grew prickly, and a wash of lightheadedness came over me.

During that hoax of a party, there had been only one instance of magic, and it was happening again.

"There's a space around the corner, about twenty feet south, where the magic is weaker. If we can get over the fence at that point, I think I can create an opening for us to get through," Micah whispered.

It didn't escape my notice that he hadn't dropped Violet's hands.

"Do you sense the same? I didn't hear anyone inside though, how about you?" Micah kept his focus on Violet.

"I don't know, I saw wavering in the air, I think. Whatever it was, I can't be sure I didn't just sense you." She seemed dejected.

She needed to remain confident—the woman I watched in the car, not the woman I'd met in the coffee shop.

"I can get us through the fence easily enough. Let's head that way, and you can open the magic barrier. We'll be exposed for about ten seconds while we run to the building. Violet, stay between me and Micah so you're concealed."

I believed hearing a solid plan would soothe her nerves. Then I thought of a better way to *ensure* she left her fears behind.

"Don't argue about it. Just do as I say."

She glared at me. "I'll be fine."

Exactly as I'd hoped, a spark of independence flashed over her countenance, and she clenched her fists.

That's the frame of mind I needed her in.

As I turned to lead us through the trees to find the weaker magic, I caught Micah's grin.

We rounded a corner and followed the fencing until we reached the spot he'd discovered.

Violet glanced about. "There's no more cameras or barbed wire. Why?"

I agreed it was odd. The building wasn't as secure where we were, yet it was the least visible from the entrance. There weren't any other buildings or roads near the rear that I could see, so it *was* the most likely spot for a breach.

"Whatever the reasons, this is the spot," Micah added. "We should hurry and get this over with."

"Haste makes mistakes. Deliberate and careful, that's how we'll get in and out safely. Remember, as soon as we get through the barriers, head to the building as quickly as possible. We'll meet to the right of that door."

I pointed out the solid metal door with only one lock.

There were no windows on that side to concern ourselves with being seen, but we'd need to stay watchful regardless.

"I don't like this," Violet said. "It seems too easy."

"Can you sense something?" Micah studied her face.

"No, it's just a feeling from years of taking care of myself. When something seems off, it usually is."

"We have to get that egg. You can *both* wait here, that will be fine. I can be in and out in record time." I wouldn't allow Violet to stay alone, and as much as it frustrated me to leave her with Micah, it would keep them out of the way.

"We need to save Jason, too." Violet pinched her lips together and met my stare. "We all go, or we all leave. Maybe we should call the cops? That way none of us needs to go inside at all."

"The police would need a reason to enter," Micah said. "We can't really provide one based on our speculation. What are we supposed to say? 'There's a magic barrier so we know they're hiding something'?"

His assessment was correct and seemed to help her.

She shrugged and looked expectantly at me.

"I'll get us through the fence, be ready to break through the magic." I met Micah's gaze and saw his determination. There wasn't time left to dawdle.

Overheating the metal fence and breaching it that way would take too long. Instead, I used my strength and twisted a section until it wrenched apart, then peeled back each side so we could slip through.

Violet and I stayed back while Micah moved ahead five strides and confronted the ward.

He raised his hands, and the blue light we'd seen from him before emanated from his palms. Spreading his hands wide, he called over his shoulder for us to run through.

We ducked around him and sprinted for the building. The magic's sizzle raced over my skin, but neither of us hesitated.

I kept Violet secured next to me until Micah arrived safely seconds later.

"Vi, let's try again to see if we can sense anyone inside. On this side of the barrier, it might work better." He took her hands again, and she didn't resist.

As close as we were, however, she leaned back into me, tickling my nose with her sweet hydrake and apple scent as I waited.

Micah popped his eyes open with a start. A hard edge lined his face, and he pressed his lips tight.

"What? What did you see?" Violet asked in a whisper.

"Jason is in a room with two others. They have him tied to a chair, and—"

"Did you see the egg?" I interrupted, more concerned with my charge than the one who betrayed his heritage, even though I knew the others were invested in his safety.

"No. But they're taking his blood into a bag like aides do at the blood bank, and there are a bunch of lit candles around the room."

"I heard one of them!" Violet's eyes sparkled with her revelation. "She said something about the power he'd give to their potion. We have to get him out of there."

"Let's go."

They lined up behind me as I wrested the door open.

Slipping inside, we slid our backs along the dark corridor in the direction Micah motioned. At each corner, Violet listened for voices, directing us to the correct room.

When we came to a plain wooden door with a blackened-out window, both Micah and Violet were convinced we'd reached the correct spot.

Two witches shouldn't be a match for Micah and me. But Violet readied her stance in the way I'd taught her to face an attacker, and I fought back a grin of pride at her resolve.

I counted down from three, and then we burst into the room.

A man and a woman spun to face us. Magic bloomed immediately in their palms, identifying them as the witches we expected.

The woman was as tall as Micah, with the same dark complexion. Her long curls hung freely down her back, and would hinder her fighting. The male was short, with the soft shape of one without an exercise regimen. The ridiculous cap he wore accentuated his bulbous nose. Neither was a match for us.

Hopefully, Violet wouldn't need to defend herself—or worse, inflict injury that would cause her regret.

As one, we charged, ducking out of the way of the magical darts flying through the air.

I reached the pudgy man first. Surprisingly, he was stronger than he appeared, but I jammed the heel of my palm into his large nose, ending him quickly. Micah grappled with the female, but managed to slam his elbow into her temple, causing her to crumple, unconscious.

Violet ran straight to Jason. She crouched down at his

side and removed the needle from his arm to stop his blood from flowing into the bag hanging from the chair.

I hurried over as she was using a small dagger she found on a nearby table to sever the ropes binding the boy.

"Where's the egg?"

Whether it was my demanding tone or how I loomed that startled him, I didn't care. He pointed to a backpack propped against a wall.

Before I could race to it, a pressure filled the air, momentarily squeezing my lungs so I couldn't breathe. The familiar cackle of the witch who'd trapped Violet and me in our previous encounter rang through the air.

Slowly, I spun to face a row of five witches standing with smug expressions beyond where a wall had been seconds ago.

Violet's earlier concerns hit me in the gut.

We'd followed a trail straight into a trap.

31

VIOLET

THE WITCHES SPREAD out and prepared to fight, although my eyes locked on just one.

Linda. She still looked like a soccer mom, but tonight, the amethyst cloak she wore gave her more of a witchy/priestess vibe.

The guy standing next to her wore the same style of robe in emerald green, marking him as her counterpart. The high priest of the Coven of Fortuna.

Considering the large, round bulge weighing down the right side of his robe, I was positive that the dragon egg was in his pocket.

Five witches to four supernaturals—one of whom was Jason, who could barely hold himself up because he'd lost so much blood. And then there was me, the girl with quaking knees, holding a pilfered dagger that she barely knew how to use.

Were we screwed? Yeah, probably, but I was holding out

hope that the dragon and the mage would be able to work some serious magic.

"Take Jason and stand back," Rone instructed. He'd inched closer to me while I was assessing the witches, clearly trying to protect me.

I did as he said, keeping hold of my dagger while I wedged my shoulder underneath Jason's armpit. Thank goodness he was skinny and shorter than me. If he were a bigger dude, I'd probably be falling over, trying to lift him.

Once I was behind Rone's bulk, I held out the dagger again.

The dragon might be protecting me, but I knew from years of barely getting by that I couldn't always depend on others. Plus, I had an audience to intimidate.

A woman with olive skin and massive, green eyes stood closest to me by the door. The dude next to her was Latino, short, and chubby. I glared at both of them.

"I told you to leave, dragon."

The high priestess spoke, and the duo I was staring down diverted their attention to the front of the room.

I followed their gazes. While she may have been speaking to Rone, she wasn't watching *him*. No, the witch was looking straight at me, her fingers tracing a line around her opposite wrist as she sneered.

My lips curled up. That asshat was rubbing in the fact that she'd trapped me with this stupid band. She was trying to intimidate me.

As if she knew exactly what I was thinking, the band shrank and tightened around my wrist.

I bit back a yelp and averted my eyes. I may not want her

to think I was weak, but I also didn't want to have my hand severed off by a shrinking, magical bracelet.

Only when I was no longer fixated on her did I notice that *all* the witches had begun to call on their magic. It radiated in front of them as shields of light or balls of energy.

Well, crap on a cracker.

This room was full of power. Rone would be smart to be diplomatic. I was considering telling him to go easy when His Majesty snorted.

"I'm Prince Egan Moray Rone Ignatius. You have no jurisdiction over me," he boasted, shattering my hope that we'd get out of here without bloodshed.

Linda sneered. "Dragons always were too prideful for their own good. Unfortunately for you, I've taken precautions so that you can't use your greatest strengths against us."

She lifted her hand, and the air began to crackle as streaks of lightning filled the room. The energy darted across my skin, electrifying me.

On the other side of Jason, Micah sucked in a breath that lifted the hairs on my neck.

What had the witch done?

The answer came with Rone's roar. "You *dare* to stifle the dragon?!"

I watched the dragon-shifter shudder, and my hands began to shake.

He couldn't shift. The witch had enchanted him, or this place, so that Rone couldn't defend himself in the most effective way possible. Of course, he was a capable warrior in human form, but still . . .

A dragon would have been *much* better.

"You didn't think I'd allow a giant beast to sneak into the headquarters of my coven, did you?"

The high priestess pouted and shook her head. "You still don't understand how things work around here. The supernaturals of this world don't revere you, lizard."

Her gaze traveled back to Jason.

"But at least you were right about one thing. I truly thought the dragonbloods of this world were extinct. Now that I know some still remain, I'll be sure to take advantage of their existence. Once I've brewed the proper potion and added the boy's blood, I'll grow even stronger. "

My stomach twisted as I recalled the needle hanging from Jason's arm.

"You will do no such thing to my kind," Rone seethed and clenched his hands.

The high priestess arched an over-plucked eyebrow. "Oh yes I will. Soon enough, I'll be unstoppable. And once our little dragon hatches," her eyes darted to her husband, confirming my belief that he held the egg, "his blood will be even more potent than the halfling's. At that point I won't need the boy, but others will pay top dollar to enhance their magic. But with my *true* dragon, my transformation will progress—"

Rone lunged, cutting her off.

The witch by the door dashed over to protect her priestess. As if he'd known what she'd do, Rone twisted, pulled his blade from his boot, and slashed her neck open.

Blood flew through the air, spattering my arms and face. A part of me instantly began flipping out, but I smothered that part, and pulled Jason to the door.

I didn't know what Rone was going to do to the witches, or how he'd save the egg, but I did know one thing: I had to get Jason out of there.

The short male witch saw me coming, and thrust his hands out in front of him. A ball of blinding white light blossomed, stopping me in my tracks.

Micah came to my rescue, barreling forth and slamming the man to the ground with a spray of power.

I rushed from the room, pulling Jason with me. Turning the direction we'd entered from, I swore.

A shimmering wall of magic stood before me. The witches had blocked the exit route.

I pivoted, and we made it precisely four steps out the door before a *crack* rang through the air behind us, followed by a loud string of curse words. The next thing I knew, the guys were at my side.

Together, they took Jason between them, and urged me to keep running.

"What happened? I thought I was supposed to get him out—"

"The cowards disappeared," Rone said, his tone a half-step above a growl. "Just popped out of existence."

Micah grunted with exertion. "They won't be gone long. I can feel magic on Jason. They knew we'd come. I'm almost certain they have a magical tracker on him."

My eyes bulged. "What does that mean?"

"We have to get him somewhere safe so I can figure out how to reverse it."

My heart, which had already been thundering like a racehorse down the track, beat impossibly faster.

"But what if—"

"No what ifs," Micah said, and my mouth snapped shut.

He was right. Questions wouldn't help. Better to save my breath than to worry about things that hadn't happened yet.

Coming to a T in the hallway, we took another left turn, and I caught sight of a streetlamp through the window. My breath hitched.

"Light! There's an outside wall over there. If we can get to it, we can find a way out." I glanced at Rone and noticed he was trembling violently. "Maybe if we leave this place you'll be able to shift."

Rone's face turned stony, prompting Micah to answer for him.

"He can't. The high priestess enchanted *him*. Don't worry, I'm working hard to figure out what she did, and reverse the spell."

"I thought you said mages were stronger than witches," I gasped between each word; even though the guys were carrying Jason, we were running freaking *fast*, and talking and running didn't mix.

"We are," Micah retorted. "But the high priestess and priest aren't like other witches. They're the most powerful in the area. Don't think they're weak opponents."

I opened my mouth to reply that I didn't think that at all, when the hallway ended, and we skidded to a stop at the edge of a massive glass atrium.

Scanning the vast space quickly, I pointed to the front door. Past it was a parking lot, and beyond that, the forest— our escape route.

"Let's go!"

"Not so fast," a voice said from somewhere in the room, freezing my blood.

The high priestess and priest stepped out of the shadows. With them was the petite blonde witch and, shockingly, the darker-skinned woman with long, curly hair. Either the latter had made a miraculous recovery, or something the other three had done had woken her quickly. We were outnumbered once again.

"What *are* you, girl?" the high priestess asked, her eyes narrowed.

That was the question of the century, wasn't it?

"I'll tell you . . ." I lifted my dagger arm to remind her of the trinket she'd bestowed on me. "If you take this off."

At my side, Rone growled.

Instead of looking intimidated, Linda released a cackle that her husband followed with a low, rumbling laugh.

"I'll get right on that," the witch mocked. "After we make a little trade."

Her eyes slid to her husband, who pulled the dragon egg from his pocket.

Rone stiffened.

Realizing that shit was about to go down, Micah scooted Jason away and propped him up against a wall.

"Stay here, dude," he whispered.

Like Jason could go *anywhere*. He couldn't even stand. At this rate, it would be a miracle if we got him out of here alive. Hell, it would probably be a miracle if any of us got out of here alive.

My jaw tightened. I'd never been one to count on miracles.

Mustering as much resolve as I could, I pointed my dagger at the witch. Rone was vibrating so hard, I wasn't sure he could talk, so I took control of the situation.

"Give me that."

"Why should we?" the high priest said. "Once this baby hatches, its blood will be used as the final ingredient in a transformation potion. In just one moon cycle we'll no longer be witches, but *mages*."

Well, crap. With a reason like that, I didn't see them giving up very easily.

"This is your last chance," I threatened. "That egg might be important to you, but there's a real dragon in here. A massive one."

Linda threw a dismissive wave. "Maybe, but that dragon's been bound. He can't—"

Rone flew into action, rushing at the witches.

The priest retaliated, flinging up a wall of power.

The dragon prince roared as he pounded on the wall. Two spells slipped through and hit him.

And then, something ripped my attention from Rone.

The dragon egg, now glowing, soared upward.

My hands flew to my mouth, but just when I thought it would crash into the glass ceiling, it stopped, hovering in midair. I frowned as what was happening became clear.

The witches were keeping the egg out of Rone's reach to enrage him.

I'd no sooner reached that conclusion, than the curly-haired witch rushed out from behind the magical barrier, coming straight at me.

I thrust my dagger out at the same time that I dropped my

barriers. I might not be the best fighter—okay, I barely had a clue what I was doing—but if I could anticipate my opponent's next move, that would give me a leg up.

I heard the witch think about attacking from above, and the next second, she leapt higher than any non-supernatural ever could.

Had I been ignorant to what was about to happen, I probably would have ducked and exposed my backside. As it was, I stood my ground and bent my knees, squatting just enough that she would clear me.

I was about to leap and slash the witch with my dagger, when a massive ball of glowing energy appeared in her hands.

Oh no you don't, I screamed inside my head. Get that magic away from me!

Her power dissolved as I exploded upward. My dagger slammed into her belly. The witch wailed as momentum threw her forward, and she collapsed onto the floor.

Violet! Micah's voice entered my head.

I gasped. He had never done that before. I swiveled around to find him battling the high priest.

What? I screamed back, as a panel of glass somewhere in the atrium shattered, and the high priestess' insane laugh rang through the air once more.

Did you just command her to stop using her power, and she did?

I stilled. Had I done that? Could I make others do as I wished with my mind?

A familiar roar cut through the question, yanking me back into the moment.

I spun to find Rone, fighting two on one.

The high priestess was holding up a shield, while the petite blonde darted from one side of him to the other, pummeling Rone. Linda enabled each attack by creating holes in the shield wherever the blonde needed them.

I shuddered as I watched her magic, spewing out of her in the form of black, inky creatures that became shadow monsters.

The dragon tried to beat them back with powerful blows that would have knocked a man unconscious, but the shadows weren't alive, and kept coming, scratching and biting him.

A pit formed in my stomach as I watched Rone stumble and nearly fall.

A tinkle of laughter flew from the blonde's mouth.

My fists clenched. That witch did *not* just laugh about hurting my dragon.

My dagger clattered to the floor, and I brought both hands to my temples. If I had mind-controlled the dark-haired witch, I could do it again. Maybe even better, if I could concentrate.

I'll help! Once again, Micah's voice rang through my head. *You get the blonde, I'll take the high priestess!*

You got it!

I zeroed in on the smaller witch. My eyes narrowed as I watched her attack Rone from behind another's shield—the freaking coward.

I pressed my fingers to my temples harder, and since I didn't really know what I'd done before, or how, I followed my instincts.

272

Freeze! I commanded.

Another shadow attacked Rone and he collapsed to the floor with a groan.

Fear gripped me.

I was about to try again when Micah screamed inside my head.

Close your eyes! Only picture your opponent! I almost have Linda!

My gaze snapped to the priestess for a second, and I saw that he was right. She was clearly fighting his influence, but judging by how red her face had become, it was taking a lot of effort.

Doing as Micah suggested, I closed my eyes and pictured the evil blonde. When she was fully formed in my mind, I tried again.

Stop moving! I screamed mentally.

The next thing I knew, Micah was back, a part of my inner monologue, and he was whooping with joy.

A thrill ran through me, and my eyes popped open.

I'd done it! The blonde witch was frozen! And the high priestess' shield was down.

Micah and I had done it together. We'd—

What the actual hell?

The high priestess was in motion again, but instead of attacking Rone, who was picking himself up off the floor, she was dashing away.

My eyebrows furrowed, and I twisted to face Micah, who should be in control of her.

A strangled sound flew from me. My friend was on the

floor, blood seeping from his head. The high priest loomed over the mage.

Terror raced through me, and I lost control of the blonde witch, who immediately went for Rone again.

This time, however, the prince was prepared, and with a powerful swipe of his arm, the woman was hurled into the wall. She moaned as she slid to the floor. Rone didn't waste a second before chasing after Linda, so I switched tack to focus on her husband.

Stop moving! Leave him alone! I commanded.

But instead of doing as I said, the high priest turned and came after me.

Fear gripped me in place.

I wasn't that far away, so he was upon me in seconds, his arms wrapping around me as he pinned my back against his chest.

"I have her!" he yelled.

"And I have the dragon between a rock and a hard place," Linda jeered.

My heart fell to my knees. Somehow, she had moved Jason closer to the front door, and a dagger was now poised over his jugular.

"Step back, dragon," the witch commanded. "Or the boy dies."

I gulped, because the egg was no longer hovering far above us. No, now it was at her shoulder, taunting and teasing Rone, whose fists were clenched into balls.

I sought to break the spell that the high priestess had over him by struggling loudly in the man's grasp.

Rone twisted slightly. When he caught sight of me, his eyes widened and blazed a bright red.

"Violet . . ."

My name had barely left his lips when the high priestess released a yelp.

I ripped my eyes from Rone in time to catch a shimmer of blue magic, Micah's, twirling around Linda. From his spot on the floor, Micah was trying to disarm her. He shook as though the effort pained him, but whatever he was doing was working.

Or at least, it was until the high priestess hurled a ball of power at him. It slammed into his side, and my friend let out a groan as his face hit the floor once again.

Spotting an opportunity, Rone took a step forward.

The witch snapped her attention back to Rone. "I warned you, dragon."

Without so much as blinking, she drew the dagger across Jason's neck.

32

RONE

MY VISION TURNED AS red as the blood spilled from the boy. Even though he'd acted foolishly, he didn't deserve to die. Violet wore a pained expression, and tears rolled down her cheeks. But my priority had to be the egg that hovered in the air.

I was worthless to stop the witch unless I could break her hold over my dragon. Her magic flogged my skin, as if shredding it bit by bit.

I needed to draw her close. Force her to make a misstep so I could surprise her and shatter the spell.

Falling down to one knee, I lowered my chin and feigned helplessness.

The witch snickered at my expense. But as I hoped, she stepped forward.

"You overestimated yourself, dragon. The arrogant leadership of your kind, is in the past. Supernaturals here will never bow to you again."

She sauntered closer. Two more steps was all I needed to endure from that woman.

"I'll admit, finding you in this realm and then receiving the knowledge that there are other dragonbloods was a disruption, but now I see that it was also an opportunity."

She made the final step in my direction, and I seized my chance. Bursting up, I grabbed her by the throat.

"Rone!" Violet's scream echoed in my ears, but I couldn't look. The magic surrounding me was weakening with each gasp of the vile creature in my grip.

My ears popped from the pressure when the spell broke, and I dropped the witch into a crumpled heap. With her energy drained, I had more pressing concerns.

I spun to search the air for the egg. My eyes snagged on Micah, staggering to his feet. He tripped and recovered twice as he rushed forward; as if in slow motion, I saw his objective.

The egg was falling. The spell that had once bound me also freed the hatchling.

My feet had barely lifted from the ground before Micah lunged through the air, and his hands slipped under the egg seconds before it hit the ground.

Relief filled me, and I slumped, my hands falling to my knees.

As I turned to search for Violet, a body slammed into my side.

The struggle against the spell, and the battle with the shadow demons had left me in a weakened state. I rolled with my attacker until we crashed into a heavy planter.

"I will destroy you," the high priest hissed between clenched teeth.

His touch sizzled with power that shook my body as he wrenched my arms into an awkward position. Without the use of my hands, it rendered my sonar power useless.

However, unlike his wife's, his power flickered, as if it was hard for him to maintain.

My temperature flared, and his face strained as he tried to keep hold of me through the heat. Sweat poured down the sides of his face.

I bucked my hips to get the momentum to lunge and smack my forehead into his nose. Blood spurted into my eyes, and he moaned as I pushed him away.

Back on my feet, I swiped the putrid residue from my face and searched for Violet.

She was again fighting the small, blonde witch who controlled the shadows and had apparently survived careening into the wall. Regardless that she seemed to be doing well, Violet wasn't strong enough to battle that woman. I knew from experience how lethal and dark she was.

The shadows she'd conjured had Violet huddled behind a pillar, ducking from one side, then the other to stay hidden.

The small female became more enveloped in her evil. It took so much of her energy to maintain the spell that it was taking over her body. Her veins turned black under her pale skin, pulsing with each step she took closer to where Violet hid. A hideous smile was etched across her face, but her laser-focused gaze didn't notice her surroundings.

I charged, smashing against her, and drove her into the ground. Emitting a scream that pierced the air like the whistling of a gale force wind, she nearly got me to let her go in favor of covering my ears. But I gritted my teeth and twisted the woman's neck until it snapped.

The black shadows briefly hung in the air before dissipating into an ash-like rain.

I rushed to Violet and lifted her to her feet.

"Are you injured?"

She shook her head.

"I don't think so. Where's Micah? I can't hear him."

My chest ached that Violet's first thoughts were for Micah. But there wasn't time for me to lament, and rushed away to aid the mage she loved.

The high priestess had risen once more and now hid behind a magic shield, striking at Micah.

With a roar, I surged forward. The man had earned my respect as a fine warrior, and he protected the egg.

My sudden appearance created another front for the witch to combat, and her face contorted from the exertion. As powerful as she was, she slipped back a step when I pushed against her green shield, and Micah blasted blue magic from his free hand.

Unfortunately it appeared that Micah's magic was reaching its limits. The blue stream grew thinner.

I had to dig deep. Dipping my shoulder, I shoved harder, edging closer to the witch. I had to get to her before Micah lost his strength altogether. I strained, teeth clenched.

A guttural scream emitted from Micah as a spike of blue power flashed in my peripheral vision. Then, the shield dropped.

I staggered—with nothing left in front of me, I fell to my knees.

Micah had broken the shield, but he lay face down on the ground. I could see his back rising and falling, so I knew he still breathed.

Where was the witch? And the egg?

I scanned the vicinity, and saw the egg rolling across the floor, with the witch chasing after it.

NO!

I scrambled to my feet, determined to beat her to the egg, but we both spun at the sound of the high priest's wails.

He'd returned to the fight after I'd broken his nose, and now it appeared that Violet was doing something to him. She held her fingers against his temples with her eyes closed. On his knees, the man screamed in agony.

The distraction was enough to keep the priestess from the egg.

I rushed for the hatchling, but before my hand could scoop up the precious cargo, my feet came out from under me, and my back slammed against the tile floor, causing all my breath to escape in a whoosh. Stars danced across my eyes as my vision shrank to small points.

Somewhere in the distance, I heard Violet scream. It wrenched my heart.

Fighting through the dizziness and pain, I rolled over.

The priest and priestess were both attacking Violet.

I glanced back at the egg from my mother's house, which sat unprotected in the middle of the floor. To rescue it meant allowing those beasts to continue hurting Violet.

I made a choice, and raced to the woman I'd sworn to protect. The woman I cared for more than I should.

Blood trickled out of her nose and ear. Her voice cracked in a scream as she wobbled, ready to fall.

My blood boiled, and my scales itched under my skin. I could char both creatures, but they were too close to Violet. I couldn't take the risk.

As I rushed to her side, I threw my dagger, impaling it in the man's arm. He screamed, and it was enough to disrupt the magic.

Violet slumped to the ground and heaved for air.

I made it to her side and crouched protectively over her, ready to take the brunt of whatever the priestess threw in our direction.

"Violet, can you stand?"

I couldn't let my attention waiver from the two in front of us. The male had dislodged my weapon from his arm and held it in his hand. Blood dripped to the floor from his wound, but he rallied.

Violet rose before she answered. "We have to stop them."

I lowered one hand and clasped hers for a brief second. A wave of reassurance crashed through me at her touch.

"Micah—"

"He's alive," I interrupted, because time was short; the two witches moved closer to each other in front of us.

They lifted their hands, and an orange cloud formed, obscuring our view of them.

"Don't let them separate us," I warned her.

"I can't hear them, my mind is fuzzy."

The fear in her voice stabbed me in the gut.

"You're strong, just fight however you can." I tried to soothe her, but the cloud grew and inched ever closer.

A prickling sensation filled the air, then the cloud exploded, assaulting us with countless magic pellets like tiny shards of glass.

I could do nothing but cover my face in the crook of my elbow. From Violet's muffled scream, she had done something similar. I heard her feet shuffle, and hoped she'd moved behind me for protection, but I couldn't feel her when I searched the space with my free hand.

When the attack lessened, I spun around only to find her missing. Twisting back, she was nowhere in sight.

The priestess' mocking laughter drew my attention. Twenty feet away, the witch held my egg in her hand, while the priest fought to drag Violet out the front doors.

The witch had what she wanted, but I believed she wouldn't harm the egg, now that I knew her vile purpose for it.

However, if they took Violet, I didn't know what they'd do. Or where they would take her. They could hide her behind their magic so I would never find her.

Once again, I followed my heart, and charged the priest. He made it three more steps before I reached him.

With a battle cry that rattled the glass around us, I grabbed the man around his wounded arm, and slammed him to the ground. He shrieked with pain, but scrambled back to his feet.

We'd never escape until both beasts were dead.

"Rone!"

Violet's scream spun me to face her. She wasn't looking at me, and no magic surrounded her.

Following her line of sight, I twisted to see the witch

holding the egg in front of her with one hand, while she raised a dagger with her other.

My dagger.

"You won't beat me, dragon," she sneered.

All sounds disappeared. Nothing existed except the sight of the witch, plunging the dagger through the shell.

No human weapon could have achieved such a thing. Hatchlings had no healing abilities, and I had given her the only blade that could destroy the descendant from my mother's house.

With a twist of her wrist, the priestess pierced the body of the hatchling inside before she let the egg fall to the ground.

The impact cracked the shell in two. Blood and the lifeless body of the innocent babe splattered against the tiles.

Rage like I'd never known shook me.

My dragon erupted with one mission—kill the witches.

33

VIOLET

THE BLACK DRAGON rose higher and higher, until Rone's back threatened to shatter the glass ceiling of the atrium.

Micah had woken up just in time and, probably sensing that Rone was about to shift, had placed some sort of protective barrier around me. I could only move a couple feet in either direction.

And seeing as Rone's nostrils were smoking, I was glad for it.

He was terrifying to behold, a total beast. There was little remnant of the man I'd come to care for. His cabernet eyes gleamed a vicious red as his chest billowed out.

But all that was nothing compared to when his maw opened, and a stream of fire spewed out.

The temperature in the atrium shot up, and the high priest, the closest adversary to Rone, attempted to scurry out of the way.

The act of fleeing only caught the dragon's attention, and unfortunately for the priest, fire moved faster than legs.

Two distinct wails, one of agony, the other of fury, rang through the room as the scent of burnt hair infiltrated my nose. My throat closed up as I watched the flames devour the man. Within seconds, his skin was gone, bubbled away to nothing. His muscles blackened and shriveled, and finally, with one last scream, the witch fell to the ground.

I glanced away, knowing I'd never be able to unsee what had just happened. What I'd been a part of—was responsible for.

My eyes went to Jason, and a sob escaped me.

I hadn't liked either man. Shit, I'd *despised* the high priest, but still . . . their deaths would hang heavy on my soul for the rest of my life.

Linda was still screaming, the sound like a wounded animal caught in a trap and about to gnaw off its own leg. As I turned to look at her, it seemed she wasn't far from her primal side. Her hands were in her hair, and her frenzied eyes were wide with fury.

I hated her too, but the pit in my stomach deepened. She'd just watched her husband get burnt alive. I wouldn't wish that on anyone.

She must have felt my gaze, because the witch paused, as if the scream had been choked out of her, and our eyes locked.

Her spine straightened, and she lifted her arms. A spray of magic flew from her fingertips, tendrils of gas that soared outside, away from us.

Needing to know what had just happened, I peeked into her mind.

The high priest has fallen. Bring reinforcements. We have a dragon to kill.

"No!" I screamed. "She called for more—*aghhh*!" I fell to the floor as the enchanted band of gold around my wrist tightened, and seared red-hot as it dug painfully into my skin.

The dragon roared, muffling my cry of pain as he beat his wings to come closer.

The heat around my wrist let up slightly.

"Get back, or she dies, dragon! I swear, I'll—"

Her threat died on her lips as Rone released an inferno. His fire poured down on the witch, and screams even louder than the ones before filled the night.

The bracelet on my wrist burned hotter and hotter. I pounded the ground with my other hand, trying to push the pain out of my mind, but it only increased exponentially.

Until finally, the pain simply ceased.

I let out a choked sob as my eyes darted to my wrist. The skin there was raw, blistered, and bloodied. But even so, my heart leapt.

The bracelet was gone.

I dragged my eyes up from the ground to see Linda lying on the floor motionless, her clothes still aflame.

Despite the relief I felt, vomit climbed up my throat, and there was no stopping it. I emptied my stomach onto the floor and then, unable to hold myself up, I collapsed and rolled away from the puddle to lay on my back.

Footsteps approached, and Micah appeared over me.

"Vi? Are you okay?"

He held out his hand, but I waved it away, not trusting myself to stand yet.

"I—I don't know. But I will be. Maybe."

His lips twisted, and he looked like he wanted to say something, but another set of footsteps—Rone's—came closer, stopping him.

I smelled the shifter seconds before he appeared above me. His natural spice scent was amplified a thousand times and bolstered by smoke.

When he appeared above me in human form, his eyes still blazed.

"Violet? Are you injured?"

All sorts of emotions swirled within me, most I couldn't identify, but something—an urge to be next to him —stood out.

With great effort, I hoisted myself up. Only when I was looking the dragon prince in the eye did I find my voice.

"My wrist is a little . . . raw, but it's nothing."

Rone's eyes snapped to where the bracelet had been, and his jaw tightened.

He wasn't fooled. My skin was wrecked, and despite my claims, I worried that the witch had seared me nearly to the bone.

"It's not so bad. I'm pretty sure she was going to kill me, or at least squeeze my hand off. This is nothing in comparison." Tears leaked from my eyes as my gaze drilled into his. "Thank you. If it wasn't for you—"

Rone closed the space between us and pulled me into an embrace.

"You did well," he said, stoic through the fury radiating off him.

His hand landed on the back of my head, and stroked my

hair. I could feel it shaking, telling of the pain he was experiencing, too.

He'd almost been bested a few times. Probably been terrified many more. And worst of all, he had seen his charge murdered.

Considering all that had happened, his touch shouldn't have calmed me. Nor should holding me have calmed him. But as the seconds passed, I was sure our connection was helping to ease both our pain. I felt the tension leave his muscles bit by bit, and his temperature cool. My body responded similarly. My breath evened out and my heartbeat slowed. Anxiety left me like a slow tide pulling away from the beach.

After half a minute that felt like an hour, I pulled back slightly.

"I'm so sorry about the egg. If I could take away your pain, I would."

I was aware that he'd chosen to save me over it. His sacrifice was something I could never repay.

The dragon prince gulped. "Thank you, but I made my choice." His voice was thick with emotion, and his cabernet eyes looked mistier than normal. "I wouldn't take it back."

My breath hitched as I tried to comprehend what that meant, but Micah coughed, breaking the spell of the moment.

"Sorry to interrupt, again, but seeing as Linda called for backup, I think we should get out of here."

Rone stiffened at Micah's words.

Belatedly, I remembered that he was the only one who didn't already know about the high priestess' call for help.

"He's right," I whispered. "I watched her make the call. We need to leave."

"I wish to gather the hatchling's body and shell for a proper ceremony. Then we can go."

"Do that. I'll go ahead and disable any wards that might be trying to keep us in here." Micah turned and made his way out the door.

"Do you want my help?"

I wasn't sure if Rone would want me touching the egg.

"Please. I don't want to miss a single bit of shell. No matter how small."

He picked up the bulk of the egg, which was miraculously, largely intact, and placed the baby dragon's body back inside. I scurried around him and gathered the smaller bits of shell. Seeing as we had nothing in which to carry them besides our pockets, which felt disrespectful, Rone deposited them into the shell halves.

The moment we were sure we had every last shard, we left to find Micah. When we reached the gates, he had already undone the spells and wards.

We dashed through the forest without incident or a single word spoken between any of us. Only once we were in the car and Micah had turned onto the main road outside coven headquarters did anyone speak again.

"The Coven of Fortuna won't stop until they find you two," Micah said, as serious as I'd ever heard him. "I wouldn't be surprised if they've enlisted the Komisio to help. Linda had an influential seat on that council. To be safe, you need to get out of the city. Do you know a place where you can go and lay low? Preferably somewhere very far away?"

I twisted to face the prince in the backseat, meeting his sorrowful eyes with the egg cradled in his lap.

He extended the hand not clutching the egg, and brushed a lock of hair behind my ear, sending shivers down my spine that made me squirm. He caught the motion, and the pain on his face broke as Rone gave me a small, weary smile.

"Are you staying to complete your mission?"

I had an idea that might keep us safe, but after what he'd gone through, seeing a babe from his mother's line murdered, I didn't want to assume anything.

"Yes." His voice was tight. "After the ceremony for the hatchling, I need to continue on. I can't let the witches deter me. My people are depending on me."

"Okay, I have an idea of a place that could be safe." My eyes flitted down to the cracked egg, and I gulped.

"Do you trust me to choose?"

The dragon prince was silent for a moment. I felt like his gaze was piercing into my soul, searching for something. Finally, he nodded, breaking the intense spell between us. "I trust you."

Reviews are vital to helping readers find new books. We would love it if you could please take a moment to review
Dragon Prince
It truly helps others when choosing their next great read.

Keep reading for a sneak peek into
Dragon Magic

DRAGON MAGIC
RONE

I CRADLED THE BROKEN, lifeless body in my lap while I stared into the darkness outside the car window. In the early morning hours, we sped away from a battle that had left me battered and bruised—emotionally more than physically.

A sweet, innocent babe was dead because of a filthy witch. I'd failed my mother's house. Her family would not have a hatchling in the human realm to preserve her lineage. My mission had been one of hope and promise, yet I'd only discovered pain and ruin.

I tightened my grip on the jagged shell pieces digging into my palms, and my thumb brushed against the icy body within. A shudder rolled through me.

"Where do you need to go to perform the ceremony?" Micah asked, peeking into the rearview mirror at where I sat next to Violet.

I was still reeling from the battle with the witches, but I focused on my duty, and considered his question. Warm sands like those in Baskara weren't available. Nowhere I'd seen in the Portland area reminded me of home. I feared it was too cold and wet here to usher my kinsman through their ascension.

"Somewhere dry with open skies. Is there such a place near here?"

Violet rubbed my arm and glanced at Micah's reflection, waiting for his reply.

After a few seconds of silence, he responded. "I think I know somewhere out of the way that will work— which is what you need, correct?"

I let out a deep exhale. "Yes, somewhere I can build a pyre."

Micah nodded without further conversation.

Minutes later, he made a series of turns that ended on a gravel road. The car's headlights burned brightly against the backdrop of tall pines we trundled past, and illuminated a sign for a state park when Micah stopped in front of a closed gate.

He twisted in his seat to stare at me. "Can you use that heat of yours to break a lock?"

I huffed at the insinuation that I couldn't, and arched a brow before glancing out the windshield.

The mixture of grief and anger flowing through me could crumble mountains; the piddly chain wouldn't take more than two seconds to dispatch. But indecision over where to place the limp body and all the shell pieces so I could get out of the car stopped me.

"I can hold it," Violet offered, answering my unspoken thoughts, and I didn't even care if she'd invaded my mind to hear me.

A lump of coal lodged in my throat, so I gently shifted the baby into her lap without a word.

The chilly air slapped against my skin when I exited my seat, and I rolled my neck; the movement a respite from the cramped quarters of the car. After a few more seconds to pull my shoulders back and inhale the clean forest scent, I strode for the gate.

I didn't even need to use any heat. The ridiculous farce of security broke between my hands with ease, and the metal bar blocking our path swung open with a bouncing groan.

"Stay there and close it behind us, so if someone passes by, they won't interrupt," Micah called from his window.

The threat seemed unlikely, but I stepped back and let the car edge by. After replacing the gate into position, I ducked back into my seat.

A few minutes later, we rolled to a stop in a flattened area among the trees. I crawled out of the vehicle once more and met Violet on the other side to take the hatchling from her. Without the car's headlights, the stars sparkled overhead like a veil of diamonds against the darkness. I'd never witnessed such a spectacular view within the buildings of the city.

"This is perfect, thank you." I turned to Micah and met his gaze.

"What do you need?" Violet let her fingers trail over my arm.

I understood that she meant it as a gesture of kindness and support, but my nerves prickled. Fire surged through my veins when my mind returned to the reason we were there.

A deep line etched its way across Violet's forehead before she removed her touch.

As I maneuvered around her, my night vision allowed me to scan the area. A small rock circle sat in a clearing next to a trestle table with benches attached. Once I built the platform, the place would work well for the ceremony.

"This is my responsibility." I glanced over my shoulder to where the other two stood in silence.

"Does that mean you don't *want* our help, or you don't believe we *can* help?"

I didn't miss the offended tone in Micah's words. He'd proven himself a warrior in our battle at the office complex.

"I can see the surroundings, but I presume that you can't." I did my best to keep the growl out of my voice, but from the way Violet's eyebrows rose, I hadn't succeeded.

Micah smirked and moved around to the back of his car. He leaned into a hatch he lifted, and when he straightened again, he clicked on a device that illuminated like a torch. "We'll be fine. Violet and I will search for dry wood, while you do what you need to."

"I will need some branches at least an inch thick . . . a lot of them, and as dry as possible."

Giving them a task would allow me a moment alone, which I needed.

Violet made a noise that crossed between frustration and amusement, but followed Micah into the trees on the opposite side of the car.

I blew out a heavy exhale. After a moment to keep myself from combusting due to all the boiling negativity still coursing through my veins after the fight, and the death of my kinsman, I scanned the area.

The circle of rocks I'd seen earlier was the perfect size to fit the hatchling body. To build the pyre, I needed to arrange the baby on the ground. Its scales were a dull gray, having lost all their luster. Its tail sprawled out of the half-shell I carried it in, so out of respect, I settled the rest of the empty shell pieces without disturbing the tiny limb.

I glanced over my shoulder to be sure that Violet and Micah were not within earshot, because I needed to voice my sorrow to my kin, my cousin, privately. The only funeral prayer I knew was for a Baskaran fallen soldier, but this was personal. It was my fault.

"The pain of your death surrounds me, and I will carry my guilt over your loss for all my days. Your flames will never glow in the night sky because I failed you, and now your house will suffer for my shame. Add your signal fire, small as it may be, to light the way for those who will fly to Zeru after you. I pledge myself to house Zimurra in your place."

Snapping brush from behind me indicated the others were returning, so I bowed and touched my fist to my heart, ending my prayer.

The night was dry, and it hadn't rained for the last two days, making it easier to collect downed branches. I'd also gathered some dried pine needles to lay under the platform I built.

"Do you have enough?" Violet knelt near me and spoke in a hushed voice.

I couldn't meet her eyes for fear she'd crack the slim margin of resolve that held me together.

"I do. If you can strip the green away, that would help."

"Here, Vi, take my pocket knife. I've got another one in the car," Micah offered.

I darted a glance at Violet.

She flashed me a tight, wincing grin as she replied, "It's alright, I have a dagger."

I'd asked her to hold onto my weapon during the drive, when I didn't want it near the hatchling.

It was appropriate that she use it on the wood for the pyre, since it was the weapon I'd supplied to the witch, Linda, who then stabbed it through the body of the baby now laying on the ground. In response, I'd become enraged and killed her and her husband.

An act I didn't regret, especially as I finished laying branches in a rectangle, cut to fit inside the stone circle. Two long sides, then two short alternated in a pattern so air could circulate and build the fire into a worthy blaze to send the little one into the afterlife.

Once I had the correct base height, I completed the platform with smaller branches laying side by side. It needed to be robust enough to hold the body and shell until the life essence had ridden away on the smoke.

"Violet, may I have my dagger?"

Her brows pinched in confusion, but she held out the weapon.

I carved the Draessonian words *adimen*, *materia*, and *arimak* on the end of three branches; the equivalent to 'mind,' 'body,' and 'soul' in human speech. I then added my name to a fourth, and rested one at an angle against each side of the pyre. When I finished, I leaned back and sat heavy on my heels.

The only thing left to do was arrange the body, then say the phrases that would guide the hatchling to those who had crossed the veil into Zeru before it.

Both Violet and Micah stood behind me, waiting. It was time.

I slipped my hands under the half-shell, and laid the body in the center, making sure the structure held before I let go. It was the first pyre I'd ever built by myself, and the only one I'd ever seen for a babe.

I arranged the rest of the shell fragments in the remaining space, then found a stick with a diameter the size of my smallest finger, and twisted to face the others.

"Step back a couple paces. Please. I need to light this." The words scraped from my throat like glass.

Neither said anything, but scooted further away.

I began the ceremony.

"From embers to ash,
"Of fire you were born, to fire you return.
"Follow the guardian sparks of those who … of me …
who offer my essence."

The ache pressed heavy on my chest, and silence bathed my senses until I steadied myself.

"Let it surround and guide you to the valley of our ancestors. Add your flames to the night sky for all to remember the life you gave. May you pass through the gates of Zeru without fear, and step into the cauldron of rebirth. You have served well. Though your fire extinguishes, your memory burns bright.
Until we soar as one."

297

In Baskara, the King's Guard would surround the pyre, and once the words were complete, they would breathe controlled flame to light the blaze from all directions. After which, they'd take to the skies and fly through all of Draessonia uttering screeches of mourning.

Those who'd added their names on the leaning boughs would wait the longest, watching the flames in respect as their symbolic gesture carried away a sliver of their own essence to guide their beloved.

Since I couldn't trust my emotional control if I shifted, I grabbed a thin branch off the ground, closed my eyes, and rolled the end of the stick between my palms, allowing my heat to build until the wood combusted.

Violet gasped when the flame burst into view. It was the only sound to penetrate our surroundings until after the fire crackled and bit into the dry branch.

I stuck the burning torch through the structure to ignite the pine needles. When the flames grew high enough, I rose to my feet.

Tears rolled down my cheeks while resolve steeled my core. I would finish this mission. No more houses would lose their chance of survival—no matter what.

The story continues ...
Dragon Magic
The Royal Quest series, Book 2

THANK YOU

Thank you to our husbands, Craig and Kurt, for your never-ending support.

Special thanks to our editor, Jen McDonnell for helping us whip this baby into shape. We love working with you.

To our pets, Bear, Flicka, and Libby, thanks for all the hard work you put in by our sides (and on our laps) as we write all the words, day in and day out.

And finally, thank you to all of our readers. Without you, we couldn't do what we love.

Ashley and Kelly

ABOUT KELLY N. JANE

Kelly writes books she loves to read. Fantasy with characters who find purpose by saving others, wielding a sword, and following epic adventures—then stir in some ancient mythology and a splash of fairytale magic!

She writes with a chihuahua on her lap and a cat nearby. Coffee always flows and she believes that dessert goes with every meal. When she's not in front of her keyboard, she's probably reading, baking, or on a wild rabbit chase down an interesting research trail!

Keep up with her for fun tidbits on interesting historical facts, mythological connections, and how it fits into what she's writing next through her Warrior Circle newsletter!

ALSO BY KELLY N JANE

The Viking Maiden Series (Completed)

Ingrid, The Viking Maiden

Amber Magic

Realm of Fate

Arcanum: Prequel Novella

The Complete Viking Maiden Boxset: includes all four books

The Royal Quest Series

Dragon Prince

Dragon Magic

Dragon Mates

The Portal Sagas: Valkyrie's Gift Series

Time Magic

Time Academy

Fairytale Retelling Collections

Once Upon A Fairytale Night

Includes *Royal Swan*, a young adult retelling of The Swan Princess

Twisted Ever After

Includes *Under the Sea*, a young adult twist on The Little Mermaid
with Vikings

ABOUT ASHLEY MCLEO

Ashley lives in Portland, OR with her husband, Kurt and their dog, Flicka.

When she's not writing she enjoys traveling the world, reading, kicking butt at board games (she recommends Splendor and Dominion), and connecting with family and friends.

For most direct access to Ashley sign up for her reader group, The Coven.

As a coven member you will receive a weekly update from Ashley and exclusive teasers, information about giveaways, and sneak peeks into her author life. You can also find her Facebook group and join in on the fun there!

ALSO BY ASHLEY MCLEO

Spellcasters Spy Academy Series (completed)

A Legacy Witch: Year One

A Rebel Witch: Year Two

A Crucible Witch: Year Three

An Academy Witch: Prequel (best read after book I or at the end of the series)

The Complete Spellcasters Spy Academy Boxset: includes an exclusive bonus short story, *A Marked Witch*

Fairytale retellings

Alice the Dagger - Wonderland Court Series

Alice the Torch - Wonderland Court Series

Fanged Fae Series - A Bonegates sister series (completed)

Blood Moon Magic

Faerie Blood

The Fanged Fae boxset

The Bonegate Series - A Fanged Fae sister series

Hawk Witch

Assassin Witch

Traitor Witch (Coming 2020)

Illuminator Witch

The Royal Quest Series

Dragon Prince

Dragon Magic

Dragon Mate

**The Starseed Universe - An Irish Witch Urban Fantasy
(completed)**

Prophecy of Three

Souls of Three

Rising of Three

Siren Falling

Rogue Fae

Anthologies

Once Upon a Fairy Tale Night -

Includes *Stealing Maid Marian's Heart*, a fox-shifter retelling of *Robin Hood*

Twisted Ever After -

Includes *The Witch and the Wolf*, a retelling of the classic Russian fairytale, *Vassalisa the Beautiful*.

Printed in Great Britain
by Amazon

37779400R00179